Kill Romeo

Andrew Diamond

Cover design by Lindsay Heider Diamond. Woman's
silhouette licensed from Deposit Photos.

ISBN (Paperback): 978-1-7341392-6-6
ISBN (e-book): 978-1-7341392-5-9

This book is dedicated to you, the reader.

1

If I had known how fast the storm was coming, or how strong it would be, I would have turned around sooner. The dog would have to find his own way home. His owner, Mrs. Jackson, told me he always did.

We were on the east side of the mountain, the storms were on the west. The peaks of the Blue Ridge muffled the rolling thunder.

The trail was muddy and the bark of the trees was still wet from yesterday's rain. Sweat plastered my jeans to my legs. The dog, an overly excitable yellow lab, had been running circles around me, snuffling through the leaves on the trail of a fox or raccoon before he disappeared.

I heard something coming fast up the trail behind me. I knew there were bears in these mountains, but I didn't think they could move that fast.

I turned, ready to fight—my instinct is never to flee—only to see the dog galloping toward me with a bright white animal clenched in his teeth.

He reached me, breathless, dropped it at my feet, and barked four times, eyes lit with excitement.

At first, I couldn't make sense of it. An animal that small, that white, dropped from the jaws of a dog, with no blood on it. You know when you stare at something you've seen a thousand times but your mind can't place it? A familiar thing in the wrong context, in a place where it doesn't belong…

I knelt and picked it up, felt the contours in my hand. It took a second to click. A woman's shoe. A white satin shoe, flat-soled and clean, except for the dog slobber. How could it be up here in these woods and not be muddy?

The dog barked loud and hard, his front legs wide and low, tail straight up. They can tell you things in their crude and primitive way. The fundamental, important things that matter to all living creatures, they can tell you.

That shoe belonged to someone.

He turned, ran down the path, stopped to see if I was following.

A violent wind raked the forest as we descended. The storm that seemed miles off five minutes ago was suddenly on top of us. The tops of giant, thick-trunked trees swayed like willows. Stray leaves blew down the mountain, flipping green over silver. I followed the dog straight down the fall line, cutting across the snaking trail. The dog veered right as the first, fat drops began to fall, and the muddy trail disappeared behind us.

We followed a narrow stream to a pond in a clearing, stopped up at the far end by a pile of branches and trees. This was the beaver dam that Mrs. Jackson had told me to avoid. It had too much water behind it and was in danger of breaking. The forest service had already removed the beaver and was going to dismantle the dam. Until they did, the trail below it was closed.

The skies opened up as the dog rounded the pond. Rain poured down in thick, deafening sheets. I slipped in the muddy leaves trying to keep up with him, went down twice and came back up just as quickly, the rain bleeding the mud out of my jeans as fast as I could dirty them.

The dog circled back, collected me, and as he led me toward the dam, the air flashed purple. The crack of lightning shook my sternum like a drum, and in the flash, I saw the dog's tail tuck between his legs as he tore off in terror.

I stood beside the dam, scanning for him. Little streams began to appear everywhere, washing leaves from the forest behind me into the clearing. The narrow creek that fed the pond began to swell and turn white.

Where was the dog? I looked toward where I'd last seen him, but my eyes couldn't pierce the grey-white curtain of rain.

There! Bolting back from the woods he'd fled to in terror, back into a grassy clearing below me, his tail still tucked, still terrified. He stopped at a figure in white by the edge of the stream forty yards below the dam and hung his head, as if he'd given up.

I slipped and slid though weeds beaten down to mud by the relentless rain. The dog, panting and somber, ears and tail down, gave me a woeful look. The woman, dressed in white, lay on her side, left arm outstretched beneath her head, like she had fallen asleep. The rain had matted her hair, exposing dark roots beneath the blond dye. I guessed she was in her late twenties.

She wore a lightweight white cardigan, white blouse, knee-length white skirt, and one white satin shoe. Her eyes were half open, light brown with a dark ring around the iris.

Her face was blue. She had no pulse. I checked her hands and forearms for defensive injuries. Not a bruise or a scratch. No wounds on her legs, face, or neck.

She wore a silver necklace with a turquoise stone. No rings. No earrings. Around her right wrist was a thin black leather strap.

The stream that had been ten feet away half a minute ago was now five feet closer and continuing to swell as water spilled over the dam above.

I circled to the woman's back side—her back was to the water—crouched, pulled at the fabric of her sweater and skirt, looking for blood. Nothing.

The dog was whining now. He pawed my knee as I stood. I think he was scared and wanted to leave.

Who dresses like this in summer? Not someone who's going into the woods. Not someone who's planning on being outside in the muggy August heat. With that thin white sweater, she was going to lunch or a movie, to some place with air conditioning. And she couldn't have walked up here in those flat treadless shoes. The muddy paths were too slippery. And this path, leading up to the beaver dam, was closed, blocked off at the bottom by the Park Service.

Her bare left foot was blue. I took the shoe off the other foot. Also blue.

I went back to her front side, knelt and rechecked her hands. Blue, like her face and feet. Like she'd been carried up here, a fireman's carry, the cyanosis setting into her extremities as she was folded over someone's shoulder.

She began to move.

The dog swatted my shoulder with his muddy paw as if to say, Come on, let's go.

How could she be moving? She was blue as death.

I reached for her wrist, checked again for a pulse before I realized it wasn't she that was moving. It was her skirt. The stream had widened five more feet in less than a minute and was pushing against her skirt.

Water poured over the top of the dam upstream, carrying branches with it. The dam was going to burst.

The dog swatted me again, hit me in the face this time as he barked his urgent warning. *Get out!*

And then the sound of wood cracking, like a building collapse. It unleashed a thunderous torrent of water.

I tried to pull her up to higher ground. I had her by the wrist, and I could have done it if we had had more time. I'm a strong man. A very strong man who used to make his living in the ring, beating up guys no one in their right mind would ever want to fight. I could have pulled her like a child pulls an empty wagon.

But the water got her before I could take a step. Pulled her down the hill and took me with her.

The first two branches from the dam hit me. One in the head, one on the right shoulder. But I didn't let go. I still had her wrist.

The next branch was a big one. Maybe a small tree. It hit the crown of her head so hard it must have broken her skull and neck. Knocked her right out of my grasp. The last I saw of her, she was tumbling head over hips through white water and black branches, her head wrenched sideways on a badly broken neck.

The rush of water slammed me into the trunk of a thick tree. I bounced off toward the outside of the stream, away from the raging center.

A branch hit me in the head and knocked me under, but I came right back up. The dog followed me down, running along the stream's edge, his frantic barks loud and sharp in my ear.

The water pushed me down another two hundred yards or so and pinned me against a couple of saplings that bent heavily under my weight and the force of the stream. I was stuck there for a few seconds before a clump of branches from the dam snagged on a rock just upstream.

The dog barked furiously at the water's edge. *Get out! Get out!*

The snag of wood diverted the flow away from me and took enough pressure off for me to move. I planted my feet, grabbed a sapling with my left hand, and pulled myself up. I didn't want to use my right. There was something in it I didn't want to let go of.

I made it to the water's edge and up a steep embankment before the catch of wood broke free, releasing a torrent that flattened the saplings I'd been pinned against.

I sat there breathing heavily, watching the world wash away as the dog licked my face. He was so happy, you'd think I'd just saved his life, not my own.

My body ached like it used to after fights, only now, parts of me were hurting that boxers aren't allowed to hit. The back of my head, my kidneys, my legs, the soles of my feet. Something had hit me hard under the right armpit. I didn't remember it happening, but I felt it now, the swelling and raw skin. A huge bruise was beginning to form.

I sat exhausted, breathing heavily, waiting for the adrenaline to wear off, waiting to regain my strength. The dog kept licking my face like he was trying to remind me I was okay. After twenty minutes, the clouds thinned and the winds calmed. The rain seemed to stop, though drops still fell from the leaves above.

The dog nudged his nose against my ear, as if to say, Come on, let's get out of here.

These woods were his stomping grounds. He knew the way back to Mrs. Jackson's. And he knew to leave me alone for a minute when I opened my right hand to look at the last piece of that poor woman I still held on to. The thin leather strap around her right wrist had come off when the stream pulled her out of my grasp.

It was the kind of strap kids use to make bracelets and necklaces at summer camp. It looked like she had tied the knot herself, and it had held, even through the flood, until it finally slipped off over her hand and into mine.

The most interesting part had been hidden from me when I found her lying in the grass. It must have been beneath her then, pressed between her skin and the wet grass. A little brass key just big enough to open a padlock or a gym locker. A key imprinted with a black seahorse and the number 212.

2

I followed the dog down a narrow trail to a gravel parking lot where a roadblock warned this trail was closed. Runoff from the woods above had carved deep trenches in the gravel. The dog wagged his tail and seemed to smile as he hopped across the watery ravines.

A hundred feet down, the lot opened out to a paved road. The clouds had broken, and the sun glared fiercely in the puddles. I followed the dog to the right. I knew where we were now. I could see Mrs. Jackson's road a quarter mile down.

Steam rose from the asphalt as we walked. The dog was finally starting to tire. He plodded head down, tongue hanging from his mouth, hips swinging loosely.

When we reached his street, he turned toward home, but I stopped. Two hundred yards down, a section of the main road had washed out. Just past the washout, the nose of a blue sedan pointed awkwardly off the right shoulder. A man stood by the trunk with hands on hips, like he didn't know what to do.

When I walked past our turnoff, toward the car, the dog tried to corral me, nudging my knee to tell me I was going the wrong way. The poor guy had worn himself out in the woods. The heat of the steaming asphalt was wilting him and he wanted to go home.

"Go on," I said. I nudged him toward the house, but he wouldn't go.

"Go home!" I commanded, pointing the way he wanted to go.

He wouldn't leave me.

He followed me toward the car, dragging behind as I picked my way across the gravelly mud of the washed-out section of pavement. The man beside the blue sedan squinted with his hand over his eyes, watching us approach. I stopped and looked at the stream that came down from the mountains to the right and then washed out across the fields to the left. I couldn't tell if it was the same stream I'd been in. Maybe there were lots of them flowing off these hills, but at some point, they all merge.

This one flowed under the road, still swollen but no longer raging. I went to the edge of what used to be the pavement and looked down. The water passed through a concrete tunnel about twelve feet wide. Part of it was blocked with debris that had washed down off the mountain. I looked for signs of the woman, a snag of white clothing in the nested mess, but there was none.

I turned my eyes back to the man by the car, who was still watching me, still shielding his eyes from the sun. He wore dark dress slacks and a white Oxford shirt. Office attire. He was average height, maybe five-ten. Average build. Brown hair and eyes. Looked like he didn't know how to jack a car.

He spoke first. "You know how to change a tire?"

That's what I figured. His right front tire had blown out.

I asked if he had a spare and he said he didn't know.

"How can you not know?" I asked.

"It's a rental."

Right. A blue Mazda 3 with a Hertz Car Rental frame around Virginia tags.

"Well, pop the trunk and let's see."

He opened it, pulled out a black garbage bag and a suitcase, and set them down on the steaming pavement. I pulled up the mat and found a scissor jack and one of those crappy temp tires that won't go over fifty miles an hour. I hate those things.

"You call the rental company?" I asked. "They might be able to send someone out."

He shook his head. "There's no cell signal. I think that storm knocked out the power. Hey uh..." He got this funny little smirk on his face, pointed his finger at me, wagged it up and down at my filthy clothes and said, "You having a rough day?"

I was soaked and covered in mud, scraped and bruised. My hair was a mess. The tears in my shirt were rimmed with watery blood.

I didn't like the way the guy asked the question, the condescending smirk, the wagging finger. Smartass can't change a tire, but he can still talk down to me.

"Not as rough as some people," I said. I was thinking of the woman, but he must have thought I was talking about him.

"Oh, it's nothing I can't handle."

I assumed he meant the car. But obviously it *was* something he couldn't handle or he wouldn't have stood there waiting for me to come along and fix it.

I told him to back it up so all four wheels were on the pavement. I called the dog, who lay panting in the shadow of the car. The poor creature didn't want to get up, but I didn't trust the driver not to run him over.

When I got the car jacked, I could see the steering rod was bent. I asked the guy what happened.

"I was coming down here pretty fast." He pointed back past the washed-out section. "The water was starting to come up over the road. I didn't want to get stuck in it, so I closed my eyes and gunned it and I hit something pretty hard on the way through."

"It wasn't a woman, was it?"

I don't know why I said that. The image of her tumbling downstream kept replaying in my mind, and when he said the water came up over the road, I pictured her in it.

The guy turned white as a ghost. "Excuse me?"

I forget what I look like sometimes, how people might perceive me. You look at my face, you can tell I've been in fights. You look at my hands, the scarred and flattened knuckles, the pinky I broke on another man's face, you know those hands have hurt people, and you know they can hurt you.

The guy was looking at my hands.

"Sorry, pal. It's been a bad day," I said. "Didn't mean to take it out on you."

I told him to return the car ASAP. "You got a crappy spare and a bent steering rod. You're going to have to wrestle the steering wheel to keep this thing straight. I wouldn't drive over thirty."

I put the flat and the jack in the trunk, he laid his garbage bag and suitcase on top. He thanked me, but when I reached to shake his hand, he wouldn't take it. My hand was covered with grime from the wheel I'd just pulled off, and there he was in his nice white Oxford, soaked in sweat but unstained.

On a normal day, I'd give him the benefit of the doubt. Maybe he had a meeting to get to. Maybe he was already late and sweat soaked and who needs filth on top of that? But after what I'd just seen and been through, it seemed petty. Small. I didn't like the man.

I turned without a word. The dog, who had only wanted to go home this whole time, stood and followed.

The guy took off in a blast of air conditioning. The dog and I trudged the other way along the sweltering road, both of us dragging in the August heat.

3

I don't know why I expected the lights to be on when I walked into Mrs. Jackson's house. If the storm had knocked out the cell towers, it would have knocked out residential power as well.

"Close the door!" Mrs. Jackson called from the dining room.

I closed it. The dog flopped onto the cool wood floor with a thud and lay on his side, panting violently.

"Sorry, Freddy, the power's out."

Mrs. Edmund Jackson stood in the dining room doorway wearing some kind of flowing robe. It was too dark to make out the color.

If Mrs. Jackson had a first name, she didn't tell anyone. She was simply the female half of a marriage that had ended twenty years ago with the death of her husband, a wealthy man who was active in state and national politics. I guessed she was around sixty-five years old. A strong-willed, strong-bodied sixty-five.

In the three days I'd been her guest, I got to know a woman who had devoted herself to her church, the local Republican party, and the legacy of her husband's family.

He had left her the old farmhouse full of dark colonial furniture, heavy oil paintings, and fancy silver. There were no crops on the farm, just rolling acres of pasture and a stable. Mrs. Jackson rode year-round, even in the heat.

She also drank whiskey. Exactly one Old Fashioned every day at five, with an orange peel but no cherry. "The cherry," she had told me on the first day of my stay, "is garish and uncouth. We're not in New Orleans, you know."

Standing there in the dark, backlit doorway, I couldn't tell if she was looking at me or the panting dog.

"This house is over two hundred years old," she said. "It's not insulated like the new ones. When the power goes out, it heats up quickly. Are you wet?"

"I got caught out in that rain," I said.

"Why don't you go up and change?"

"I will. And then I need to talk to the police."

"About what?"

"I found a woman up in the woods."

"Oh? Well if you found her up there, she probably isn't your type."

"No, she was dead."

"Oh, dear! Are you sure?"

"I'm sure. Her body got caught in the stream. We both did. The beaver dam broke in the storm and washed her away."

"You're not making this up, are you?"

"Why would I make up something like that?"

"What were you doing by the dam? That trail is closed."

"The dog led me there."

"Buster?"

"He found her lying in the grass, brought me her shoe and then led me to her."

Mrs. Jackson sucked in a breath. She came closer in the dark. I think she wanted to examine me. The panting dog thumped his tail on the floor as his mistress approached.

"Are you okay?" she asked.

"I'm okay."

"Describe this woman."

"She was... Mid to late twenties. Dyed blond hair."

"You're sure it was dyed?"

"It was darker at the roots."

"How dark?"

"Dark. Like mine." I pointed to my hair. "Mediterranean dark."

"How tall?"

"Maybe five-five, five-six."

"Fat?"

"No, but womanly."

"What does that mean?"

Mrs. Jackson was a sharp interviewer.

"You know."

"I know," she said, "but tell me."

"Shaped like a woman."

"You don't have to be a prude about it. She had hips and boobs."

"Yeah. But not fat. Why do you ask?"

"I'm trying to match her to the local girls I know. What color were her eyes?"

"Brown."

"Dark or light?"

"Light. With a dark ring around the iris."

"Tattoos?"

"Not that I saw."

"How did she die?"

I shrugged. "I don't know. I didn't see any sign of violence or injury."

"A broken heart, perhaps? Wouldn't that be sad? What was she wearing?"

"White. All white."

"In the woods?"

"Yeah. White blouse, white skirt, white sweater."

"A sweater? She must have been indoors. No one would wear that in this heat. Sweaters are for restaurants and movie theaters where they blast the air conditioning like they're trying to refrigerate you. Was she wearing jewelry?"

"A necklace. And this." I handed her the black leather strap with the key. "It was on her wrist."

"I can't see it. Let's have a look in the kitchen."

We walked to the kitchen at the rear of the ancient house, where light streamed in through renovated windows.

"You recognize that?" I asked. "That seahorse?"

She shook her head. "Not from anything around here."

She turned to look at me as she returned the key. "You look awful, Freddy. Why don't you wash and change while there's still some hot water left in the tank? Then you can drive into town and talk to the police."

I was going to suggest we call, and she seemed to read my mind.

"The phones are out. Cell and landlines both. Go change. You're not hurt, are you?"

"A little banged up, but nothing's broken."

4

On the road from the old farmhouse to Route 29, I started to see the storm's damage. Lots of trees down. Phone and power lines down. Watery canyons gouged out of the brick-red earth by torrents of runoff. A trampoline standing on its side in the middle of the road. The nearest house was a quarter mile down, so it must have blown quite a ways.

The traffic lights on 29 were out. The gas stations near Lovingston were empty, unable to pump. Even in town, the roads were strewn with branches, leaves, garbage, and debris.

The police station was hot and stuffy. Two workers, a middle-aged woman in uniform and a skinny old man in civilian clothes, had set up a makeshift desk near the entrance, where there was natural light. Behind them, all was dark.

A young woman, Mexican maybe, paced in front of them, bouncing a sweaty baby.

The uniformed woman was running dispatch off a handheld radio. The base station that plugged into the wall wouldn't have power.

The Mexican woman said something in Spanish, calmly, politely, and the woman in uniform snapped back, "Dammit, I told you I don't understand you. Comprende? Can you wait? Wait till Bill gets here, okay? Is someone dying?"

The woman continued to pace as if she hadn't heard.

"Okay then, you wait your turn. Everyone's out right now. Everyone's got problems."

A voice came over the radio, loud, sharp, and cheerful.

"We got all four out of the car, safe on dry ground. These kids got a story they can tell their grandkids."

I pictured a car stuck in high water, electric windows not working, doors unopenable without help.

The uniformed woman told him through the radio where to go next. Some house where a tree had fallen. It smelled like a gas leak. Elderly owners had been sitting outside for two hours. Could he go shut off the gas?

"And you can't get up that road," she added. "A big oak came down, so you'll have to hoof it. Be quick, 'cause I got more for you."

"Yes, ma'am."

A dutiful cop. Doesn't complain, just takes everything the world throws at him.

The old man sitting next to the dispatch woman had a cell phone to his ear and three more on the desk in front of him. He seemed to have calls going on all four of them at once.

I checked my phone. There was a weak signal here. Fifteen miles north there had been none.

"The generator's out," the old man shouted. He glanced up at me, raised a finger as if to say *one minute*, and then barked, "It won't start. Come on, we're in the dark here."

Another radio call, this time from a different voice, a different cop. A man attempting to clear debris from the road stepped on a power line. No need for an ambulance, but someone would have to get the body to the morgue.

"I don't care what's going on up there," the old man barked into the phone. "You come down here and get this gennie started so we can do our jobs."

The uniformed woman put down her radio, looked up at me, and snapped, "What is it?"

She was stressed, red faced, smothering in the stuffy, humid air.

"I want to report a death."

"You want to— What? This from the storm?"

"No."

"I'm sorry, sir, we got—" She cut herself off and pointed to the door behind me. "Talk to the sheriff."

I turned to see a man in uniform on his way through the door. He looked to be about fifty. Maybe six feet tall, burly, with a big belly.

"I was calling you," the woman said.

The sheriff dropped his radio on the table. "Thing's dead. Which of these work?" He pointed to the four silent units lined up on the table.

"Take any one," the woman said. "And talk to this guy." As she pointed at me, the radio sparked to life again. Man pinned in bed by a tree that crashed through his roof.

The old man with the phones said, "Lovingston, Norwood, Arrington have cell service. North and west of twenty-nine—" He shook his head gravely. "However bad things are in the places we *can* hear from, they're probably worse in the places we *can't.*"

"Yeah, I just run into a truck from Nellysford," the sheriff said. "Sounds bad up there. What's up with the gennie?"

The old man with the phones told him help was on the way.

"If that ain't the phrase of the day," the sheriff muttered. "You got something for me? Let's talk outside." The sheriff put his hand on my shoulder and nudged me toward the exit.

Outside, the sun was bright and hot.

"What can I do you for?" the sheriff asked.

I sized him up instantly. Smart and competent, friendly, with the kind of take-it-as-it-comes attitude a cop needs to do a cop's job without going crazy.

"Hey," I said, "I know you're busy."

"So, cut to the chase." He was headed back to his cruiser. I followed, not wanting to slow him down.

"I found a body up in the woods."

"Shit," he muttered. "You know who?"

"No. I don't think she's from around here."

"A woman?" He twisted the knob on the radio he'd just taken from the table inside and it squawked with static.

"Yeah," I said.

A male voice on the radio reported an accident. Two cars going through an intersection where the traffic lights were out. He was asking for two ambulances.

The sheriff shook his head. "Dammit! Why the hell's anyone out driving now anyway?"

"Maybe this isn't the right time," I said.

"What happened to this woman? She drown?"

"No. She was lying in the grass."

"Lightning?"

"I don't think so."

"You sure she's dead?"

"I'm sure."

"Well I gotta help the living right now. She can wait. Write out a description of the woman and her location. Leave it on the desk in there with your name and phone number. And thank you for taking the time."

"I don't know where the body is. It washed away."

The sheriff stared at me for a second, annoyed. "Look, pal, there's nothing I can do for you right now. Leave your statement on the desk. We'll see if your woman turns up. How do you know she's not from around here?"

"I described her to Mrs. Jackson. She said—"

"Oh, you're the detective." The sheriff grinned and shook my hand. "If Mrs. Edmund Jackson says she wasn't from here, then she probably wasn't. Leave your statement. If she's local, we'll get a missing person report soon enough and we can match her to the description. If she's not from here... Well, God, I hope she ain't. We got enough of a mess on our hands already. I gotta get up to Massies Mill. What that fella in the truck told me, it's like The Cataclysm all over again up there."

5

The reason I was down here, in this out-of-the-way place, was work. I was wrapping up a background check on a politician who'd risen quickly through the Republican ranks—so quickly, no one had a chance to really dig into his past.

The party thought Ken Harper might someday be a viable candidate for governor. Before they threw their weight behind him, they wanted to make sure he had no skeletons in his closet, nothing the news media or his enemies could ambush him with in a close election.

I started in Richmond, interviewing his colleagues in the State Senate. No skeletons there. Even his political enemies testified to his character. I backtracked through Roanoke, where he ran a business, and ended up in Nelson County, where he'd grown up. His schoolteachers had nothing but praise for the guy.

He had married his high school sweetheart. Didn't gamble, didn't go after women, and his business associates were clean. As long as his financials checked out, we could tell the party they had nothing to worry about. Claire was working on that part back in DC, digging through his personal taxes and business records.

As an investigative firm in DC, we did a lot of this kind of work, vetting candidates for both sides. Some of them are not as crooked as you think. Some are worse.

I had wrapped up my part of the investigation the day before the storm. Mrs. Jackson, the party ambassador who had offered her house as my base of operations here in Nelson County, had convinced me to spend an extra day in the shadow of the Blue Ridge for some rest and relaxation.

This is what I got.

6

I stopped at a gas station on my way back from Lovingston and picked up two bags of ice and a cooler for Mrs. Jackson. With power out, she could at least keep a few things fresh and have some ice water to drink.

I reached the house around four and found Mrs. Jackson in the kitchen, dressed for riding. She had pulled the fridge away from the wall and was plugging it into a long orange extension cord that ran out the back door. She was sweating. Her hands were dirty, and her nails were black underneath.

The fridge kicked on when she plugged it in. She looked up at me and smiled.

"I had to change the oil in the generator. You can't even hear it, can you? Those Hondas just purr." She nodded toward the red and black Honda humming in the damp green grass.

"That'll give us a fridge and some lights," she said. "Not much more. It's only two thousand watts. I'm going to clean up, and then we'll have happy hour. You'll join me, right? You're not heading back to DC?"

"Actually, I was thinking—"

"You were thinking how nice it is to be in the country, roughing it without electricity. You city folk romanticize everything. Wait here. I'll clean up and— What's in the cooler?"

"Ice."

"You got that for me? How thoughtful! Hold tight, and I'll make you a drink."

It took her an hour to clean up. When she returned, her nails were clean. Not a trace of black beneath them.

Mixing the five o'clock Old Fashioned was something of a ceremony. She apologized for not doing it in the dining room, by the silver tray, but the light was better in the kitchen.

She set two bottles on the counter, then opened the cooler and picked through the ice, putting some cubes into a glass, rejecting others.

"You want the clear ones," she said. "The cloudy ones release air when they melt and change the flavor of the whiskey. You spoke with the sheriff?"

"Briefly," I said. "He couldn't take a statement."

"No, I imagine he was busy. What did you do?"

"Wrote a statement. Left it on a table with a couple of harried dispatchers."

She picked up the whiskey bottle and showed it to me.

"Bowman," she said. "John J. Have you had it?"

"I'm not much of a drinker."

"Well, tonight you are. This is Virginia whiskey, and a good one."

She brought in two tumblers from the dining room, dropped a sugar cube into each, added a dash of bitters, and mashed it all together. Then she carefully measured a jigger of whiskey in a silver cup. She dumped that into one glass, dumped another jigger into the other glass, then added a generous extra splash of Bowman to each. She dropped in a few of the clear ice cubes that had passed her inspection, carved two peels of orange, garnished, and served.

"Cheers!"

She took a seat at the kitchen table and described her tour of the property. She'd taken one of the horses out while I was in Lovingston and done a full inspection. A fallen tree took out a section of fence, the stable roof lost some shingles, and lots of little things needed to be cleaned up. But she was happy to report there was no major damage.

"Grace of God," she said, tipping her glass toward me. "Others, I'm sure, were not as fortunate, and now it's our job to help them. Are you a Republican, Freddy?"

"No."

"A Democrat?" She put her hand to her heart, feigning shock. "Don't tell me I've been squandering all this hospitality on a liberal heathen! The thought of it makes me feel dirty. And I just got out of the shower!"

"I'm not a Democrat either."

"You couldn't be. You're too sensible. Who do you vote for then?"

"The honest candidate."

"There isn't one."

"I know."

"So, you just sit it out?"

I knew she was toying with me, and I could tell she was enjoying it. But political conversations never end well, so I cut it off.

"Let's not talk politics, okay?"

"Yes, Freddy. Let's not. Have I told you how nice it is to have a man in the house? I mean a real man. Not a weakling or a pleaser."

"You haven't told me, but I got the vibe. Hey, what did the sheriff mean when he mentioned The Cataclysm?"

"The Cataclysm?"

"He said this storm was like The Cataclysm all over again. The way he said it, it was like he was referring to something specific."

"The Cataclysm," she said softly. "Oh goodness, it's August nineteenth, isn't it? Is that the date?"

"That mean something?" I asked.

She sucked in a breath. "Dear, what a question! This is going to require another drink. You'll join me, won't you?"

She emptied her glass in one big gulp and went to the counter to mix another. There was no ceremony this time, no measuring. She just dumped everything in and stirred it with a silver spoon.

Mrs. Edmund Jackson had lived near Nellysford when The Cataclysm occurred on August 19, 1969. She was thirteen years old. She told me that much and then she clammed up. For a long minute she sat in silence. I could see her processing the memories.

When her glass was half-empty, she said, "Did you ever see the Woodstock movie?"

I nodded.

"You know on one day of the festival they had torrential rains? The hippies were wallowing in the mud like filthy drug-addled hippopotamuses. If you want a symbol of America's decline, there it is, in Technicolor."

"What's that got to do with a cataclysm in Virginia?"

She raised her finger to make a point. "In Nelson County. The Cataclysm was here in Nelson County. The storm that brought all that rain to Woodstock was a nor'easter. One of those huge, sprawling storms that rakes the East Coast from south to north. They can be a thousand miles long, battering the humble farmers of Georgia and the proud Boston intellectuals at the same time. A true testament to the power of God."

"It hit here?"

"It did." She nodded as she swallowed a sip of her drink. Other than loosening her tongue, the drink didn't seem to affect her. She sat tall and upright. Her mind and speech were clear.

"It did," she repeated, "but it got us worse than anyone because— Do you remember Hurricane Camille? It struck the Gulf Coast in sixty-nine. A category five. One of the strongest storms ever to hit land."

"I haven't heard of it."

"It destroyed the Mississippi coast and went up north into Missouri, then it turned east and came over the mountains. Hurricanes usually fall apart over land, but that one didn't, it was so strong and so tightly wound. The last place you expect a hurricane to come from is the west, from across the mountains. They're supposed to come from the sea, not the plains.

"But Camille came in from the west. It crossed the mountains and came up against the nor'easter and got stuck.

Two monster storms ran smack into each other, and that hurricane just parked itself right over Nelson County. Do you know who wins when a hurricane meets a nor'easter?"

I shook my head.

"Nobody," she said flatly. "But between the two storms, the hurricane wins because it's organized. It has an eye and a circular flow." She spun her finger to illustrate her point. "It sucked up all the moisture from the nor'easter, pulled it in from the ocean, up the mountainsides into its eye, and dumped it all down on Nelson County. Thirty-nine inches of rain in one night. No one who lives through something like that ever forgets it.

"Whole towns were washed away. Davis Creek was gone. Homes, roads, every bridge in the county was gone, overnight. Literally every one. This isn't the flatlands, where water just pools on the ground. It comes down the hills in torrents. When the US Geological Survey came to assess the damage, they found the mountains had suffered three thousand years of erosion in a single night. The rain drowned the birds in the trees and washed the forests off the hills.

"Weeks after the storm, crews were clearing out huge piles of trees, and underneath them, they'd find houses. Houses with people inside, dead in their beds, houses that had been washed miles from their foundations. It was traumatic. Everyone who was here remembers. That's why the sheriff takes this seriously. This is the hour of need. This is when the public servants have to come through for the community. And he does. That's why he's sheriff."

She continued for a while, describing the damage to her family home, how she lost a cousin four miles away.

"You can still see the plaques," she said, "by the roadsides. The silver plaques that describe places that were underwater during The Cataclysm. You're standing fifty, sixty feet above a streambed reading that plaque, and you think there's no way in the world the water could have ever gotten this high. Well, it did.

"Some of the homes washed into the Tye and from there into the James. They broke into pieces and floated past Richmond, past Williamsburg and Hampton Roads, into the Bay and out to sea. It was awful, Freddy. It was truly awful. The memory of it upsets me. And I've had too much to drink. I need to shut up now, don't I?"

She stood and got two bottles of water from the fridge. She set mine on the table in front of me and stood with her hand on her hip, chugging hers. She got about halfway through it then wiped her mouth and screwed the cap back on.

She glanced at me and read my mind. "You're thinking about her again."

"The woman?"

"I can see it." She took her seat at the kitchen table and eyed the remains of her Old Fashioned. There was one watery sip left in the bottom of the glass.

"Go for it," I said. "Finish what you start."

She did. And then she said, "You too."

I shook my head. "I'm not really a drinker."

"I don't mean your drink. I mean the woman. You want to find out who she is, don't you? You're an investigator, right? So, don't give up. That would be acting against your nature."

"I have to go back to DC."

"Really? You have to? Or are you just saying that?"

"This is a case for the sheriff."

"Which is why you can't stop thinking about it. Tell me where your mind is. What are you thinking?"

I took a breath, looked out the window at two horses grazing in the pasture.

"Okay," I said, "let's assume you're right. She's not from here. That means she probably left a car somewhere, or she might have been renting a room. If she left a car, it'll turn up. Someone will report it to the sheriff, and he'll figure out who she was. If she didn't leave a car..."

Mrs. Jackson had a very sharp eye. She didn't just look at you, she looked into you. "Go on," she said. "I can see the wheels turning. Finish your sentence."

"Well, I'd check the hotels and inns. The bed and breakfasts."

"But not the motels?"

I shook my head. "I'd check the motels last. The way she was dressed, she'd be in a hotel or a bed and breakfast."

"Those are spread out all over the county," Mrs. Jackson said.

"And the power is out and the phones are out and the roads are a mess. So, what's the point? I'm going back to DC."

"But we have cell service."

"They have it down in Lovingston."

"Here too."

"Since when?"

"An hour ago. And I know two inn owners. I know their cell numbers. And they know the cell numbers of other inn owners. Would you like me to make some calls for you?"

"I think *you* want to make some calls."

"You think I'm a busybody?"

"Pretty much, yeah."

"Well, you're absolutely right, and I don't mind saying so. Busybodies are information aggregators. We're essential to the social fabric of society. I'm going to call a few places. I know some restaurants too. I'll make the calls, and you'll make me a promise."

"Will I?"

"Absolutely."

"What, exactly, am I promising?"

"If I find one lead, you'll look into it."

"That's it?"

"That's it. You have nothing to do in DC anyway. You just wrapped up an investigation confirming that our up-and-coming political star has no skeletons in his closet. You can write up your final report in two words. *He's clean.* So, don't give me that excuse about needing to rush back to the city. If I find a lead, just one, you'll look into it. Then you can go."

"You know what that will lead to."

"I most certainly do. Once an investigator gets hold of a clue, he can't let go."

"You want to hook me."

"I spent half my adolescence figuring out how to hook a man. I'd hate to let that hard-won knowledge go to waste. And you wouldn't deprive an old widow of her fun, now would you, Freddy?"

"No, ma'am."

She smiled. "Good answer."

7

August 20
Nelson County, VA

The house was brutally hot that night. At midnight, I tried opening the window, but the air outside was even more humid than the air in my room.

At one, I took a cold shower by candlelight. It cooled me off, but it also invigorated me and made it harder to sleep. By the time the energy from the shower wore off, I was hot again, sticking to my sheets.

At three, I filled a jar of ice cubes from the cooler, went back to the bathroom, and soaked my feet in the tub while I crunched the ice.

Sometime around four, I fell asleep.

At a quarter to ten, I heard Mrs. Jackson walking softly down the hall outside my door. When she reached the end, she turned and walked back. She paused but didn't knock. I had a feeling she wanted me up. And if she did, I knew why.

I got up and washed my face, dressed, and went downstairs.

I found her by the stove, beside a bowl of uncracked eggs and a skillet of bacon. She was bursting with excitement.

"I have something for you!"

"A lead?"

She lit the burner beneath the bacon with a match.

"A lead indeed," she said proudly. "But first, do you like your bacon soft or crispy?"

"Crispy."

"Eggs over easy?"

"That sounds great."

She lit a second burner and dropped a pat of butter into a pan. She scooped coffee into a percolator and heated it on the back of the stove.

A smile lit her face and she passed me a slip of paper.

Philip Nikander, Olympic Inn, Afton, VA.

It had an address and phone number.

"I got his cell from a friend of a friend of a friend."

She explained her process over breakfast.

"I didn't think she'd be staying in Lovingston, because no one really does. I figured a visitor would stay at Wintergreen. It's beautiful there. Have you been?"

I shook my head.

"Well, I couldn't make much progress with Wintergreen, because so many of the places are Airbnbs. Who do you even call? And I don't think all the cell towers up there are back online anyway. What do you think of this coffee?"

"It's excellent."

"I forget how good it is when you make it in the percolator. We lived in Paris, you know. Edmund and I, when the kids were young. And before that, in Uruguay. My husband was twelve years older than me. He raised a lot of money for George Bush—the father, not the son—and the president rewarded him with an ambassadorship. To Uruguay, not France. But in France, this was how we made the coffee. It tastes so much better this way, but I hardly ever make it like this because the electric coffeemaker is so much easier. How is your bacon?"

"Very good, thanks."

"I hope so. The pig lived just up the road."

I looked at her for a second to see if she was serious. She read my mind.

"Yes, I'm serious. You live in a city, so you think bacon comes from supermarkets. It comes from animals. Listen, when I was collecting phone numbers, I got a few in Afton, and that one panned out." She tapped the slip of paper she had written. "It's an inn with eight rooms and a restaurant. A good restaurant. They serve Greek food."

She was getting more excited. She hadn't touched her food, but she was downing the coffee pretty fast, adding fuel to the fire in her mind.

"They had a guest there matching your description. She left yesterday morning dressed in white and never came back."

"Why would they expect her back?" I asked through a mouthful of eggs. I was hungry despite the heat.

"She never checked out. Her bags are still in her room."

I frowned.

"What?" she said. "What's wrong?"

"This is really a job for the sheriff."

"Of course it is. But didn't I do well? Didn't I?"

"You did great."

"Now remember your part of the bargain."

"What part?"

"You promised to investigate."

"I told you, this is a job for the sheriff. Or one of his deputies."

"So?" She shrugged. "It doesn't mean you can't also have a look."

"Cops don't like people butting into their investigations. Especially private investigators from out of town."

She leaned forward and asked with the earnestness of a young girl, "Do you think someone killed her, Freddy?"

"I think..."

In my mind, I saw the unstained white shoes, the spotless sweater and skirt. Not only had she not gone up that path under her own power, she had never intended to be out in the woods in the first place. The blue of her hands and feet—she was carried up there over someone's shoulder, up a path that was closed, where no wandering day-hiker would find her.

Mrs. Jackson was baiting me, leading me to thoughts she wanted me to think.

"It's possible someone killed her," I admitted. "I can't speculate, but it is possible."

"And would you want her killer to walk free?"

"No, I— Look, we don't know if she was killed."

"What does your gut say?"

"My gut says if it's homicide, it's for the police to investigate. They can get warrants. They have legal means to investigate that private investigators just don't have. They can compel people to talk, to turn over evidence."

Nothing I said dampened her enthusiasm.

"Would you want her killer to walk free?" she asked again.

"Come on now! We're just speculating. We don't know what happened."

Mrs. Jackson leaned farther forward, almost into her food, as she reached for my hand, which I slid across the table for her to squeeze.

"One more question, Freddy."

I could tell by the look in her eyes she was going to pull out her trump card, her last, best weapon to force me to play her game.

"Have you ever, in any investigation, found evidence that the police did not find?"

I wasn't going to respond to that, but the answer was yes, and she could read it on my face.

"Well then, why not give the poor girl every chance of bringing her killer to justice?"

"Stop saying she was killed."

"I know the sheriff, Freddy. I'll call him, and he'll meet you there. At the inn. You want me to call him?"

"Does it matter?" I asked. "Is this really about what I want?"

Her face beamed with satisfaction. "My goodness, Freddy, some woman trained you well. It took ten years of marriage to teach my husband to respond like that!"

8

Sheriff Earl Kessler had business in Afton that afternoon. Mrs. Edmund Jackson arranged for us to meet at the Olympic Inn at 2:00 p.m.

I arrived a few minutes early to find the driveway in front of the converted Edwardian mansion blocked by a fallen elm. A shirtless, rail-thin kid of twenty or so was dismantling it branch by branch with an orange chainsaw. He had an intense, manic energy about him, climbing barefoot over the tree, a cigarette clamped between his lips, oversized baseball cap clapped on his head.

He stared through clear goggles at the chain as it shredded the wood, working his jaw like he was chewing or grinding his teeth. His face and neck were covered with acne. Or flea bites. Or something else.

It took me a second to put it all together: the wiry physique, the manic intensity, the sores from picking at himself. Crystal meth.

When the sheriff pulled up, the kid hopped down off the tree and retreated to the side of his red Ford pickup, eyeing the lawman warily, like a dog watching a stranger pass its property.

The sheriff parked and got out, glanced at the tree and the kid, who nodded silently. When I got out of my car, the sheriff shook my hand and apologized for being distracted yesterday.

"No need to apologize," I said.

"I don't like to be unfriendly. My job is to help. That woman you found—seems like she's got a second life inside the active mind of Mrs. Edmund Jackson."

"What *is* her name?" The question burst out of me. I never understood why any woman wouldn't want to be called by her own name.

The sheriff laughed, more at the way I asked than at the question itself.

"She was Jessica Warner as a girl. Went by Jessie before she became Mrs. Edmund Jackson. Her husband was in politics for a while. It's a hard thing for a southern white Republican to be called Jessie Jackson. Remember, the reverend made a big splash in the Democratic primaries back in eighty-eight, the same year that she and her husband worked to get Bush Senior into the White House. She roped you into this, huh?"

"How could you tell?"

"Only one person runs the show when she's around. You licensed?"

"I am."

"All right. You let me start with Nikander. Feel free to throw in any questions you want, but let me lead. Also, don't stare at his wife."

"Why would I stare at his wife?"

"You'll see. If our mystery woman was staying here, we'll check her room. Let me and Sherri go in first."

"Who's Sherri?"

"My investigator. She'll be along in a few. Don't touch anything in the hall, don't come in unless we tell you to. We'll take some photos. If we find anything interesting, I can't let you handle it, but I can show you. You did some work for Mrs. Jackson?"

"For the Republicans. Vetting a political candidate. She let me stay at her house while I interviewed his old teachers and neighbors."

"Candidate? Ken Harper?"

"That's the one."

The sheriff broke into a friendly grin. "Didn't find nothing on him, did you?"

"Nope."

"The man's just what he says he is. Nothing more, nothing less. Sharp too. He's one I wish I had on my force. But I guess the Lord made him for a higher calling. They're talking about governor. He'd be a good one. What's Mrs. Jackson want you to find up here in this room?"

"A murder weapon. A motive. A suspect."

"Not likely," said the sheriff with a smile. "But we'll walk it through and we'll come up with something to tell her, and then you can be on your way back to DC. But I sure can't imagine why anyone in their right mind would be in a hurry to get back *there*."

We entered the property through an iron gate between two rows of boxwoods. When we passed the bushes, the chainsaw kicked up again behind us.

The house was wood, three stories high, with a wraparound porch that had stairways on two sides. We entered through double doors into a carpeted hall. Someone had tracked mud onto the dark red carpet, and someone had tried unsuccessfully to get it out. To the left was the front desk, dark wood and unmanned. To the right, a dining room with six white-clothed tables and windows that looked out on the fallen tree in the front drive.

The lights were on. The inn must have had its own generator, though I wouldn't have been able to hear it over the buzz of the chainsaw.

The sole figure in the restaurant, a striking blond-haired girl of seventeen, sat erect, sipping tea, looking out the window at the chainsaw kid. When she heard us enter, she turned and stared at me—a brazen, suggestive stare through ice-blue eyes. She took no notice of the sheriff, just locked her eyes on mine, and I couldn't look away.

A short, dark-haired man entered through the kitchen doors at the far end of the dining room, clapped his hands with a loud crack, and shouted, "What are you doing? Eh? Get up! Go upstairs and clean."

She ignored the man, kept her eyes fixed on mine, deliberately, as if she was trying to provoke him. Then slowly she rose, tall and slim, muttered a curse in what sounded like Russian, dropped her napkin on her chair, and walked out.

She gave me a pointed look as she passed. A full up-and-down that enraged the little man. He glared at me with undisguised hatred for a second. And then, when the woman was gone, he wiped the anger away, smiled, and greeted Sheriff Kessler like an old friend.

"Have you come to eat? We have fresh lamb today!"

"No, Phil, I'm afraid it's business."

Philip Nikander looked crestfallen. His face seemed to be capable only of extremes.

"You talked to Mrs. Jackson?" asked the sheriff.

"Ah, yes!" His face lit up. "She asked about a guest."

"We have some questions about her too," the sheriff said.

Philip Nikander didn't seem to like the word *we*. His smile faded and he worked hard to hide his scowl when he looked at me.

His warm tone gave way to a voice that was all business. "Yes, well, I put down her name after Mrs. Jackson called. It was Rachel. And her room is open if you want to look." Nikander's dirty glance told me the sheriff was welcome to search the room, but I was not.

"She have a last name?" the sheriff asked.

Nikander shrugged.

"You didn't take her last name?"

"Why would I?"

"Because you're supposed to know who your guests are. It would have been on her credit card anyway."

Nikander's look seemed to say, "Credit card?"

"She did use a card, didn't she?" asked the sheriff.

"It was a prepaid card. No name."

"She show you a license?"

"Why would I intrude on the privacy of a paying customer by asking to see her personal documents?"

The sheriff looked annoyed. "Dammit, Phil. When's the last time you saw her?"

"Yesterday morning. She went out the front walk. A car picked her up."

Nikander was looking me up and down, the way the girl had done, only he liked what he saw a lot less than she did.

"What kind of car?" Sheriff Kessler asked.

"What kind? I don't know. A car. Maybe it was a truck. Maybe I don't look at such things."

"Something eating you, Phil?"

"Nothing eats me. Who is this man?" He pointed at me like I was something dirty.

"An investigator," Kessler said. "What was the woman wearing when she left?"

"Clothing, I'm sure. If she was naked, I would have noticed." Nikander stared arrogantly at me for a moment, then added, "Let's talk in my office."

9

The sheriff and I sat alone in Nikander's office at the back of the inn. The innkeeper had supposedly gone to get us coffee, but we could hear him upstairs, screaming in Greek at a woman who responded coldly in Russian.

"I told you not to stare at his wife," said the sheriff.

"That's his wife? How old is she?"

"Twenty-two. She doesn't look it, does she?"

"How old is he?"

"Fifty-one."

He gave me the lowdown. Nikander had been in the US over twenty years. He was a citizen and a widower. A year and a half ago, he dropped twenty pounds and started dying his grey hair black. He had a new spring in his step. You could hear him whistling as he trimmed the hedges in front of the inn.

"He flew away for a couple weeks and came back with her," Kessler said. "She's younger than his daughter. His daughter used to do some of the cooking and a lot of the administrative work. She left in disgust three months after Natasha showed up. You gotta wonder what goes through a man's mind when he does something like this."

"Do you really have to wonder?" I asked. "Seems pretty obvious."

The sheriff grinned. "Ben Franklin said if a man had half of what he wished for, he'd double his troubles. Nikander got everything he wished for, and he's miserable. I've never seen anyone so jealous. She tortures him for fun. Like the way she looked at you. It drives him crazy. The man runs an inn, for Pete's sake. He's got people coming and going day and night, looking at his wife, his wife looking back at them. There are beds to fall into behind every door. The man is mad with jealousy, and he did it to himself. What kind of foolishness makes a person choose a life like that? He yells at her to clean the rooms and then he watches her like a hawk because he doesn't trust her out of his sight. She resents him for all of it."

I tried to picture the online courtship that preceded the marriage. Him selling himself as a hotelier, her picturing the Hilton in Manhattan. Her sending nude selfies. Him picturing her in his bed.

Sheriff Kessler stopped talking when the fighting stopped. Philip Nikander walked in a moment later carrying a tray of coffee, milk, sugar, and cups, his bright, friendly smile pasted on with violent determination. A flap of dark hair stood straight up from his forehead, waving as he walked. His face was red and moist with sweat.

"Sheriff," he oozed. "Cream and two sugars, yes? Yes! An innkeeper remembers his customers' favorites. So you feel at home. And you?" He dropped the forced smile.

"Straight black," I said.

"Black, eh? Black is good. Simple tastes for simple people." His hostile tone made it clear he meant that as an insult.

His hand shook as he poured the cups. I noticed he took his black too.

"This woman," he said, handing the sheriff his coffee. "What do you want to know?" He pushed a cup to me, then took a seat across the desk, holding his coffee with both hands. His right pinky stuck out but his left didn't.

"When did she check in?" Kessler asked.

"Mmm... Four days ago." Nikander opened a drawer and pulled out a printed page. He slid it across the desk to Sheriff Kessler.

Kessler read it and frowned. "That's all you got?" He handed the page to me, an act which seemed to offend Nikander, whose nostrils flared in anger.

"If you wanted me to spy on her, you should have told me ahead of time."

"Did she act strange at all while she was here?"

"Define strange," Nikander countered. "What you Americans think is strange is quite normal in some parts of the world."

"Like she was scared or nervous or depressed?"

"What would be strange about that? Are you never scared? Too much coffee makes people nervous. And it's easy to be depressed when your wife is a slut."

"Just answer the question, Phil."

"Very well. She was not scared. Nervous? I would say no. Depressed? Well, if I had any understanding of women's psychology, perhaps I could answer that. But this I know. She did seem to be waiting for someone."

"What makes you say that?"

"She came down for breakfast every morning at eight. She sat by the window and looked outside. She checked her phone constantly. After breakfast, she'd be in her room or in the garden. She never went far. Lunch? By the window, looking out. Dinner? By the window, looking out. And she dressed like she meant to go on a date."

"She ever go into town?" asked the sheriff.

"What town?" he huffed. He didn't seem to think much of Afton.

"Did she drive anywhere?"

"She didn't have a car."

"You sure about that?"

"I didn't see one."

"What time did she leave yesterday morning?"

Nikander shrugged. "Nine? Ten? I don't know. My guests come and go as they please. I am not their chaperone."

"But you said she was wearing white when she left," Kessler reminded him.

"When did I say that?"

Kessler took Nikander's paper from my hand and passed it back to him. "You said it to Mrs. Jackson on the phone this morning."

"Yes, well that is what Natasha told me, but I don't believe anything she says."

Sheriff Kessler was doing a good job keeping his cool. If I was here alone trying to get information out of this guy, my temper would be rising fast.

"Let me talk to Natasha," Kessler said.

"You." Nikander pointed fiercely at the sheriff. "You talk to her. Not him." He made a vague eye motion in my direction.

Kessler rose from his seat. "She upstairs?"

Nikander rose as well. "How did you know that?"

"I didn't," Kessler lied. "I'm just asking where she is."

"You wait," Nikander said. "I'll get her and you can talk on the porch. But the only English she knows is lies."

Nikander left and the fighting upstairs resumed. He came back a minute later, sweaty, and Kessler's investigator, Sherri Prescott, was with him. They must have run into each other in the hall.

"She is on the porch waiting for you," Nikander told the sheriff with the most gracious veneer of a smile he could muster.

Kessler introduced me to Deputy Prescott and went outside. She took his seat and set her bag on the floor. I knew what was in it. A camera, baggies, tags, labels, seals, fingerprint powder. She probably wouldn't use any of it other than the camera. If the woman in white left the inn under her own power, her room wasn't a crime scene.

Nikander took his seat across the desk and glared at me.

"You're a very strong man, eh? That's what you want people to think?"

"I don't really care what people think." And I didn't care about his wife either, but if I said so, it would probably set him off.

"Do you beat people up to enforce the law?"

"I'm not a cop, so I don't do law enforcement. Why'd you ask if I beat people up?"

He nodded toward my hands, which were folded across my stomach.

44

"I used to box," I told him.

"It's a crude, cruel sport," he observed.

"In some ways, it is."

"A low sport, for low people. Beating up others for money. What kind of life is that?"

"You don't see a lot of rich kids going into it."

"That's what I mean. It's low."

"It's a way out for people who don't have a lot of choices," I said. "And for people who don't know what else to do with their aggression. Or their heartache."

I could have told him more. That it's a way of learning discipline and self-mastery. That for some people whose worlds are so chaotic and so out of control, who live in circumstances where nothing can be mastered, the act of mastering the self is a kind of deliverance. It changes your perspective, your identity, your understanding of who you are and what you can accomplish.

Most people are terrified of having the crap beat out of them in front of a bloodthirsty crowd. As a fighter, you learn to tune out the fear, tune out the pain, stick to your discipline, and trust your skills.

You have a trainer in the corner who's watching from the outside, who knows your strengths and weaknesses, sees opportunities you can't always see in the heat of battle. You go into the corner and the cut men are jamming cotton swabs up your nose, pressing End-Swell into the throbbing welt above your eye, and you look to your trainer. You listen. You take his advice back into the fight.

Most people can't follow advice even when there's no pressure. A boxer has to do it while he's getting his face beat in. He has to be patient when he's losing. He has to have faith in his heart and his abilities. And he needs discipline to stick to his plan long enough to turn the tide, even when the battle seems hopeless.

Sure, it's a savage sport. But life is a savage affair. When you learn to navigate the worst of it, you know you can get through *any* of it.

I could have told Nikander all that and more. But I didn't want to waste my words, however strongly I believed in them, on someone who was determined not to listen, who prided himself on his refusal to understand. People like him have a knack for building their own hells, and for stubbornly staying in them.

Nikander looked at me like he had won, like he saw all the words I didn't say, and interpreted my silence as an admission of defeat. He turned to Deputy Prescott and said, "Are you going to put fingerprint dust all over my inn?"

"I'm not planning on it."

"Good," he huffed. "Because my wife is a terrible cleaner."

10

I stood in the hall while Sheriff Kessler and Deputy Prescott toured the room with Natasha. Philip Nikander stood a few feet behind me, arms crossed, watching. Watching me, that is. Not the room.

I could hear the sheriff's questions, Natasha's heavily accented responses, the click of Prescott's digital camera.

They were in there ten minutes, tops. They didn't bring anything out with them, but the sheriff gave me a summary in the air conditioning of his car a few minutes later.

"First off, we don't know for sure whether the woman in this room is the same one you saw in the woods. It looks like she may have come back."

"What makes you think that?"

"Natasha found her key in the door."

"How does she know it was her key?"

"They only gave out one. And it was there in the door yesterday afternoon, after the storm, when Natasha walked past."

"That's weird. Who leaves their key in the door? That doesn't make sense."

"No, it doesn't. But I'm not going to pick the place apart and haul all this stuff into evidence for what might not even be a crime. If the occupant of that room returns..."

"So, what are you gonna do?"

"I asked Phil to close it up. Lock the room and keep everyone out for a few days, until we know more."

"You think you can trust him?"

"He's pissed about the money he'll lose, not being able to rent it out, but he's not gonna go against me. Plus, I have some suspicions. I don't like the feel of this, and I let him know. He's wary of crossing the law. I don't think he'll mess with anything. Let me show you something."

Kessler pulled out his phone and showed me a photo of the woman's suitcase.

"Whoever went into the room went through her clothes. But look here." He zoomed in on a wad of cash. "That's three hundred and thirty dollars. Not enough to raise a cop's eyebrows, but if there was foul play and the perpetrator came back to the room to go through her stuff, he probably wouldn't have left the cash. The clothes, by the way, are all expensive. There's no reason to dress like that in the country. She might have been from a city, or on her way to a city. Now look at this."

He swiped ahead to the next photo and put the phone in my hand. It was a letter on the desk, written by hand in blue ink.

> Carlo,
>
> I can't tell you how surprising it was, after a lifetime of disappointments, to see so many hopes fulfilled in one person. To peel back the layers of you one by one only to find again and again a person I thought I'd never meet. The surprise of you never wore off.
>
> So how did we come to this? I understand a liar. I understand a fraud. But I do not understand you.
>
> You really did love me. I know you did.

"I think there was more to the letter," Sheriff Kessler said. "Natasha said she'd emptied the wastebasket a couple of times during the woman's stay and it was filled with crumpled paper. Trash was picked up this morning. Nikander had to wheel the cans out through the front gate. Whatever else she wrote, we're not going to find it. Except this."

Kessler reached over and swiped to the next photo. "This was on the floor, crumpled up."

I could see the wrinkles on the page. Kessler or Deputy Prescott must have smoothed it out before snapping the picture.

> I lied, just like you. They're not here.
> Disappointment is a bitter pill, isn't it?

"That was on the floor of the closet," Kessler said. "Below the safe. The safe was open, but Natasha said it had been locked the other day. What's that make you think?"

"It could be nothing," I said, rereading the words. "Maybe part of some other letter she had written."

Kessler shook his head. "Look at the paper. It's torn off in a neat, clean strip. Like she meant it to be a note. Like that's the whole of it."

"Let's say this note was in the safe," I offered. "Let's say someone killed her and took her room key and came back here looking for something."

"How would he get the safe combination?" asked the sheriff.

"The same way he got the key. He took it."

"Well, he'd have to ask."

"Maybe she left the safe open on purpose. She seems to have known someone wanted something from her. She seems to have wanted him to know she was angry or hurt. She was thwarting him. She leaves a taunting note in the safe, knowing he'll come for it. He crumples it up and throws it on the floor. I mean, that's just hypothetical. You have to think through all the angles."

"Hmm..." The sheriff drummed his fingers on the steering wheel.

"There's something else," I said.

"What?"

"I don't know, but you do. You're holding something back."

He sat poker faced for a while, rubbing his chin. At last, he said, "I appreciate a detective who can see that. Did she have a purse? The woman in the woods?"

"Not that I saw."

"Mmm..." He thought again for a minute. "Natasha said she left with a purse, but that's not the part that bothers me. What bothers me is that when Natasha came to clean the room around eleven yesterday morning, there was a passport on the desk. Today, there wasn't."

"What do you think that means?"

Kessler shrugged. "Dunno. Maybe we got one dead woman in the woods and a different woman in the same outfit who decided to leave the country."

"You really think it's that complicated?" I asked. "Maybe whoever came into the room took the passport because her name was on it. It's hard to crack a murder case when you can't identify the victim."

Kessler shrugged. "I don't know. Most crimes come down to love, greed, or revenge. This one... Well, we don't even know if there was a crime. We'll have to wait and see where the pieces fall."

"All right," I said. "I appreciate you looking into this. And I'm sorry for that woman. I—" The image came back again. Her tumbling down that violent stream. Abusing a corpse is a crime. Societies passed laws against it because it's so disturbing, so insulting and wrong to treat a body like that, even when it's dead.

Kessler was reading me. "This one's eating at you, huh?"

"Yeah. Listen, if I didn't know it was against the rules, I'd ask you to forward those photos to me."

"And if I didn't know that official evidence goes on the official police camera, I wouldn't have snapped these with my personal phone. What's your number?"

I gave it to him, and he sent the photos.

"Show 'em to Mrs. Jackson. If she sent you out on a mission, she'll expect you to come back with something. Trust me."

11

Mrs. Edmund Jackson studied the photos over her five o'clock Old Fashioned. She examined them quietly and deeply for such a long time I think she forgot I was there.

"It's so sad," she said at last. "People pity me because I'm a widow. But I had the best marriage anyone could ever ask for. I can't imagine how it would hurt to lay my heart on the line for someone and be betrayed. Who do you think he is? This Carlo?"

"I'll leave that to your imagination. And the Nelson County sheriff."

The lights flicked on, then the air conditioning kicked in with a rattle and hum.

"Oh, thank God!" Mrs. Jackson cried. "Thank you, thank you, thank you!"

"Hey, um, if you're all good here—" I stood from my seat at the kitchen table.

"You're going to run off to the bustling city."

"DC isn't really bustling in August."

"Then what's the hurry?"

"Just time. Time for me to get back. Thank you for your hospitality. I'll have the report on Ken Harper to the party bosses as soon as Claire finishes her review of the finances. As long as those check out, there's not much to tell. I'll shoot you a copy too. He seems like a good guy. The press can't smear him unless they start making things up."

"The press would never make anything up," she said sarcastically. "Thank you, Freddy."

"Let me know if Sheriff Kessler finds anything."

"I won't have to." Her tone was distant. She was staring out at the horses in the pasture, lost in thought.

"Why not?"

"You'll contact him yourself."

"No. I'm done here."

"Are you?" She turned to me with a questioning gaze, quietly self-assured. "Can you really unsee her, Freddy? Can you unsee your final glimpse of her and be at peace?"

12

August 21
Washington, DC

Why did she have to say that?

13

August 25, 26, 27...
Washington, DC

Why?

Why?

Why...

14

August 28
Washington, DC

Saturday. I was supposed to take my son, Lenny, to a Nationals Game. At 3:00 p.m., I got a call from Miriam—his mom, my ex. Lenny was throwing up. He wasn't going anywhere.

"He eat something bad?" I asked.

"Not bad. Just a lot. A whole chocolate cake."

"Why'd you let him do that? You know how he is with sweets."

"What do you mean, why did I *let* him? You think I put it on a plate and told him to eat it? I was in the garden. He was in the kitchen."

"You left him alone in the kitchen?"

"He's seven, Freddy. He can be in the kitchen while I'm in the garden."

"Yeah, and look what he gets into."

"Freddy! Ugh!"

There was that note of exasperation. I knew I should stop, but I was really looking forward to this game.

"Why'd you even have a cake in the house to begin with?"

"Because we're irresponsible," she huffed. "We're horrible parents. It was for Milos's friend's birthday. What's wrong with you?"

"Just disappointed, that's all."

"Well you have every right to be. I'm sorry, Freddy."

"You give him some Pepto?"

"Yeah, I'm on it. How about you come by after work on Monday?"

"All right. Don't let him eat any crap."

"Freddy," she sighed.

That "why does it always have to be this way" tone said it all. I wondered the same thing.

This was how it was when we were married. This was why we stopped being married. I love the woman. I really do. But we can only stand each other in small doses. Something in our nature rubs the wrong way and every conversation turns into an argument.

Now what was I going to do with my Saturday? Go to a baseball game alone?

I called Ed. Ed founded the agency as a solo operation then brought me on a few years later as employee number one. Now we were partners, fifty-fifty. He did less footwork these days, spent more time working his contacts to find new jobs for me and Bethany and Leon and Claire. A long career with the FBI left him well connected, and maybe a little burnt out. He was pushing sixty now, looking forward to retirement.

We'd been to a few football games together. Never baseball. I gave him a call, asked if he wanted to see the Nationals. He told me he was busy with family today.

Family, more and more. That's how it's been with him the past few years. Guy's got four grandkids and two more on the way. I'd do the same if I were him. Spend my time with the ones who matter.

What about Claire? Did she like baseball?

Who knows?

Bethany?

No.

Leon?

I've never met a guy less interested in sports. Going with him might be worse than going by myself.

I called him anyway.

"Hey, you want to see the Nats play the Braves?"

"Why would I want to do that?"

See what I mean about Leon?

I like the kid, but he has no social skills and no filter. I think he's autistic, which is what makes him so good at his job. A lot of detective work these days is done in the office, on the computer. When Leon's digging for information on the internet, he has a kind of focused attention I can't even fathom. Wading through pages and pages of information, he has a superhuman tolerance for tedium. You ask him to do a background check on someone, he'll give you a full biography, including the guy's favorite foods and the color of his underwear.

Bethany is fascinated with him, maybe because they're opposites. Leon is tall, thin, dark-skinned, with a high-top fade that went out of style with Kid 'n Play. I don't think it was even in style then.

Bethany is tall and thin with fair skin, pale blue eyes, and straight strawberry-blond hair. She came to us from the library school at Catholic University. She's as good a researcher as Leon, but she comes at it from another angle. She has that librarian's discipline. Everything in its place. She's also good at digging information out of sources that most people don't know exist. Microfiche collections in the basements of government buildings. Out-of-print phone books. Indexes and reference books you'd only find in university libraries.

When I say they're opposites, I mean the way they perceive the world. Leon sees a collection of facts and details that never add up to the whole that Bethany sees. He can't seem to read the most obvious social cues. Bethany reads them before they even happen. Her social antennas go out in every direction. Leon dissects the world. Bethany vibes it with uncanny accuracy. Sometimes I think she's psychic.

I pulled out my phone to text her, ask her if she wanted to go to the game with me. But as I was typing, I thought better of it. I knew how it would go with her. At some point—maybe in the third inning, or maybe in the first five minutes—she'd start reading my mind and asking questions that annoy me.

Just because I'm thinking something doesn't mean I want to talk about it.

I hit backspace, erased the invitation, and asked a different question instead.

Does Claire like baseball?

Five seconds later, she wrote back.

Why do you ask?

You see why she gets under my skin? I ask her a yes or no question. A yes or no or I don't know question. You ask a guy, and you'll get one of those three answers.

You ask Bethany, and she responds with that.

I don't know why I bother with her sometimes.

15

Five-thirty, I was on my way out to Nationals Park. Claire called. Did I have time to talk? In person?

"What's up?"

"I want to talk to you about the Temple case."

"You like baseball?"

"What's that got to do with it?"

What the hell? Was she autistic too? Why can't people just say yes or no?

"I'm going to a baseball game. Would you like to join me?"

Her sigh told me she wanted to talk, not sit in a loud stadium.

"Where are you now?" I asked.

"On my way back into the city from Mclean."

"You know where The Salt Line is? By the stadium in Southeast?"

"I'll find it."

"I'll see you there in half an hour."

Claire was doing contract work for us, a three-month try-before-you-buy. We wanted to see whether she was a good fit and how she handled different kinds of cases. Ed was already sold, wanted to bring her on full time, if we had the work.

She came from the corporate world, and she dressed like it. Wore pants, women's suits.

I had met her on a job I did for a lawyer in Montgomery County. Claire was the client. She was in trouble for a crime she insisted she didn't commit. The evidence looked bad, and her lawyer was angling for a plea bargain with the prosecutor. She would have none of that.

She carried out most of the investigation herself and did a damn good job. Cleared her name and helped bring the right people to justice. I helped out here and there, tailing a lowlife gambler out in Vegas who she'd managed to track down through sheer tenacity and hard work. I was impressed.

When she wrapped up that case, I asked her if she was looking for work. She said yes, and I brought her in. Ed was impressed with her right off the bat. She had good financial and business knowledge. That filled a hole in the firm's skill set. We used to have to hire contractors to help us analyze information in white collar investigations—fraud, embezzlement, money laundering. With her, we have the expertise in-house.

She agreed to come on board only if I'd mentor her. I didn't think she needed mentoring. Her instincts were as good as mine, her intelligence was off the charts, and she had an education I never had the chance to get.

What could I teach her?

But she was serious about the mentor thing. We put her on a few cases, in various roles. Follow someone, interview leads, find out what's in a guy's trash can. She liked to work outside the office.

Every bit of work she did—every tail, every interview, every source she went after—she'd come back and explain to me what she'd done, why she did it, how she did it, and she'd ask, "Was this the right thing to do? Was it the right time to do it? Was there more I could have done? Would another approach have yielded more information?"

At first, I was surprised she asked so many questions. I mean, she was already doing everything right. And if you're that smart, why do you need to ask questions at all?

It took a few weeks for me to understand. She's that smart *because* she asks questions. Because she never *stops* asking questions.

I had always thought—without realizing it, I guess—that what made a person interesting was the things they could tell you. The stories they shared, the knowledge. It hadn't occurred to me how interesting a person could be just by the nature of their questions. When they ask you something, you see where their mind is going, and your mind goes there too.

It starts to seep into you, the way they see the world. You're walking down the street by yourself, you see a building you wouldn't have remarked on yesterday, and in your mind, you hear her asking questions about the architecture, the building's history, what kind of people live there. Now you're seeing everything from two perspectives. Sights that had been so familiar for so long you'd stopped seeing them—suddenly they appear again through another set of eyes, fresh and new.

I asked Bethany in a roundabout way if she'd felt a change in the office since Claire arrived. I was fishing for hints of an *uncomfortable* change. Bethany said, "No. Claire is great."

I asked Leon, even though I knew it was pointless. All he could tell me was that Claire smelled good, knew a lot about spreadsheets, and never had wrinkles in her clothes. Factually correct and completely worthless information.

In my mind, I kept going back to our first meeting in the airport in Vegas. She was there to interview a guy on the Reisman case. I was there for support, in case she got into physical danger.

Was there something there? I asked myself. Some spark?

No.

It was a job, and on the job, all I think about is work.

My impression of her then: She was sharp, but tightly wound. Headstrong, maybe a little reckless. I thought she was getting in over her head, going alone to interview a violent felon who'd just come out of prison.

The interview was in a restaurant near The Strip. I watched from a table nearby, looking like some random tourist on a long solo lunch.

The guy was a real hardass. Cagey too. She handled him brilliantly, got more information out of him than he knew he'd given.

She didn't need me to chaperone.

Next time I saw her in person was at Anton Durant's office in Maryland. We were reviewing the case. That's when I asked her to work for us.

It was a business decision. Ed and I had worked with contractors in the past, licensed investigators, and some of them had caused more trouble than they were worth. The ones we did want to work with again, the good ones, were never available.

Claire was a good one, and if we didn't get her, someone else would.

The last few weeks I'd been asking myself if my motives were pure when I asked her to work with us. Was there some attraction, conscious or not, that day in Anton's office?

No.

I'm certain of that.

But I didn't know her then, and now I was starting to. That was the problem.

16

The Salt Line was a bad idea. Saturday evening, right before the start of a game, and it was across the street from the stadium. There was no way we'd get a table. I don't know what I was thinking.

I walked out of the Navy Yard station and it was hotter than hell. My clothes would be soaked by the time I got to the restaurant.

I pulled out my phone, texted Claire: *We might want to pick a different spot.*

She texted back: *I already have a table.*

How the hell did she swing that?

It was inside too. In the air conditioning. She had a glass of ice water waiting for me. Always on top of things.

"You dress like that even on Saturday?" I asked.

She was wearing a suit. Blue jacket, which she'd removed and folded over the back of her chair. Crisp white shirt, blue slacks. No wrinkles, as Leon noted.

"Yeah, and hello to you too, Freddy. I just came from a meeting with a client."

"In Mclean? The lobbyist's wife?"

"Her name is Laura. She happens to be married to a lobbyist who's cheating on her."

This was the assignment that had kept her out of the office most of last week. Crawford Temple, two-term former congressman from Alabama, now a lobbyist for the corporate interests he vowed to regulate when he ran for office.

Temple could easily have won a third term, but he chose not to run. It took his wife a year to figure out why.

Elected officials can't be too flagrant with their affairs because they live in the public eye. Lobbyists make more money with less scrutiny. They work the same hours on K Street as on the Hill, which is to say, if a guy has to go to dinners and late meetings six nights a week to influence public officials and seal deals, his wife isn't going to get too suspicious about it.

Until she does.

Someone referred Laura Temple to Ed. Probably the wife of one of her husband's colleagues. Ed gave the case to Claire. Find out who the guy is sleeping with.

"Who is he *not* sleeping with," Claire said. "That's the better question."

I can't tell you how many of these cases we get. It's always a guy in his forties who has it all. Big house, kids in private school, cush job. The investigation business is recession-proof because greed and lust are built into human nature.

"What did you get?" I asked.

The restaurant was too loud for cross-table conversation. She came around the table, sat next to me. Too close for my comfort, but there was no way to talk otherwise.

She showed me photos on her phone. Temple in a restaurant with a forty-something redhead. She was dressed for business. Looked like a strategy meeting. Only when they got to his car, they kissed.

"Where'd they go after that?"

"To a townhouse in Georgetown."

Claire showed me the photo.

"It's hers," she said. "I looked up the records while I waited outside."

"He spend the night?"

"No. He came out around eleven-thirty. You know, the sad thing is, he called his wife while he was in there. Told her he was in a meeting. She texted me right after they hung up. She asked where I was. I told her, in my car, in front of a house on Dumbarton Street. She asked if he was inside. It was heartbreaking, Freddy. When I said yes, she was just silent. I mean, the woman has children."

A waitress glided through the crowd, slipped a tray of oysters onto our table. A dozen raw, on the half shell with lemon wedges. She smiled at us, like we were a couple.

"Everything okay here?"

"Fine," Claire said. She looks people in the eye when she talks. I like that about her.

The waitress moved on.

"You order those?" I asked.

"You okay with oysters?"

"Yeah."

I picked one up, gave it some lemon and Tabasco. It glided off the shell into my mouth.

Claire did the same, only without looking. She kept her eyes on the phone, didn't notice how much hot sauce she put on.

"Look at this," she said. Another photo.

This one was in his office. He was standing beside a young woman, holding papers, like they were reviewing them together, only his hand was on the small of her back.

"How'd you get that one?" I asked.

"From the office across the street."

"They let you in? To take pictures?"

"I told them it was for an architecture magazine. Now look." She swiped ahead to another photo. Same woman, same outfit, but now she was outside, alone, on the corner of 19th and K.

Claire turned to me. "How old do you think she is?"

"Twenty-three."

"Twenty-two," she said. "She's an intern. Not his. But he seems to have her in his office a lot." She dumped the oyster into her mouth, the one she unwittingly drowned in hot sauce. "And on the street, she had this glow. This dreamy look that made my heart sink. I mean, why? You look intelligent. Why would you get involved with him?"

I was waiting for her reaction to the spice. Her expression didn't change, but her cheeks flushed and the skin on her brow moistened with sweat. She's like me. Doesn't like to show what's going on inside. Suppress the natural reaction. A good boxer learns that lesson before he gets into the ring. Your opponent will attack your weaknesses, so don't show them.

I didn't know much about her past because I didn't ask and she didn't offer. I didn't need to ask, anyway. She had a hard shell, and hard shells come from hard lives. Someone broke her trust at a time when she couldn't defend herself, and now she was built to make sure that didn't happen again. If you've lived that life yourself, you recognize it in others.

After the oyster, she picked up her beer. Three big, long sips. She felt the heat.

She told me recently that she used to be angry. I don't know what she meant by "used to be." Her tone was pretty sharp earlier when she corrected me about Laura Temple being a woman and not someone's wife. When she was working with Anton Durant, trying to clear herself of a murder charge, she was pretty damn pissed.

I used to be angry too. Most of my life, in fact. I looked calm on the outside because I had trained myself that way. But inside, I was full of bitterness and resentment, and with good reason. There came a point where I understood that anger and bitterness are poisons to the heart that bears them, that my most closely held feelings were killing me, but still I couldn't let them go.

Not until a guy down in Texas put a few bullets in me and forced me to let go of just about everything. He did me a favor, even though he wasn't trying to. When I woke from a coma a few days later, I thought, Here's your second chance, Freddy. Don't screw it up. Don't be such an ass this time around.

I sometimes wonder why it had to come to that. Why did I have to almost die to break out of a way of living that I *knew* I could no longer endure?

I don't know. A spirit in the world is like a baby in the womb: All the pieces need time to form. Even when the outcome is inevitable, there's no shortcutting the process.

"What?" Claire said.

"What what?"

"You're staring at me."

"Sorry. I got lost in thought."

She was sitting so close, her knee bumped against mine. This meant nothing to her. Didn't register.

It shouldn't have with me either.

"You want to know the worst part of this?" she said.

"Of what?"

I slid away from her, a couple inches to the left, where her magnetic field wasn't so strong.

"This case. What else have we been talking about?"

I shook my head, shook the thoughts out, reoriented myself to the conversation.

"The worst thing is, I ran into him."

"Temple?"

"Yeah. I followed him to a meeting, an actual honest-to-goodness meeting at the Hawk 'n' Dove up on the Hill. Six people, including him. Four men, two women, but neither of the women were near him. I had to go inside to get a good view of them."

She took another oyster, added lemon, and measured the Tabasco carefully this time. A single drop.

"He laid some papers on the table. Got signatures from two of the men and one of the women. Five minutes later, they're all up and ready to leave. I wanted to get out of there, but I needed to get my check from the bartender."

"You pay up front in situations like that."

"I didn't think they'd be leaving so soon. Besides, the bartender walked off as soon as he gave me my drink."

"What did you order?"

"What difference does it make?"

"Just curious what you drink."

"On the job? Ginger ale. Anyway, I turned to look for the bartender as soon as I saw them get up, but I caught Temple's eye as I was turning. He could tell I was looking his way."

"Caught red-handed. Over time, you learn how to avoid that."

"How do you avoid it?"

"Don't look right at people."

She smirked. "Smartass. Anyway, a guy like him, if he catches a woman looking, he's going to follow up. Sure enough, his friends all leave, and as the bartender is handing me the check, Temple slides up next to me. Puts his hand on my back and asks what I'm drinking. I can't stand it when men think they have a right to touch me. He doesn't even know me. I mean, yeah, I looked at him, and in his world that means come put your hands on me. Creep!"

"You let him buy you a drink?"

"I wanted to see if he would hit on me."

"Did he?"

"There, and at the Tabard."

"You went to Dupont Circle?"

"I wanted a quieter place."

"Why?"

"So I could record him."

"On your phone?"

"Yeah. I wanted his wife to hear how he operates. He's not very smooth. He feeds you drinks and compliments, talks about himself more than he knows, drops names. None of that impresses me. After twenty minutes, he just asked me outright if I wanted to get a room upstairs."

"What did you say?"

"I asked him what his wife would think of that. He said, What makes you think I'm married?"

I wondered if she was able, on their date, to suppress the look of disgust she was showing now.

"You have to be careful recording people," I told her.

"DC has one-party consent for audio recordings."

"Not every place does. You have to be aware of local laws when you're working."

She waved the issue off. "Regardless, I was in the right, was I not? In this particular case? In this jurisdiction? I wanted something to bring back to his wife. This wasn't for a court case."

"You send her the recording?"

"I went to her house to talk with her about it. That's why I'm dressed like this." She tugged at her clean white shirt. "Do you want to go to the game? I mean, you invited me and I don't want to keep you from it."

"No," I said. "It's hot as hell out there. We can watch it in here on TV."

She smiled. "I was hoping you'd say that."

She gave me a summary of her talk with Laura Temple. Her two-hour talk. They had the house to themselves because the kids were out and the husband was on a business trip in New York.

"With the redhead from Georgetown," Claire noted.

The photos didn't surprise Temple's wife, but they upset her. Same with the recording.

"Throughout this investigation, I thought I was gathering evidence to initiate a divorce. But she loves him, Freddy. She showed me photos of him and her together, of him with the kids.

"The whole time, I thought this guy was pure scum, and then I see there's another side to him. He's another person at home, and she wants to hang on to that person. She told me she went through a pill addiction years ago. She was horrible to her husband and the kids. But he stuck with her, got her into treatment, never gave up on her no matter how awful she was.

"And she's not going to give up on him. She's going to use the evidence to force him to go to counseling with her."

The waitress came and cleared the oysters. Claire ordered another beer and a plate of fries. For me, ice water.

"A few years ago," Claire continued, "I would have told that woman to leave her husband, and I would have been disgusted with her if she didn't. I would have seen nothing but weakness in her, because the issue was black and white. But a marriage is a terrible thing to break. I know, because I've done it."

"You were married?"

"Almost. But that's not the point. The point is that if you have something in your life that means that much to you, and if you're willing to fight for it even when it hurts that badly—

and this woman was hurting, Freddy, I saw it—well then, you must have a lot of courage and a lot of faith and a lot of hope. Those things are harder to hold on to than anger."

What did she expect me to say to that? I thought we were going to review the mechanics of the case, how she followed him, how she could avoid rookie mistakes like getting caught looking at the guy in a restaurant. Of course, she turned that mistake to her advantage because she's resourceful. Always thinking on her feet.

"Well, you did good work," I said.

"I actually don't care about the work. I wanted to talk because I was upset. The whole thing upset me. That someone would bring that much hurt into his family's life. That his wife loves him enough to want him back. That I wanted her to feel as angry and disgusted as I did, and instead... Well, it humbled me, Freddy. My moral certainty, my self-righteousness and pride and indignation, in the face of a love like that—it made me feel small."

"You can't get wrapped up in your client's problems," I said. "Not in this line of work."

She looked me in the eye. "Freddy, I switched from corporate investigations to human investigations *because* the cases matter. Because it's not just about money, it's about people, lives, things that are actually important. And I know I shouldn't get wrapped up. Just deliver the facts and move on. But I'm human, Freddy, and so is she, and so are you, and I guess I just needed to vent."

She paused, thought for a second, then added, "It's uncomfortable when someone opens your eyes like that and you realize what an awful person you've been in the past. How all the certainties you took such pride in were really just defenses, how judgment is an excuse to keep from feeling, how much harder it is to truly care, and to take the beating life will give you for caring. Sorry to dump on you but... You understand that, don't you?"

I didn't respond. I couldn't untangle everything that was going through my head just then. Miss Professional, Miss Cut-to-the-Chase, No-Nonsense Efficiency—sorry—Mizz. Ms. Just-the-Cold-Hard-Facts just unloaded on me with a shot I didn't see coming.

This wasn't the first time, either. She had a way of catching me off guard, hitting me where I felt it.

"It's okay, Freddy. You don't have to answer." She lifted her beer, took a sip, and then delivered the final blow softly, almost as an afterthought. "I know you understand."

17

Nine-thirty p.m., I was back at home. I had the game on in the background, no sound. The Nats and Braves were tied at six in the eleventh inning, and it looked like they were headed for twelve.

Claire bailed from The Salt Line a few minutes after our talk. Said she had to take care of some things in her apartment. She hit me with an emotional dump and run. The flip side of what men do to women.

I hung around the bar for a while, had a beer, watched Juan Soto hit a two-run homer in the fifth.

On the way home, I called Miriam, checked in on Lenny. He was watching the game on TV, scanning the stands for a glimpse of me. I talked to him for a few minutes, asked how his stomach was feeling. He said he'd never eat another piece of chocolate cake again, ever. At his age, that meant two weeks.

"I'll see you Monday, Lenny?"

"You're coming over?"

"Didn't Mom tell you? To make up for missing out on the game today."

When we hung up, he was happy. I was happy.

The TV caught my eye. Soto was at bat again. Swung at a low fastball and even with the sound off, I can tell he crushed it. The ball sailed a mile over the centerfield wall. There would be no twelfth inning tonight.

I turned the TV off, looked for a clean towel and the soap I bought the other day. I swore I bought a bar of soap.

It might be in the fridge, I thought. Things had a way of winding up in there when I got distracted.

On the way to the kitchen, my phone chimed.

A text from Sheriff Kessler in Nelson County. Not a text, a photo. A scrap of grease-stained paper that looked like it was pulled from the garbage. Same handwriting as the notes in the mystery-woman's room from the Olympic Inn. Same cream paper, same blue ink.

...out of the frying pan, into the fire. You're
everything I wanted to get away from when I left Del...

I puzzled over that for a minute. The letter in her room was written to a guy named Carlo. Carlo, the liar and the fraud who let her down. Carlo, who she taunted with the note in the safe that said, "I lied, just like you. They're not here. Disappointment is a bitter pill, isn't it?"

So, who was Del? Why did she leave him? Did she have a pattern of bad boyfriends? Abusive relationships?

I was about to call Kessler but he beat me to it. I picked up on the first ring.

"What's up?"

"Just wanted to let you know the occupant of that room never returned. Philip Nikander was pestering us to get her stuff so he could rent the place out again. We brought her belongings into the station. Sherri took prints from the room, the letter, and the suitcase. There was nothing in the suitcase to identify the woman. The clothing was from Anthropologie. They have stores around the country, and they sell online, so that doesn't help us know where she came from. Sherri will do an official inventory on Monday."

"Where'd the note come from? The one you just sent?"

"Natasha found it in a garbage bin behind the inn. The bin had been emptied, but that scrap was stuck to the side with grease."

"Any idea who Del might be?"

"No clue. Sherri talked to Philip and Natasha again, but they never saw the woman in white with anyone. We tracked down a couple of guests who had spoken with her. The woman never mentioned her name or where she was from, but both said she seemed intelligent, well educated, and anxious. On edge, like she was waiting for something important to happen."

"Could they tell where she was from? She have an accent?"

"Nothing that stood out. American, but not Southern."

"All right, well, let me know if anything new comes through."

"Tell you the truth, Freddy, we're not chasing this one too hard. There's no evidence of a crime and no one has filed a missing person report. We're still cleaning up from the storm down here, trying to track down some looters. Some people—Well, there's nothing too low for them. Stealing from the stores when the whole county is reeling."

"I don't envy you, Kessler."

He hung up and I opened the fridge, immediately forgetting what I was looking for. I closed the door, left the kitchen, then remembered when I got to the bedroom. Soap.

Back to the fridge, and there it was, next to the orange juice. A bar of Irish Spring with the wrapper half torn off. I must have been in the middle of something when I did that.

I put the soap in the shower and went back to the bedroom, sat on the edge of the bed, picked up the key from my nightstand—the little seahorse key on the black leather strap.

I reread the note.

...out of the frying pan, into the fire.

She'd been in trouble before. Around trouble, at least. Del was the frying pan, Carlo the fire.

You're everything I wanted to get away from...

She knew where she didn't want to be, what she didn't want, but she didn't seem to recognize that she was walking back into it.

My phone chimed again. A text from Mrs. Jackson.

What do you make of that?

I should have known she was behind this. She prodded Kessler to send me that photo and she was on me already. Busybody.

I think you need to find a hobby.

She texted right back.

I already have a dozen, and this is the best of the lot. Sleep well, Freddy.

I looked again at the note.

> ...everything I wanted to get away from when I left
> Del...

I wonder why she left him.
What was wrong with Del?

18

August 30
Washington, DC

Today was a rarity for August, neither hot nor humid. We had lunch outside, all five of us—Ed, Bethany, Leon, Claire, and I—at a sidewalk cafe a few blocks from the office.

I spent the hour after lunch going through a folder Claire had left on my desk. She had printed out some business documents from that candidate we were vetting and wrote an eight-page report describing things his political enemies might seize on to whip up a controversy.

A refund from one of his company's suppliers looked like a kickback. But there was a clause in the contract that said unit prices would drop if the candidate's company purchased more than a certain amount of materials. The refund was legit. Claire even included a copy of the contract with the relevant clause highlighted.

She pointed out a few other things, intricate financial details that made my eyes glaze over. The folder included tax documents and regulatory filings that showed why all these potentially shady dealings were legit.

I read her report three times because I was so impressed by the clarity of her thought. If I had written that report—and I couldn't have, because I don't have her business knowledge—it would have been at least twice as long. She expressed ideas with a minimum of words and no ambiguity. That's an art.

The last two pages of the report covered the sexual harassment case at the politician's manufacturing company. The case had gone to court and was a matter of public record.

The jury ruled in the company's favor, saying there was not enough evidence of a pattern of behavior, or an environment of pervasive harassment or hostility. But still, it didn't look good. Political opponents would harp on this to paint the candidate as sexist or misogynist, to try to siphon off the women's vote.

Claire didn't give any recommendations on how to deal with this. That would be the party's job.

When I finished my third pass of the document, Claire and Bethany were at Claire's desk discussing the harassment case. I shut the folder and carried it back to them. Claire was leaning, hip on desk, arms crossed, listening to Bethany.

"It's just icky," Bethany said. "I've been through that, and it's uncomfortable and gross and... icky." She seemed to shiver at the memory.

"Someone harassed you?" I asked.

"In grad school. One of the TAs. It wasn't like he was groping me or anything. Just, you know, these little touches. Like, he'd hold the door for me and as I walked through, he'd touch my shoulder, like I needed to be guided or something."

"That's harassment?" I asked. "I've done that."

"I know, but— Okay, it starts like this. He does it once. I figure, like, maybe I was going to bump into the doorframe or something. Because I do that sometimes. He wasn't copping a feel. It was just a touch. I didn't think much of it.

"A couple days later, he does it again. Touches my shoulder as I go through the door. Then he does it as I'm taking a seat. Like, I don't need your guidance. I'm not going to miss the chair.

"All this happens slowly, by degrees. One day he starts putting his hand on the small of my back as I go through the door. He starts coming over to me when I'm studying, talking, super familiar, like we're picking up a conversation we left off earlier. Probably a conversation he was having in his head. And I'm like—I don't know—I go along. Because I work with this guy. I have to get along with him."

Claire gave a subtle nod, her eyes focused on Bethany.

"And after a while, it's like, everywhere he sees me, he comes up and talks. About nothing I'm interested in. And there are always these little touches. Like he has a right to waste my time with all his pointless chatter and a right to touch my body. And I'm looking back, trying to think when exactly did this become uncomfortable? When did it stop being okay? I can't find the line. I can't put my finger on the day or the time or the specific thing he did. But I'm conditioned now to let this happen because it all started off so naturally. And if I try to tell someone, if I imagine someone looking at this behavior from the outside, it doesn't look wrong. How do I tell someone I don't like him leaning over me, looking at my work? Yes, he's my advisor, but he doesn't have to stand that close. How do I say that without coming off as rude when he's doing something that, by itself, doesn't look wrong?"

"You just tell him flat out," Claire said. "Because some men don't get it."

"But then I'm rude."

"*You're* rude? For letting him know he's making you uncomfortable?"

"Yeah. I mean, I know that sounds perverse but—"

"It *is* perverse. His sense of entitlement is *his* problem. Don't let him make it yours. If he's really a man he can deal with your feelings. You say, 'I don't like this. Stop.' And if he doesn't respect that, then there's the crossing of the line. Clear as day. There's the thing you can point to."

This was the sharpness of mind I admired. Intelligence isn't just having a command of the facts. It's the ability to separate what's important from what's not. Claire cut through all the BS, got right to the heart of the matter, and explained it clearly.

"Freddy," she said.

"Huh?"

"What if I told you to stop touching me?"

"When have I ever touched you?"

"I mean, hypothetically. If I said, Freddy, you don't need to touch me when we're having a conversation. You don't need to stand so close. You don't need to tell me every detail of your weekend when I'm trying to get my work done. How would you react?"

"I never did any of those things."

If anything, I thought, I did the opposite, and consciously so. I stood farther from her than I did from anyone else. I didn't tell her anything unless she asked.

"See," said Bethany. "This is what I mean. You try to tell a guy something about your own feelings, and they take it personally and get defensive."

"I'm not being defensive!" I protested.

"Oh my God, Freddy, listen to your tone! How do you deal with that?"

She was asking Claire.

"When I worked in New York," Claire said, "in that corporate environment, it was a very male culture. A real boys' club. I took this posture from day one: You do not touch me, you do not talk down to me, you do not even look at me like someone you'd ever think of touching. If I got a look from someone, I'd give it right back, let them know I wasn't friendly. I swear, it was like prison sometimes, everyone testing you to see if you're weak."

"I wish I could do that," Bethany said.

"In the long run," Claire said, "I wish I hadn't. I became that person. Defensive, unapproachable. Like a porcupine. That chip on my shoulder ruined a lot of relationships. I didn't even like myself after a while. No one should ever *have* to be like that, but sometimes it seems like the only options are to fight all the time or get stepped on. There has to be a middle way. For sanity's sake, and for decency..."

Another thing I liked about her: She knew exactly who she was and what her flaws were, and she worked to fix them. Nothing happens in life unless you show up and put in the work. A lot of people flake out on that and they wonder why their lives aren't going right.

Bethany said, "Show me the look you'd give the guys in New York."

Claire turned this gaze on me that was absolutely withering.

I wasn't ready for it, and it stung. This was the woman who had opened up to me at the restaurant on Saturday. How could she look at me like that? I knew it wasn't rational—I knew it even when it was happening—but what went through my mind was, What did I do to deserve that kind of contempt?

"You wouldn't need that hard shell," I said angrily, "if you weren't so soft inside."

Now *she* looked hurt, like I had taken information she had given me in confidence and used it against her. And I had. I should have stopped myself. I should not have said those words.

This kind of atmosphere didn't exist before she arrived. This conversation never would have happened between any combination of Bethany, Leon, Ed, and me.

"Sorry," I said. "Not professional. My bad."

I was going to leave it at that, because commenting on a coworker's emotional traits in that tone, in front of other employees—that's harassment. That's wrong. Especially when a man says it to a woman. Especially when an owner says it to a contractor he hired. Especially when a person says it to someone who asked them to mentor her. It's wrong on every level.

But I couldn't stop there. I had to throw in something to make up for being rude.

"It's not a bad thing, you know. To have a heart."

I should have kept my mouth shut. Sometimes, trying to make up for a faux pas just makes everything more awkward.

Now, they were both staring at me.

Good God, could one of you please show some expression so I have some idea how bad I screwed this up? It drives me crazy, that unreadable look she sometimes gets. Claire, I mean. How could she look at me like that?

"Dammit!" I slammed the folder on her desk and turned away.

As I walked back to my desk, I heard Claire ask, "What's with him?"

And Bethany said, "He's having his period."

19

I was supposed to take Lenny to the park after work to play whiffle ball, and then out for ice cream. But when I got to Miriam's house in Bethesda, he was still out with her husband, Milos. They had gone looking for crayfish in Rock Creek, and Milos either didn't bring his phone, or he left it in the car.

"I can't get ahold of him," Miriam said. "He knew you were coming. Or at least, I thought he did."

I knew how this would end. Lenny would get hot and cranky and Milos would get him a popsicle or a Sno-Cone. When they got back, Lenny would be too tired for whiffle ball, and too sugared-up for ice cream.

"It bothers you that Lenny is closer to Milos now, doesn't it?" Miriam asked.

"It does."

We were standing on the porch. I noticed Milos had put up a porch swing. He'd sit there on summer nights, I imagined, kissing my ex-wife. He'd sit there on fall afternoons, reading to my son.

"But you're still special," Miriam said. "I mean, to Lenny."

"I know. But I'm not his father. Not like his 'dad dad.'"

"You never were. Not biologically."

"Thanks for reminding me."

Lenny was the product of one of Miriam's affairs. Though I know she's ultimately responsible for her own actions, I still blame myself for some of what happened. She told me again and again she didn't like me going away on jobs. She didn't like not knowing when I'd be home. To me, it sounded like nagging. I had a lot on my plate already. Why couldn't she take care of herself?

Not a helpful way of thinking, but that's how it was. When we were married, it was the first time in my life I had to think about someone else, and I wasn't used to it. I had learned to look out for myself, learned that young, because no one else was looking out for me.

I figured everyone had that ability. I figured she could take care of herself while I was away on work. It never occurred to me that she just missed me, that she just liked having me around.

How could I have thought that when no one had ever missed me before? When no one else had ever cared if I was there or not? How could I have known she liked having me there when it seemed like all we did was fight?

"It's good for the home," Miriam said. "Those two getting close. I didn't think Milos would ever warm up to him like this. It makes the house feel different, when everyone bonds. You know?"

"I wish I knew."

I had a chance and I blew it. Not that I could ever imagine living with Miriam again. We'd kill each other. But as friends, we work. The trick is to take each other in small doses. Talk for fifteen minutes every couple of weeks. That's usually not enough time to get on each other's nerves.

"You look sad, Freddy."

"I'm not sad. I just feel like the years are wearing me down. Like everything's getting away from me."

"Everything?" Her voice had that leading tone that used to always piss me off, that tone that says, Are you sure you really mean *everything*?

"Yeah, everything. I have no wife. No family. I go to work and I come home to an empty apartment."

"Is work getting away from you?"

"No, actually. Work is going well. It's slow right now, so I'm thinking through a case that I'm not even really assigned to. It's an interesting one, even if I wish it didn't exist. Work, you know... Overall, work is fine."

I was picturing Claire in the blue suit she'd been wearing that day, leaning over her desk, reading. She gets this intense look on her face when she reads. Intense focus. And at the same time, it's natural, completely natural for her mind to be that engaged with what's in front of her.

"Who is she?" Miriam's question startled me out of my train of thought.

"Who is..." I saw the woman in white, tumbling down the rapids. "I don't know."

"You don't know? But you're in love with her?"

"In love with who?"

"That's what I'm asking. You tell me."

"I'm not in love."

"Yes, you are."

"Who would I be in love with?"

"I don't know, Freddy. I always wondered that myself. But I can see it."

"You're hallucinating."

"Promise you'll introduce me, okay? I want to meet her, give her some instructions on the proper care and maintenance of Freddy Ferguson."

If I was in love with anyone, I'm not sure I'd want them taking advice from Miriam. In our time together, we had lots of fights, another man's baby, and a divorce. If I ever do get another chance to make a life with someone, I hope to hell it goes better than that.

20

September 1

From the *Richmond Times-Dispatch*, Richmond, VA:

> Police recovered the body of a woman from the James River yesterday afternoon after kayakers discovered it in a snag of branches near Belle Isle. The woman, believed to be in her twenties, has not been identified. Investigators say the body may have been in the water for more than a week.

21

September 3
Washington, DC

Work was so slow, I was only in the office a few hours a day. Bethany came over to my desk, and we went through credit card charges line by line. She wanted to know which charges belong to which jobs so she could get the billing right.

Ed kept disappearing, which meant he was out networking. Which usually meant we'd have a job coming in soon. Maybe after Labor Day, when DC started to come back to life.

The whole office stank because Leon set one of his computers on fire. Or just about. He set up an old desktop machine on the floor by his desk. He hacked into it from his laptop, and then—his words—he "got root-level access" and disabled the fan that cools the central processor.

"There are op codes for that level of hardware access," he told us, "but you have to be root."

I nodded like Miriam used to do when I talked about boxing.

"I disabled the fan and the temperature monitor and kicked off a CPU-intensive job."

Translation: He made the machine work hard and overheat to the point where it started smoking. Now the thing was ruined and the office smelled like burnt chemicals. He was proud of himself. He called it "a successful proof of concept of a remote exploit causing physical damage."

Leon described this as "cyber-security research." My mother used to call it "too much time on your hands." Now,

Leon went on eBay looking for another cheap desktop to replace the one he just ruined.

Claire was at her desk by the window, staring quietly at her monitor. I had no idea what she was working on.

When Bethany and I finished the credit card bills, I went back to what I'd been doing on and off for more than ten days: combing through images on the internet.

The key was in my pocket, the one that came off the wrist of the woman in the woods. I should have given it to Sheriff Kessler. It should have gone into evidence, with the rest of her belongings. But they were still cleaning up from the storm down there, the police were short staffed, and Kessler didn't have time to pursue a case no one was asking about.

The cops in Richmond had the body. Or the coroner did. If this turned out to be a homicide, I'd give Kessler the key. Just then, I was the only one who knew it existed.

Well, me and Bethany. Whenever I started obsessing over something, she knew. And she knew that I knew that she knew. She wouldn't say anything for a long time, and then, out of the blue, she'd ask how it's going. Meaning, how is this thing that's been preoccupying you going? She was a good listener. Her attention encouraged me to talk, and as I talked, my thoughts would become more clear. That's the gift a good listener gives.

I told her about the woman, how she was dressed, how she went downstream. I showed her on a map how the streams from the eastern Blue Ridge feed into the Tye, and the Tye feeds into the James. The James flows through Richmond and that woman who washed up on Belle Isle is the right age, the right height and build. I know because I called Richmond and asked.

Claire got drawn in as I was telling the story. She drifted over to my desk, listened, asked about the woman's clothing, her physical condition, asked how I knew her hair wasn't really blond.

That was yesterday.

Today, I was scrolling through seahorse logos on Google, trying to find a match for my key.

I heard her stand and stretch behind me. Claire. I heard the swish of her pants as she approached. She crouched down beside me, a little too close, I thought, but no closer than Bethany or Leon would be. The field of her presence was just stronger than theirs.

She pointed to an image on my screen. This one was the wrong color. It was blue. It was wrong in other ways too.

"You see the spikes?" Claire said. She touched the monitor. She had to lean in to do that, and I leaned away. "Four spikes, on the back of the neck."

She picked up the key from my desk, said, "Yours has three spikes, and they're on the head."

Because her desk was behind me, she could see my monitor. I was sensitive about that usually, because with Bethany, I knew she watched, kept tabs on what I was looking at, figured out what I was up to, and then we'd play our game of I know and you know and when are we going to talk about it. That could sometimes get on my nerves because I don't like to answer questions until I'm good and ready. Kudos to Bethany for having the sense to know when to approach me and when not to.

Claire didn't have that sense yet. We hadn't been around each other long enough. And she was a different kind of person. More confident. More forward. If something grabbed her attention, she pursued it. If you didn't like that, well, that was your problem.

"The curl in the tail is different," she said as she examined the key. "This one is tight. That one," pointing to the screen, "has a looser curl."

Bethany was keeping tabs on our interaction. She was facing the other way, but she had eyes in the back of her head. And she eavesdropped on everything.

"What do you think the key goes to?" Claire asked.

She has a smooth voice. She enunciates clearly. What Leon said about her clothes, that they never have any wrinkles—that's true about the way she talks too. Her speech is a crisply tailored expression of her thought. I don't know how else to explain it.

Her skin is clear. She has tiny freckles on the bridge of her nose, very faint. Things I shouldn't notice. Bethany has freckles too, but I don't look at them because I don't care.

"I don't know what it goes to," I said. "That's what I'm trying to figure out."

Her hand was on the desk. She was standing, leaning with her hand on the desk. Slim fingers and smooth skin and—

"Go away," I said. "Leave me alone."

"Jeez, Freddy!"

She took that in stride. Kinda smiled. Touched my shoulder as she turned. Her way of saying, No hard feelings.

Her touch made me tense. What she and Bethany were talking about the other day—unwanted touch—it goes both ways, you know.

Don't put your spark in my gunpowder. I'm trying to keep this professional, and that takes a lot of discipline.

I thought about telling her, but how? What would I say?

"Look, I have a problem with you. A lot of feelings I didn't ask for and don't want, and you're not helping the situation by being yourself."

Who wants to be told that? How would that not be awkward? And then we'd both be second-guessing every gesture, every word.

I swear, between her and the woman in the woods, I thought I'd go nuts.

I put my elbows on the desk, dropped my head in my hands, and closed my eyes.

I knew Bethany was watching me. Even with my eyes shut, I could see her, twisted in her chair, looking over her shoulder at me.

Wait for it. Wait for it... Three, two, one.

"Why don't you go take a walk, Freddy?"

I knew she would say that.

She was right. I needed some air.

22

September 8
Washington, DC

The coroner's report from Richmond:

> White female, age 25–30. Multiple skull fractures, six
> broken vertebra, broken collar bone, 11 broken ribs...

All of that must have happened after I saw her, nature's final insult to her remains.

I read on... Yes, the report confirmed trauma likely occurred after death.

> Mechanism of Death: Respiratory Arrest
>
> Cause: Acute Intoxication.

From what? If she'd been drinking, I would have smelled it.
There it was, on the next line: Rohypnol and phenobarbital.
People can take Rohypnol without knowing it. It's the date rape drug. People get roofied all the time.

> Manner of Death: Undetermined.

Not natural, not accidental, not suicide or homicide.
Undetermined. Like her age, her identity, why she was there, what she was doing, who she was last with, why she had to die.
Undetermined is not an answer the human mind was built to accept.

Someone gave birth to her. Somebody somewhere loved her and didn't know she was gone.

Godammit, I couldn't unsee her.

23

At six fifteen, Claire and I were the last two in the office. I should have left an hour earlier, when Bethany and Leon left, but I got caught up in reading some old notes, stuff Ed had written about a case we did for an airline a few years back. I had forgotten Claire was there, and that's saying something, because usually I was hyperaware of her.

She snuck up on me while I was reading. I felt her before I heard her.

"I'm heading out," she said. "You want a ride?"

"You drove?"

"Yeah. It's raining."

I told her I had a date. Not a romantic one, not one I was looking forward to. It was a setup, courtesy of Miriam's husband. His boss's niece, a twenty-nine-year-old woman from Missouri, was new to town and I was supposed to be part of the welcome committee. Or a solo welcome committee. I had the feeling that Miriam was ultimately behind the whole thing, and my only interest in going was to see what kind of woman she'd pick for me.

I was supposed to have met Kendall when she first arrived in DC in June, but that got put off because I had to travel. In July, she had to go out of town. In August, I was in Central Virginia, drinking Old Fashioneds with Mrs. Jackson and finding corpses.

Now it was September, and after three months in town, she couldn't need much showing around. But a date was a date. I wasn't going to stand her up.

"You don't want to show up wet," Claire said.

"We're meeting on H Street, Northeast. I don't want you to go out of your way."

Claire lived up near the Woodley Park Metro, a few minutes north of the office. The place I was going was miles to the east.

"I don't mind."

"You sure?"

"It'll give me a chance to pick your brain."

When we got in the car, I texted Kendall, told her I'd be a few minutes late. Not that anyone cares about a few minutes these days, but it's a decent thing to do, to tell someone you still intend to show up, so they don't sit there wondering. Ten seconds of my time to save someone else ten minutes of angst is a good investment.

Claire asked me about Ed's days in the Bureau, how he kept his connections.

"He works at it, that's how. This is DC. The whole city is about connections."

"How'd you come to work for him?"

I told her the story. It was chance, really. Ed overheard me gently interrogating a guy—so gently, the guy didn't even know I was interrogating him. I got the information I needed. Ed was impressed. We ran into each other a few days later, got to talking, and the rest is history.

I pinged Kendall again when we were a few blocks from the bar. No response.

A minute later, Claire pulled into an empty parking space and asked if "my date" had responded to either of my texts.

"No. And don't call her a date."

"That's what you called her."

"Yeah, well, I don't need that kind of pressure when I'm about to hang out with someone I'm not even interested in."

"How do you know you're not interested?"

"I'm just not."

"Have you met her?"

"No."

"Jeez, Freddy, what kind of attitude is that? That's my nightmare date. A guy who hates me before I even show up."

She was smiling.

"I don't hate her. I'm just not interested."

"Mind if I come in with you? Keep you company until she arrives?"

"Yeah, that'll be great. When she walks in and sees me with another woman, she'll know the score."

Claire cut the engine and we went in.

I was afraid the place would be loud, but the jazz coming through the speakers was quiet enough for people to talk. And the place was surprisingly empty.

We took two stools at the bar. Claire ordered a glass of wine. I got ice water.

"Is that what you usually drink on dates?" she asked.

"I don't go on dates."

"No? Did marriage turn you sour?"

"How'd you know I was married?"

"Bethany told me."

"You guys talk about me behind my back?"

She shrugged as the bartender set our drinks down and asked if we were interested in seeing the menu.

I said no and Claire said yes.

"What, you're gonna sit here and eat while I'm on a date with someone else?"

"I just want to see what they serve here," she said. "Besides, you said it wasn't a date."

"Yeah, well, in answer to your question, no, marriage did not make me bitter."

"But you don't date?"

"What do you care?"

"Just asking. Why are you so touchy about it?"

"Why does every woman I know have to pry?"

"Because you don't tell people things. You don't say anything."

"When I have something to say, I say it."

"And I'm supposed to just sit quietly and wait for that to happen? What kind of date are you?"

"Are we on a date here? You and I?"

She shrugged.

"'Cause I don't think my other date is going to like that."

"She's not a date," Claire said.

"Jesus! I can't win with you."

The next thing she said—I wasn't sure I heard it right, because a busboy behind the bar set down a case of beer too hard and rattled all the bottles together. And she said it kind of softly, into her wine glass as she was about to take a sip. What I heard was, "Oh, I think you can."

"What?"

My reaction was so sharp, she almost spilled her wine. She looked at me wide-eyed, like a deer in the headlights.

"What what?" she asked. "What did I say?"

"What *did* you say?"

And then I heard it again. "Oh, I think you can."

The voice coming through the speakers, the woman singing jazz. It was part of the song.

The worst part was, she got it. Claire put it together. Me saying I couldn't win with her and then hearing "Oh, I think you can." She got this big smile and said, "Did you think I said that? That you could win?"

She took a sip of wine, right through her smile, her eyes laughing at me the whole time.

The bartender came back and she ordered a plate of vegetables and hummus, and one of fried calamari.

"Why'd you do that?" I asked.

"Order food?"

"Yeah. You'll still be eating when she walks in."

"Your girlfriend was supposed to meet you fifteen minutes ago and she hasn't even texted. She's not going to show."

"What makes you so sure?"

"Freddy... You really haven't been dating, have you? Haven't you ever been ghosted?"

"Yeah, but that was so long ago, ghosting wasn't even a word."

We got dinner after the appetizers. Salmon for her, a steak for me.

She told me about her grandmother who had raised her, how Claire had to get her into a home for dementia care, watch her go downhill, sell her house, wrap up her affairs, bury her, deal with lawyers and the estate.

She told me about her years in New York, the corporate life, and the first case she'd worked on, the one that made her want to be an investigator. She made some mistakes, but in the end, she managed to bring down some people that the DEA had been after for some time.

I asked if there was anything she's *not* good at.

"Life."

"That can't be true."

School and jobs, she said, were easy because the goals were defined. All you had to do was put in the time and effort and you'd make it.

"There's more to it than that," I said.

"Like what?"

"Skill. Ability."

She shrugged. "Well, whatever the case, work always came easy. The rest of life, not so much."

The couple beside us was on their first date. It was obvious, and it was awkward. The guy was maybe thirty. The woman, a little younger. The guy kept trying to force the conversation, talking mostly about himself. Bragging about his job, his condo, his two cars. The woman just sat there quietly, nodded, tried to change the subject now and then, but the only thing the guy could talk about with any enthusiasm was himself.

When they left, Claire said, "That's why I don't date."

"'Cause of guys like him?"

She shook her head. "Because I'm like her."

"How do you mean?"

"I'm an awful date. If a guy doesn't have something interesting to say, I just tune out. I can't fake it. I can't just smile and nod. I get angry when people waste my time."

That first sentence rang in my head the whole night.

I'm an awful date.

How could she think that about herself? I wanted to tell here right then and there, "You're an awesome date. You're real. You don't bullshit or play games. You're actually *here*, present and engaged, and everything you say has real thought behind it. How much more can a man ask for in a date? How often does he even get that?"

But I didn't say that. I was co-owner of the business that employed her. She was a coworker, a subordinate, a contractor looking for full-time employment, and I had a say in whether or not she'd get it. I had experience in the field. She didn't. She had asked me to mentor her. I was in a position of trust. Trust and power, and those are two things you don't abuse.

But it killed me to hear her put herself down like that.

If she put herself side by side against another woman—any other woman—how could she think she came up short? How could she even remotely think that?

I was up for hours after she dropped me off. I kept picking up the phone, kept almost calling her, because I couldn't stand the thought of anyone putting her down. Not even her. I wanted to set her straight.

But each time, I stopped myself. It wasn't my place to say such things to her. She didn't come to work to be evaluated as date material.

Every time I put the phone down, the cycle started again. I had to tell her what a standout she was, because she was the only person in the world who didn't see it, and that was a shame.

That's what I did that night. Picked up the phone, put it down. Picked it up, put it down.

The problem was me, and I knew it, but I couldn't stop. Finally, I had enough. I knew exactly who to call to fix this problem. A risk-averse, rule-following librarian who never colors outside the lines; the antidote to passion, always ready to stick the pin of her cautious pragmatism into the balloon of my enthusiasm.

She sounded groggy when she picked up.

"Freddy?"

"Hey, Bethany, what you were talking about in the office the other day—where is that line?"

"Freddy, what the fuck? It's like two a.m."

"It is?"

"What are you talking about? What line?"

"You were talking about harassment. Like, there's a point where it's okay, where a compliment is an honest compliment, and there's a point where it's not okay. Where it's too familiar. Where even though it's well intentioned, it's not appropriate. Where is that line?"

"What the hell are you talking about?"

"I don't know."

"Are you intoxicated?"

What a funny choice of word. Intoxicated.

She could have asked if I was drunk, and I could have given her a definite no.

But intoxicated?

I think I was.

"Freddy," she said, "if you're worried about harassing someone and you're not sure where the line is, the best advice I can give you is *don't*. Whatever action you think might cross that line, don't do it. Because if you're not a hundred percent sure you're on the right side of the line, there's a pretty good chance you're on the wrong side. Now go to sleep."

See what I mean about her? They ought to put her in a chapel in Vegas to dissuade love-drunk couples from wrecking their lives on the wings of passion. She'd have them all sobered up in no time, getting fitted for chastity belts.

She hung up, and I took her advice. That night I made a choice. A very difficult and painful choice.

Whatever I felt about Claire Chastain, I would keep to myself. And that sucked. It just plain sucked.

If I like a woman, I have no problem showing it. Unless it's not allowed. When there's no acceptable outlet for your feelings, what are you supposed to do with them?

Same thing you do in the ring when someone's punching you in the face. You suck it up and keep going because crying isn't going to help.

I would build a dam, and all the feelings that flowed through me when she walked past, when I looked at her, when she talked to me, they'd all go behind the dam.

If I was infatuated, it would be my problem, not hers. I wasn't going to put that on anyone else.

Someday, this love would pass, like everything else in life, and it would pass with a minimum of grief, without troubling her or my coworkers or anyone else.

Oh, and Kendall. She texted back while Claire and I were finishing dinner. She got caught in a meeting, left her phone on her desk, forgot all about our date on H Street. I told her we'd catch up some other time.

24

September 10

Slow day at the office. I called the police in Richmond to follow up on that body. No missing person reports matched her description.

The beating she took in the river destroyed her teeth. Her whole face, actually. Like nature joined in the conspiracy to erase her. They couldn't identify her through dental records.

The Richmond police sent her DNA to a number of registries in hopes of a match. 23andMe, My Heritage, Ancestry DNA, Living DNA, and some specialists too. Places that test for rare genetic conditions, research labs to which she or a relative might have submitted samples. They were waiting to hear back.

After talking to Richmond, I called Sheriff Kessler in Nelson County.

"Hey," he said, "I was gonna call you."

"You got something?"

"A little something."

"Lay it on me."

"Remember the letter? On the desk in her room? It had only one set of prints on it, so I think it's safe to assume they're hers. We ran a check on them and it came up empty. No arrests. She didn't hold any kind of job that required a background check either, or her prints would have been on file. A lot of states fingerprint teachers and other workers before they're cleared. Not her. She was in some other line of work.

"But get this. The cops in Richmond submitted a print from the body that washed up on Belle Isle. They had a hell of a time getting one because she was so waterlogged. You ever see how the coroner does this? First, they drain fluids from the body to reduce the bloating, then they pump some back in to try to restore the plasticity of living flesh. Then they ink her.

"The only usable print they could get was her left ring finger. It matched one we pulled from the letter in the hotel room. A sharp-eyed technician in the BCI lab noticed because both requests came in on the same day. The girl who washed up on Belle Isle is the one who disappeared from the Olympic. Oh—and one other thing."

"What's that?"

"I'll text it to you. A little something Sherri found inside the suitcase, stuck to a piece of clothing. Nothing to get excited about, but maybe you can make something of it."

My phone chimed a minute later with photos showing the front and back of a printed sticker. Or, really, just a small piece of what had been a sticker. It was part of a baggage tag.

On one side was the letter I. Airport codes are three letters, and this was the rightmost, the last of the three. On the other side was a fragment of barcode. Not enough for a barcode scanner to make sense of.

There's a whole website dedicated to airport codes. I know because I looked at it many times when Ed and I worked on cases for a major airline.

How many airports in US have a three-letter code ending in I?

Survey says... thirty-two, starting with Abilene, Texas (ABI) and ending with West Palm Beach, Florida (PBI). Our mystery woman passed through one of them. I was hoping it wasn't a busy one like Baltimore (BWI) or Kansas City (MCI).

The sticker meant the airport ending in I was her destination. She'd pick up the bag at baggage claim, and the next time she came to the airport, they'd remove that tag and put on a new one for the new destination.

I showed Claire the photo, gave her some background, asked what she thought.

She said she always tore the tag off herself. "They put it right on the handle and it gets in my way."

"Sometimes they're hard to tear," I said. "Our mystery woman rips it off, maybe it takes a few tries. A piece of it sticks to her pants or her sweater, winds up back in the suitcase later."

"Okay," Claire said, "where do you go from here?"

"You tell me."

"Scan the code?"

Now Leon dropped in on the powwow. He took a look and said the barcode wasn't scannable. There wasn't enough of it left.

So, I asked Claire, "What next?"

"The letter I."

"Yeah?"

"We go online and find a list of all the airport codes that end with I."

"Done," I said. "We have thirty-two in the US. What next?"

I could see the wheels turning, but I seemed to have her stumped.

"Where do you even start with something as vague as 'an unidentified woman flew into a US commercial airport sometime before August nineteenth?'"

I told her that was a pessimistic way of looking at it.

"Well, where *do* you start?"

"We've already started. The airport won't tell us anything other than where she might have been, and that's just one more piece of the puzzle. There might be a hundred pieces, or a thousand, but each one adds to the picture."

Bethany couldn't resist the sight of Claire, Leon, and me in conversation. Her instincts told her she was missing out on something. She made a beeline for my desk. She didn't ask for a summary of the talk so far because she'd been listening the whole time. She always listened.

"What codes you got?" Leon asked. "What are the thirty-two airports?"

I showed them the list I had cut and pasted from airportcodes.org.

For a few seconds, everyone was silent. Then Claire said, "West Palm. Start there."

I told her that's what I was thinking.

"What? How?" asked Bethany.

"The seahorse," Claire said. "Try to connect the new clue to one we already have. Palm Beach is the only airport on that list that's by the sea."

I love the way her mind works.

"What if that doesn't pan out?" I asked. "What next?"

"Smaller airports."

"Why?"

"Fewer people flying in means a smaller pool of travelers to scan through. But how could we even scan through them? That would be weeks of TSA videos and tens of thousands of people. And you'd have to do all the looking because you're the only one who knows what she looks like."

I shook my head. "TSA isn't going to give us access to their videos."

"Not even for a murder investigation?"

"If it was a confirmed murder—and it's not—they might give the Nelson County sheriff access to the videos. Not a private firm. Not a private firm that isn't even technically on the case of a death whose cause is still classified as undetermined."

"Okay," Claire sighed. "So, we start with what we have. A seahorse. A letter. Photos of her clothing. That's it?"

"This isn't the corporate world, Claire. There's no accounting department keeping a neat ledger of events with dated receipts for us to inspect and verify. We're the accountants. We build the ledger with whatever scraps we can find, before the winds of time blow them all away."

"That's very poetic, Freddy."

"Don't encourage him," Bethany says.

25

September 17

After a week of fruitless searches, the airport codes led us nowhere. We couldn't get information from TSA, and even if we could have, there was no way to formulate a question specific enough for them to answer. We were looking for a woman with dyed blond hair and dark roots who passed through an airport ending in I on her way to Central Virginia.

Finding a needle in a haystack was one thing. Finding a needle in thirty-two haystacks when you couldn't adequately describe the needle was hopeless.

I told Claire, Bethany, and Leon not to waste any more time on this. It wasn't our case, and we weren't getting paid.

I told myself the same thing, but a fat lot of good that did. All it took to break my resolve was a call from a cop in Richmond named Willy Banks.

"Just wanted to pass this along to you, because you seemed concerned. We heard back from all the DNA places. No one has a record of her."

"So, what do you do with a case like this?"

"Put it on ice. Wait for someone who misses her to step forward. Which gets less and less likely as time goes by. But there's one thing..."

"What?"

"None of the DNA companies had a record of her, but one had a tombstone."

"A tombstone? Like a rock to put on her grave?"

"No. It means something different in archival record systems. You have a pen? I'll give you a name and phone number, and a case number too. You'll have to reference that since we don't have a name attached to the DNA sample."

I wrote it down. Vivek Parmar at a company called Mitogenic. He had a 737 area code. That would be Austin, Texas, or thereabouts.

"He's a tech guy," said the cop. "Talk to him. We don't have the resources to pursue this any further. If you learn anything, let us know."

I called as soon as I hung up with Banks. It was six thirty on a Friday in DC, five thirty in Austin. Vivek Parmar had left for the weekend. I'd have to wait till Monday.

26

Six thirty-five, I got up to leave. I was supposed to meet the elusive Kendall in Adams Morgan later for dinner. And now I knew Miriam was behind this whole setup because she texted me not to stand the poor woman up this time. I don't know where she gets her information. I never stood her up.

Bethany stopped me at the door on my way out.

"What are you doing here? I thought you left at five with everyone else."

"Where are you going?" she asked.

"Do you always have to answer a question with a question?"

"Do you?"

"I'm going to Adams Morgan, smartass. Why do you ask?"

"Drop this off at Claire's."

She handed me Claire's phone.

I was thinking I could go home, shower, and change before meeting Kendall. An extra stop to drop off the phone would throw a wrench into that plan.

"Why do you look hesitant?" Bethany asked.

Because I've been doing everything I can to avoid that woman. Why torture myself?

"I had other plans," I said.

"It's not far out of your way. I mean, if you're going up there anyway."

"No. I'll give it to her."

I knew before I even saw it what her apartment would look like. Tastefully decorated, but spare. Not the kind of place with piles of pillows on the couch and tables cluttered with knickknacks. Not the kind with posters all over the walls. More like one artwork per wall, framed. Maybe one table with some rocks piled up, like Zen rocks, if that's what they're called.

Three or four flat oval-shape stones neatly balanced. The kind of thing I'd bump into and knock over.

The whole place would be spotless and dust free. Everything in its place. That's what happens to a room when a perfectionist lives in it.

She'd hate my place. Not that it's cluttered or dirty. Okay, it's probably dirty by her standards. But it's not cluttered because I don't keep stuff I don't need. And so what if I don't always put things back?

As for colors? For her place? Blue, white, green. But pale green, not bright. Nothing too garish and nothing too heavy. This is what was going through my mind as I got off the elevator.

I smelled seafood in the hall outside her door. Shrimp, and maybe clams. She pulled the door open just as I raised my fist to knock, and I just about punched her in the face. So far, so good.

"Hello, Freddy."

"I have your phone." I shoved it at her, but she didn't take it.

She was wearing a white apron, freshly pressed, over a dark blue t-shirt. Her hair was tied back. Dark strips of it fell on either side of her face, accentuating the soft angle of her cheekbones.

A normal woman, she dresses okay at work. And then in the evening, if she's going out, she turns it up a notch. Looks really good, maybe for a guy, maybe just for her girlfriends.

This was the opposite. Claire dressed professionally at work. Very sharp. It inspired confidence and respect. Here I saw her for the first time dressed down, and it had this effect on me that was deeper than if she'd dressed up. This was her with her guard down, her natural self, at home and at ease. There's a feeling of intimacy, honor even, when a guarded person lets you see them like that.

She didn't take the phone, just stepped back and told me to put it on the table.

The little side table there against the wall with the flat oval rocks balanced on top of each other. Didn't I tell you?

And didn't I tell you I'd knock them down? Walked right into the corner of that table. Got a nice sharp poke in the thigh.

She knelt to pick up the rocks before I could get a start. So I didn't kneel. I didn't want to be that close to her.

She handed the stones up to me and I tried to restack them, but they were all off balance. It looked like the work of a toddler, or a late-stage Jenga tower built by a drunk. She took one look at it, and I could tell exactly what her perfectionist mind thought of that mess.

"You like Italian food?" she asked. She was smiling. A warm, white smile. I had to get out of there before she offered me something to eat.

"Love it."

"Frutti di mare?"

"My wife used to make the best."

Oops. That took the starch out of her for a second. Fucking Miriam finds a way to ruin everything.

"Well I'm just a beginner," she said. "You hungry?"

Leave, Freddy. Get out of here while you can.

"Sure."

"Sure?" she repeated uncertainly. "You don't sound sure."

"Are you offering?"

"I'm offering." Her smile was back. She shut the door, and I felt trapped.

The apartment was lighter than I expected. Good natural light from the windows.

"Come here."

We went to the kitchen. I felt awkward walking behind her. She's five foot six and 135 pounds. I know because she showed her license when she was filling out papers for the job. I know her birthday too. She's thirty-three.

But five-six, 135... I'm six-three, 240. I felt like an elephant.

She has very straight posture, light steps, grace in every movement.

In the kitchen she turned around, caught me looking. I mean, I was looking at her shoulders. I could see the frame of the bones, perfectly level. I was looking at her shoulders, and she turned around, and then I'm looking at her front, at about the height of her collar bones, and my eyes went down instead of up, because—that's just what happens sometimes. Try being a man if you're not one already. You'll see what I mean.

I forced my eyes up, looked her in the face, and she just looked friendly. An honest, open, friendly person. That wasn't how she came off when we first met in Vegas. She was tough, all business, which was the right way to be in the situation. This side didn't show.

Bright smile, warm brown eyes, smooth skin. She didn't need to be this friendly or this close. I didn't need to be in her kitchen. I had no business here.

This happened once when I was married to Miriam. I was on a case out of town, and I wound up in an unexpectedly tight place with a woman I had grown to like. I kept reminding myself I was married. That pulled me through. The thought of Miriam waiting at home kept me on the straight and narrow. Ironically, that was the week she was conceiving Lenny with another man whose identity I still don't know.

I couldn't tell myself I was married now. I couldn't play that card because the dealer took it back.

So, what do I do? What do I do?

"What's in frutti di mare?" she said. Like a little quiz. She was relaxed, cheerful.

"Clams, mussels, shrimp."

"Uh huh." Her eyes had a dark, warm luster. They flashed when they catch the light. Her tone invited me to go on.

I took a step back, because I could smell the scent of her skin. We were in this little kitchen with all this stuff cooking, and what I smelled was her.

"What about herbs?" she asked.

"Depends," I said. "Parsley. Basil if you want."

"Taste mine."

She put some linguine in a bowl, seafood on top, and handed it to me.

"You can eat over the sink if you want."

How did she know where I like to eat?

She made a bowl for herself. A strip of linguine dropped from her mouth as she ate. She smiled.

"This is good," I said. Like I couldn't remember the word *great*. "The pasta is just right. Al dente."

"Yeah?"

"I don't like it too soft. The shrimp—" Don't say it, Freddy! "The shrimp is overcooked."

Jesus, you asshole!

But it didn't faze her. She said, "I know." There was a simple brightness in her voice.

"I know what you did," I said.

"What?"

"You sautéed them first, then you threw them in with the sauce."

"You're right. I like them sautéed, because they stay firm."

"But they were done after you sautéed them. Then the heat in the saucepan overcooked them."

She looked thoughtfully into the pot of seafood, sucking a bit of sauce off her finger. "You're right," she said. "Next time I'll keep the shrimp separate and add them on top when I serve."

Next time? Was she planning on inviting me back? No, wait. She didn't invite me here in the first place. I was returning her phone.

Maybe she meant next time she cooked this dish. Did that mean this was a practice run for someone else? Was I helping her refine her recipe for the man she really liked? The thought made me jealous, but I told myself it was just as well. If she had a man in her life, it would give me more incentive to back off, to stop thinking about her.

Why did she have to invite me in? Why couldn't she have just taken the phone and said thanks?

In my head, I heard Miriam scolding, "She's your coworker! Act like Ed is watching. And don't forget about Kendall! If you stand her up again…"

I banged my bowl down on the counter. The fork went flying into the sink.

"Shit! I have a date."

"Now?"

"Yeah. I totally forgot."

I felt like an ass for being so rude. For not even finishing the meal she cooked.

I turned to leave the kitchen and she slid in front of me, adjusted my collar.

"It was folded over," she said. "You don't want to show up for a date like that."

I went past her without saying thanks, and inwardly rebuked myself for my rudeness.

She slipped by me again, got to the front door first, held it open.

"Good luck, Freddy!"

I bumped the table, knocked the rocks off, said goodbye from out in the hall, turning to look once more at her while I still could. She was looking down at the stones on the floor, trying hard to keep her smile from breaking into a laugh.

27

I got to the restaurant early, but I wasn't hungry. I was too rattled.

And wouldn't you know it, Kendall was beautiful. Smart, funny, down to earth, and just all-around lovely.

Her vibe told me that Miriam *did* set this up as a date. She asked earnest questions and awaited my answers with bright-eyed expectation. She heard I was a detective. She heard I used to box.

Kendall had been waiting since June to meet me. That's when Miriam first hatched this scheme. Before Claire came into the picture.

What kind of hopes had been brewing in poor Kendall all these months? She kept searching my face for signs of approval. On any other night, in any other lifetime, she'd be a better date than I ever would have hoped for.

But not tonight. She just couldn't measure up—no one could—to what I just left behind.

I felt horrible for this woman across the table. She had it all, but I wasn't responding to any of it, and it was killing her confidence. I could see it take the wind right out of her. She was going to leave this meal feeling like a failure.

What could I do to salvage her self-esteem? I couldn't compliment her because all my compliments just then were reserved for someone else. So, what then? Buy her a drink? She was already drinking her wine too fast because she was foundering.

I couldn't do this to her. How could I give her what she deserved? Let her know what a ray of sunshine she was?

When I lapsed into silence, she looked glum and lost heart. She stared quietly at her plate for a long time, but to her credit, she did not pick up her phone. She did not try to distract herself.

Finally, she asked, "What's wrong?"

"I think I'm in love."

She lit up instantly. "Oh my God, tell me!"

How is it that for years and years there's not a single person of interest on the horizon, and then two of the best women you could hope to meet cross your path in the same night?

We ditched the meal. Neither of us was hungry.

We walked to Kalorama Park and talked for an hour. It scared the crap out of me, the way I went on about Claire. I knew I was lost because I'd made a vow less than ten days earlier to keep this to myself, and I'd already blown it.

Kendall was delighted.

"Oh my God! So, there is still hope! People *do* still fall for each other!"

"I don't know about the *each other* part. All I know is one person fell."

"And you weren't even trying!"

"Trying?" I said. "I'm trying to avoid it. I'm trying to make it *not* happen."

"But why?"

I told her about the agency, me being a fifty-percent partner. I told her about bringing Claire on board. I had invited her in. I was technically her boss. That put me in a position of power. I was her mentor too. She asked me to teach her. That put me in a position of trust.

Claire was a consummate professional, one hundred percent dedicated to developing her career. How could I be anything less?

"What if you'd met outside of work?" Kendall asked. "What if the power thing and professional trust wasn't an issue?"

Funny, I had never thought of that.

"I don't think anything would have happened."

"Why not?"

"I wouldn't have got to know her. I wasn't looking for anyone, so I wouldn't have tried. We would have been two ships passing in the night. But you know what really sucks? Work is the only thing I do. And I think it's the only thing she does. Where else would either of us meet anyone? And I think that's true for a lot of people.

"There's no in-person interaction anymore. Hardly anyone goes to church—at least around here. Hardly anyone belongs to leagues or social clubs, like our grandparents did. Work is the one place where people spend enough time together to actually get to know each other, and it's the one place where developing a deep, meaningful relationship is forbidden. What kind of world is this?"

"There's a reason for that," she said. "I've been on the wrong side of that equation and it was so uncomfortable, I left the company. I mean, that's part of why I moved to DC. I wanted to get far away from that whole mess. If a woman's not interested in a guy, and she has to work in an office with him, and he's persistent, it's just..." She shivered. "No! It's just no, is what it is. You haven't, like, hit on her, have you?"

"No," I said. "The dynamics are all wrong. I put myself in her shoes, ask what if I was the new person coming on board and my boss is also my teacher, and I really want to do well, and I really want this job? Whenever I think of it like that, which is about fifteen times a day, I come up with the same answer as you. No. It's just a flat-out no."

"Yeah, well... I think you're doing the right thing. This is the kind of thing where, if it turned bad, it would be *really* bad. Lots of fallout. For her, for you, for the company. How many people work there?"

"Five."

"Yeah, definitely no. A big corporation could absorb something like that, but a group of five? Uh-uh. God, that sucks."

"Tell me about it."

"So, what do you do if you can't let her know how you feel?"

"Burn in hell."

"Ooh!" she teased. "So dramatic!"

"Seriously, though, that's what it feels like. But it'll pass. Everything does."

"And you're just going to let it?"

28

Kendall's question rang through my head all night.

You're just going to let it?

It was the same challenge I had heard from Mrs. Jackson a few weeks earlier.

Can you really unsee her, Freddy? Can you unsee your final glimpse of her and be at peace?

I cannot unsee the woman in white.

I cannot unknow Claire Chastain.

So—no, Kendall. No, Mrs. Jackson.

I am not at peace.

Thanks for asking.

29

Monday, September 20
Washington, DC

Vivek Parmar, the lead I'd gotten from the police in Richmond, struck me right off the bat as an intelligent guy. His speech was crisp, clear, and direct. He was Indian, but his accent told me he had spent time in England.

He said that when Mitogenic was founded more than twenty years ago, they did only specialized testing for rare genetic conditions. Over time, they expanded to do all kinds of testing. Then they put up a consumer website where anyone could submit their DNA and learn about their genetic heritage, their ancestors, even living relatives.

"We also warn people if they have genetic markers for things like breast cancer and Alzheimer's, but only if they check the box that says they want to know. Some people don't want to know. Why ruin today with worries of tomorrow?"

I gave him the case number from Richmond, the woman who washed up on Belle Isle. He was familiar with it. Cops trying to track down the family of a Jane Doe.

"You're with the police?" he asked.

"I'm an investigator." Which was true. "Detective Banks gave me the case number and asked me to follow up." That was also true.

If Parmar had asked flat out whether I was an officer of the law, whether I had any legal standing to compel him to turn over what amounted to protected medical information, I would have had to say no.

Luckily, it didn't come to that. He wanted to help, and if I sounded like I was officially connected to the Richmond police... Well, it was an honest mistake on his part. A forgivable assumption.

"Let me just pull it up on my monitor," he said.

After some typing and a brief pause: "Yeah, right. White female. Found in a river in Virginia. Sad case."

"How do you know she was white?" I asked. "From the case report or the DNA?"

"The case report. And the DNA that Richmond sent. We don't have the prior DNA sample she submitted. All we have is a tombstone."

"She submitted?" That was news to me. "She submitted a sample herself?"

"A year and a half ago. But all that's left is the tombstone."

"What's a tombstone?"

"It's a marker that tells us we once had the record, but it's been deleted. At least, it was supposed to be deleted. We still have some fragments in a database of rare genetic sequences that some of our researchers in Chicago are using to study gene therapy treatments. Our AI matched her sample against those."

"But you don't have any other info on her? No name? No demographic info?"

"Nope. Technically, those remaining fragments should have been erased too. It's hard to weed everything out of the system when these lab guys are copying bits of data all over the place. We have labs in seven states. Some of these researchers load up a workstation with twenty terabytes of data and do analysis on their own. We're trying to stop that because it leads to problems like this."

Parmar explained that when the company received a request to delete DNA records, they had a legal responsibility to fully delete them. At the same time, to satisfy auditing requirements, they had to keep a record of the fact that they once did have the info. That was the tombstone.

Like the kind in graveyards, this tombstone had dates. Our Jane Doe had submitted her DNA eighteen months ago, and then deleted it six weeks after submission. Why?

I asked Parmar.

"That's a good question," he said.

"Is that common?"

"Not really. We occasionally get deletion requests from on high. Someone gets put in the witness protection program. The government doesn't want them to be identified by saliva left on a coffee cup at Starbucks. Someone is doing sensitive government work— Wait, can you see I'm doing air quotes? If they're doing 'Sensitive Government Work,' their whole family gets wiped from our database. Think about it. A foreign government wants to control an American agent. Identify their family and go after them. The US doesn't want to make it easy for them, and DNA searches are easy."

"You think she might have been doing government work?"

"I don't know. I know no more than you do about her. And the government isn't the only one to request deletions. We've had a few Hollywood celebs twist our arms to remove data. They're scared of being cloned."

"Are you serious?"

"Yeah. A celebrity is their own brand. You steal their DNA, it's like stealing the plans for a secret fighter jet. Now you can make your own copy, get rich off it. Theoretically, anyway."

"Celebrities worry about being cloned?"

"What else do they have to worry about? Give an anxious person enough free time, they'll invent something to fear."

"If she was a celebrity," I said, "someone would have reported her missing by now."

"And if she was doing government work," Parmar said, "she may never be claimed."

Those words made my heart sink.

"Is there anything else you can give me? Anything at all? Because I have a feeling that somebody somewhere loved this person and doesn't know she's dead."

"There is one thing."

"What?"

"These deletion requests usually have a corresponding administrative record showing who requested the deletion and when. Hers doesn't. The data was just wiped. We have no record of who ordered it or why."

"How could that happen?"

"I don't know. Maybe whoever wanted to get rid of her DNA record had a contact inside the company."

30

At 10:30, Ed called the team together for an informal meeting. We gathered around Bethany's desk as Ed described upcoming work. We had a couple traces to start on right away. One was a man, the other a couple. Both skipped out on some hefty debts.

Ed assigned the couple to Bethany. Leon got the guy. Claire would work with both of them to see how the process worked. It's mostly done online these days. You can track people through public databases, social media, sites that sell information about their cell phone location history. If you're a licensed investigator, you have access to a few other tools as well.

It's not the most exciting work, but it can pay pretty well, depending on how much money the person owes and how bad the creditor wants to find them.

We rarely have to leave the office for this kind of work. If we think we've located someone in New York or Chicago or Nacogdoches, we'd contact someone there to try to make a positive identification. If we didn't have a contact in the town, Ed or I would go find the person. And we'd try to cultivate a contact so we didn't have to travel there again.

Ed mentioned a potentially bigger job coming down the pike. He was still ironing out the details on that one.

I could read him though. Whatever it was, it wasn't in the bag yet. He wanted to keep the team's spirit up after what had been an unusually long dry spell.

After the pep talk, we met privately in his office.

Ed stood by the wall behind his desk with a thoughtful look. If this was going to be a serious talk, if anything worrisome was going on, he'd have been sitting.

"What's your confidence on this big gig?" I asked.

"It's just a question of when they want to pull the trigger. Not yet, but maybe in two weeks or a month. A company out on the Dulles Corridor is leaking data. They have a couple employees in mind, but they're not sure. The data isn't going out through the internet. Their guys are carrying it out the door and probably delivering it in person."

"So why do they want to wait?"

"Nothing's happened in the past couple of months. They're watching some people internally. If they see something fishy, they'll call us to follow them outside of work."

"And till then?"

"I have my ears open. I'm working my contacts. It's never been this dry. Things usually pick up after Labor Day."

"Well maybe things are running a little late this year. You want me to go down to half pay?"

"Do you mind? I took the cut the first week of August."

"Why didn't you tell me? Knock me down to half pay and you can bring me back up when we get busy again."

He asked how Claire was working out.

"Great."

Ed told me he wanted to put her in front of this potential client. "The company out by Dulles. I think she'll impress them."

That told me something right there. That told me Ed had already decided to keep Claire. Her three-month contract would be ending in a few weeks and we had to either hire her or let her go. If he wanted to put her in front of a client whose job wouldn't even start for a few weeks—a job that could run for a couple months—that was an implicit promise to the customer. He was telling them this is what you'll be getting when you hire us.

Of course, he still needed my agreement on all hiring decisions. On the basis of her work so far, I could raise no objections. There wasn't a single argument I could make to say she wasn't good for the company.

"I heard you have a hobby," Ed said.

That was his word for cases I looked into on my own time.

"A woman in white," he added. "Bethany told me. How wrapped up are you this time?"

"Do I seem distracted?"

"Very."

"I didn't know it was showing."

Ed flashed a rare smile. "You always show it and you never seem to know."

"Yeah, I guess this one's pretty bad."

And Ed didn't know the half of it.

"Why don't you take some time off?" he said.

"Whenever I do that, I start to go crazy. You know I need something to work on."

"Work on that," he said.

"On what?"

"On not going crazy."

Eleven fifteen, I left for the day. Left Claire and Bethany and Leon huddled around Leon's computer.

I went to the gym, hit the heavy bag, felt the shock of the punches travel up my arms. The dent in the side of the bag grew deeper with each hook.

When I finished, soaked in sweat, I turned to see two young guys and a woman staring wide-eyed. If I looked like I was trying to murder the thing, it's because I was.

You always show it and you never seem to know.

31

Back in my apartment with a couple of cartons of Chinese food, I opened up my laptop. What Claire had said about trying to tie our clues together stuck with me. We had a key with a seahorse and an airport code ending in I. Claire said look at PBI, Palm Beach International. It's by the sea.

You're more likely to find a business with a seahorse logo there than in landlocked cities like ABI-Abilene or BOI-Boise. Of course, there's Bellingham too. BLI. That's on Puget Sound.

I asked Google a simple question. Where do seahorses live? The best answer was short and to the point: "They prefer shallow tropical and temperate waters close to the coastline."

Score one for Claire. I'd start with Palm Beach, where the water is warm.

I pulled up Palm Beach on Google maps. What was I looking for? I didn't know yet. I was just poking around. Like when someone hires us to follow a suspect. How do we learn about him? Just watch. See where he goes, who he talks so. Live in his world long enough, you start to get to know him.

The beating I put on the heavy bag made me hungry. I'd been trying to eat the Chinese food with chopsticks so I wouldn't wolf it all down, but it was so damn greasy, I couldn't keep hold of it.

I caved, grabbed a fork, started eating too much too fast.

PBI, according to the map, was about a mile and a half east of the Atlantic, in Palm Beach proper. The ritzy resort area was West Palm Beach, which was an island.

Huh! I'd learned something already. Not that it had any bearing on the case, but I felt smarter now than I had five minutes before. Now I knew that seahorses like warm shallow water and West Palm Beach is an island. I tucked those facts away, in case I ever wound up sitting next to someone on a plane who needed to know these things.

I zoomed in on the map. Golf courses, lakes, marinas. The train ran along Route 95. To the east, Dixie Highway cut through the city from north to south.

I zoomed out to see what else was in the area. Palm Beach Gardens and Jupiter to the north. Boynton Beach and Delray Beach to the south.

That got me thinking...

I grabbed my phone, found the photo Sheriff Kessler sent of that scrap of paper recovered from the garbage can.

> ...out of the frying pan, into the fire. You're
> everything I wanted to get away from when I left Del...

What if Del wasn't a person, but a place?

The paper was torn there, right at the letter "l," but what if Del was Delray?

Our mystery woman flew into an airport whose code ended in "I" because that "I" was on a destination tag in her suitcase. I knew she left that place too, because she ended up in Virginia.

Did she fly into Palm Beach, do something in Delray, and then leave?

What the hell did Delray look like anyway?

I zoomed in. The map view showed the usual South Florida sprawl. I knew without having to visit that the rich people lived closer to the coast and the standard of living went down as you moved inland.

It looked like Atlantic Avenue had the restaurants and shops.

I switched to street view where I could see the palm-lined sidewalks, the storefronts, tourists drinking coffee at outdoor tables in the shade.

Street view let me cruise down the sidewalks with a click, spin the whole view around, see a guy in pink shorts midstride as he crossed the street eating an ice cream cone.

When I was a kid, I used to wonder what it would be like to stop time. To walk through a scene like this where everyone was frozen. Doing it now was kind of cool.

A few more clicks on Atlantic Avenue and I was crossing a bridge. The beach was up ahead, but on the left...

I sat up straight, clicked again. There on the left, on the sunny side of the street beneath the palms...

I ran to the bedroom, got the key off the nightstand, came back to the monitor.

The woman jogging on the sidewalk by the green bench, she was dark skinned. Indian maybe. Short black ponytail swinging above her left shoulder. She was wearing a yellow t-shirt with my seahorse.

I held up the key to compare them. Three spikes. On the head, not the neck. Tightly wound tail.

The back of the shirt had no words, but the front might. I dragged the mouse sideways to rotate the image, but I couldn't get in front of her.

I clicked ahead, jumping farther up the street then panned around, trying to look back.

The front of the shirt showed the same seahorse, only smaller. The woman was midstride, both feet off the ground, her right arm swinging in front of her belly, obscuring the words. All I could see were the last three letters. APE.

I kept going. Raced down Atlantic Avenue to the coast, turned left on State Route A1A where the sidewalks were empty.

I turned around, went back to my jogger, and had a little think.

Time to call Leon.

"Whassup, Champ?"

He calls me that sometimes. I think boxer and champ are synonymous in his mind.

"How are those traces going?"

"Slow."

"Give yours to Claire."

"What?"

"Tell Claire to work on the guy you're tracing. I got something else for you. Check your email."

I sent him a map of Delray Beach with a pin stuck in the intersection of Atlantic Avenue and I-95. I sent him a screenshot of the jogger's t-shirt too, front and back.

"What's this, Freddy?"

"Go to Google street view and start looking for that seahorse. A virtual canvas, digital dragnet, whatever you want to call it. Look at storefronts, signs on buildings, ads on bus stops, anything that might show a name to go with the logo. Start at the pin on Atlantic and move north. I'll go south. We're going to walk every street, okay?"

"Sure thing, Freddy."

I wouldn't have assigned this task to Bethany, Claire, or Ed. It's too mind-numbing. Half an hour of it would be enough to strain your eyes and give you a headache. It's the kind of work I hate, but Leon excels at it.

After a couple hours, my eyes were starting to dry out. Something about staring at a screen makes me forget to blink.

I was noting the blocks I'd covered so I wouldn't go through them twice. Leon did the same. I didn't have to tell him.

After almost three hours, I had to take a break, go outside, get some air.

I took a walk around the block and I was back at the building entrance before I knew it. This is what happens when my mind gets going.

I grabbed a club soda from the fridge, sat back down, checked the email from Leon.

Two screenshots. A guy with the same seahorse shirt walking into a deli. A woman in front of a house, bent over a plant, her hands in the soil. Same shirt. Both photos showed just the back, with no words, and there was no way to get a front view on these two. But we were on the right track.

Five p.m., I told Leon to knock off. Go home.

He said no.

Eight thirty-three, he said he's done, sent me a map of the grid he had covered. I don't know how he made that. It was a map of the streets with a light red overlay.

He had covered three times as much territory as me, but I didn't worry about him going too fast and missing things. The kid has the eyes of a hawk.

I thanked him for his work, told him to get some rest.

I kept plodding. First time ever I'd outlasted Leon on a search like this.

32

Twelve sixteen a.m., I booked a morning flight to Palm Beach.

The last three letters on the woman's shirt, APE—I had found them five minutes earlier. Ship Shape. Big yellow sign over a gym in an upscale mall just a couple of miles from where she was jogging. Seahorse on the left, words on the right.

That key with number 212, it went to a gym locker. And whatever our mystery woman *didn't* bring to her lover Carlo in Virginia, whatever he thought was going to be in that safe where she left the taunting note—I had a feeling it might still be waiting inside locker 212.

33

September 21
Delray Beach, Florida

The gym was just off one of the main boulevards, a mile or so inland, in the same mall as Bed, Bath & Beyond, Blue Mercury, and a few restaurants with outdoor seating. No one was eating at the outside tables when I pulled into the lot. South Florida hadn't gotten the message that summer was over. The temperature was still in the nineties and the sun was stronger than in DC in July.

Delray, from what I could tell, was quieter than Miami and richer than some of the towns I'd seen on the Gulf Coast. Lots of new condos, high-end restaurants, art galleries, and golf courses.

The sliding glass doors leading into Ship Shape made me think it was once a supermarket. Inside was a sitting area, cafe, and reception desk. Beyond that was the floor with exercise equipment, a track, and basketball courts. I could hear the puck and thwack of racquetball courts off to the left.

Or were they squash courts? I still get them confused. I grew up in a boxing gym, not the kind of place where women in Lululemon drink super green smoothies between their workout and their massage. That's what this was. An indoor country club for people who don't like golf. The cafe was a meeting place for tennis wives who like getting yelled at by the spin instructor as they pedal a bike that goes nowhere.

There were two people behind the reception desk. A woman and a man. Ken and Barbie, tall and tan and perfectly fit. As I approached the desk, a fifty-something woman who had come through the doors behind me approached as well. She was on my left, heading for Barbie. I was on the right. Ken's side.

Funny thing: They switched stations. Ken went to her side, flashed a perfect white smile, asked how he could be of help. Ms. Fifty-Something reacted to the smile. Like it knocked her back half a step.

Barbie had the same teeth, impossibly white and straight. The two of them could have been an advertisement for oral hygiene.

"Can I help you?" she chirped.

I told her I wanted a tour. She gave me a description of the facilities. They had everything I had already seen and heard, plus saunas, steam rooms, an indoor pool, and a spa with massage and Reiki. Their other facility had outdoor tennis and two outdoor pools. A single membership got you into both.

We could do the walking tour now if I was ready.

Sure.

On the way in, one of the guys in the sitting area reminded me of people I used to know in New York. Guys who did collections. Guys who extracted payments from hardworking people who owed money to not-so-hardworking people they never should have borrowed from.

This one was standing about thirty feet behind me, wearing a black polo shirt and black shorts, leaning against the wall, reading a magazine. His posture made him look out of place. Standing and leaning, instead of sitting like all the other members in chairs with lattes or smoothies, talking or looking at their phones. The way he held the magazine in one hand instead of two... The way he scratched his crotch with his free hand and snorted loudly instead of blowing his nose...

If his manner didn't give him away, his build would have. He was about my height, six-three or so, but close to three hundred pounds. I used to see this kind of guy in the gyms in New York. They go in and bench 350 pounds, sometimes more. The rest of the day, they're eating donuts and drinking Pepsi.

They're top heavy, and it's as much fat as muscle. They look in the mirror, they see Dwayne "The Rock" Johnson. Everyone else sees the donuts and Pepsi. They're strong, but they tire easily from carrying all that weight. I know, because I use to watch them get sweaty and winded beating the crap out of people they were collecting from.

The other thing about guys like him—they can't really fight. They think they can because they have all that muscle, but when it comes down to it, they don't have the skill or the discipline to beat a real fighter. When they come up against someone who fights back hard, who takes their best shots and returns it even worse, they panic. They come in thinking they'll overpower you, and if that doesn't work, they don't have a Plan B because most of the guys they pick on succumb to Plan A.

I know that panic. I've seen it in the eyes of a lot of guys who thought they could fight me. It got to the point back in New York where even the organization I was working with— and I'm ashamed to say I ever worked with them, that I ever did that kind of stuff—even they wanted to get rid of me.

I left New York because I had to. I'd been around guys like this one with the magazine and the fat muscles long enough to develop a hatred. I hurt one of them pretty bad, a guy in my own organization, because I don't like bullies. The higher-ups, the ones who used to tell us both what to do, didn't like what I'd done. While Muscles was recovering in the hospital, they pulled me off the street and gave me the message to leave town in the most effective way they could, which was to beat me within an inch of my life.

When I run into guys like this, my hackles go up, like a dog who knows from fifty feet away when another dog is bad news. He starts putting out the warning. Like, you get any closer, this is not going to end well.

Before I got shot, I was an angry guy. Now, not so much. But guys like him—anything that reminds me of my years in New York and the people I fell in with up there, the loan sharks and extortionists, the fight fixers who ruined my boxing career when it was still on the upswing—I have no patience for those people. No sympathy. The anger is still there. Every ounce of it. That won't ever go away. It just doesn't come up anymore until someone like him sets it off.

I followed Barbie off to the right, toward the weights and machines. Something funny happened when we turned. There was this other guy in the cafe by the smoothie counter. Tall, like six foot six. White guy, clean cut. Wearing khakis and a white shirt. Light brown hair with a nerdy-looking side part. I never would have tagged him as the type, but he was looking at me. An unfriendly sizing-up look, like he was trying to figure out how much trouble I'd be if we had to mix it up.

It hit me then. While I was sizing up the guy with the magazine, the tall one was watching me. Probably wondering why the hell I was staring at his friend like that. People who have been in the life recognize each other. If he knew anything at all—and I could tell he did—he would recognize me as someone who'd been around.

One last thing about the tall guy. He was pretty damn sure of himself. He didn't look like a fighter, or like anyone who would even bother using his fists. Which told me he was probably carrying. Florida has liberal gun laws. The only people who can't legally get guns are the ones who use them to make the kind of living that Florida cops don't approve of. And even those people have guns.

Barbie walked me out through the treadmills, stair steppers, rowing machines. Then the weight machines, then the free weights.

"You lift?" she asked.

"Yeah, but not enough to bulk up. I don't like the bulk."

"That's good," she said. "Too much muscle and you lose your range of motion."

I looked back to see if my friends were following. They weren't.

I fingered the key in my pocket like a rosary, the key to locker 212.

We took a few shots on the basketball court. Barbie made three straight, told me she played in high school. I missed three, told her it wasn't my game.

We made it to the pool in back, went through the glass doors. It was steamy in there. People swimming laps. Lots of echoes.

She told me the hours for lap swim, which lanes were reserved, and when and for whom. At the locker rooms, we parted ways.

"Go straight through," she said. "Check out the showers and the steam room. I'll meet you on the other side."

It was all pretty high class. Clean. Nice tile. The showers had soap and shampoo dispensers. You didn't have to bring your own.

The lockers used old-fashioned keys, not the new number pads. They were made of wood, not metal. Each had a small metal plate in the center, a little bigger than a quarter, with the seahorse logo and the locker number. The numbering for the men's lockers started at 400.

That meant 212 would be in the women's locker room. I was already thinking how I might get Barbie to open it for me. But then again, that could be a bad idea. What if there were drugs in there? A big wad of cash? Maybe she'd take one look and not even come back to me. Maybe she'd go straight to management and tell them this guy came in with a women's locker key, asked me to open it up, and look what I found.

I had thought about this on the plane as I flew in.

This was where Claire could really help. Claire could go in there and open it. I'd call her if I needed her.

Barbie was waiting for me by the locker room exit. She showed me the courts— squash *and* racquetball, it turns out— and then we went back to the front desk. And that's when I noticed the day lockers. They were off to the side of reception. Numbers 200 to 248. The empty ones were open a crack; 212 was shut tight, and the key was in my pocket.

While Barbie was stacking a pile of brochures for me to take home, I took a look at the cafe. The tall guy was still standing there. Magazine guy was with him. They were joking about something. Neither one seemed interested in me, but I noticed they did watch everyone who came through the entrance, like they were looking for someone.

Barbie gave me the rundown on rates, the discount for paying annually versus month-to-month, the thirty-day cancellation policy, the add-ons like personal training, yoga, and the rest.

I thanked her and she turned to her attention to the next guest.

I took one more look around the place. No one watching, everyone busy exercising, talking, drinking smoothies, texting. The two goons in the cafe had their eyes on someone coming through the door. Like, riveted. Whoever it was was so fascinating, I had to turn to see.

A dark-haired woman in Spandex shorts and exercise bra with giant fake boobs. Why would someone do that to themselves? My back ached just looking at her.

I slid the key into locker 212, gave it a turn. Inside was a black canvas bag. I pulled it out, turned, headed for the exit.

I was right about Donuts and Slim. They *had* been waiting for someone. They were right on my tail as I left the building, closing fast.

Two steps outside the door, the muscular guy pulled an old grade school trick. Stepped on the back of my shoe. It breaks your stride. A normal person would turn around instinctively, see who did it. I turned and swung. Caught him on the chin and he went down hard.

His tall friend pressed a gun into my side and told me to keep walking.

That was stupid. I should have hit the guy with the gun. The other one I knew I could take care of. Always disable the dangerous one first, and Slim was the dangerous one because he was armed.

Anger is the source of a lot of stupid mistakes. I didn't like these people. I got mad and made a mistake.

He marched me to a white Chevy Suburban. We walked past four people in the lot. It was obvious to anyone with their eyes open that this scene wasn't right. A man does not walk half a step behind another man with his hand in the guy's back. People saw it and looked away.

What the hell is wrong with South Florida?

When we reached the Chevy, the guy said, "Give me your phone."

I gave it to him.

"Put your hands up, asshole."

I did as he said. He patted me down with one hand, keeping the gun pointed at my face, his eyes fixed on mine. Any move, he'd put a bullet up under my chin.

He opened the back door of the Suburban and told me to get in. It was about two hundred degrees in there, and I had to roast in the back seat for a couple of minutes while he stood outside and waited for Donuts to get up off the asphalt.

The big guy finally made it. He took the driver's seat, moaning about his head and his chin, while Slim sat in the passenger seat with his gun on me. The big guy started the engine, then turned around and punched me in the face. I couldn't do anything about it because of the gun. The punch didn't hurt too bad because he threw it from an awkward angle and he had no leverage.

Slim kept his gun on me while the big guy drove. Instead of going out onto the main road, he drove farther into the parking lot, around the back of Ship Shape, and stopped by a metal door at the rear of the building.

Slim got out and ushered me toward the door.

"Seriously?" I said. "We could have walked here."

He told me to shut up and bring the bag.

Why would they want me to bring the bag if they already had it in a locker in the front of their own gym?

This was making less and less sense.

When I pulled open the office door, the big guy clocked me in the back of the head with something. It hurt, but more than that, it pissed me off. This was exactly the kind of cowardly shit the enforcers in New York used to do. They'd wait till you're in a position where you couldn't defend yourself and they couldn't lose. Like me with both hands occupied and my back to him. Then he hits me. I don't like cheap shots.

I dropped the bag and spun on the ball of my foot. Dug a left hook into his gut and watched him double over in agony.

Again, not smart. But that's for all the shit I had to put up with in New York. And guess what? Whatever the hell you pricks are up to, you're not going to shoot me in broad daylight in the parking lot of your own damn club. You're not going to draw that kind of attention to whatever operation you're running here. No one is that stupid.

Slim clocked me in the head with the gun, hard. It opened up a cut on my forehead. Then he just stood there blinking at me, wondering why I didn't go down.

I picked up the bag and went inside.

34

The receptionist sitting at the desk inside was not the kind I expected. Not like Barbie out front. More like someone's sixty-year-old mother. She didn't ask my name, just looked at the bag, startled like it meant something, picked up the phone, and said, "Come out here. Now."

Slim came in through the outside door. Another guy opened the inside door, the door of the office just past the reception desk.

This was a dark-haired guy. Maybe fifty, wearing light grey suit pants, a white dress shirt with rolled-up sleeves, no tie. Hairy arms and a gold Rolex watch.

He was chewing a mouthful of something, wiping his hands on a cloth napkin. He looked at the bag in my hand and then he gave me the funniest look. The kind of look a man who has no manners gives a woman he wants to screw. A full up and down, followed by this sort of "meh" reaction, like he's not impressed.

"You're Romeo?" he said. He sounded underwhelmed.

I felt a blast of hot air behind me as Donuts entered. He had finally got up off the pavement after that gut punch.

The guy with the Rolex said, "She leaves here because she doesn't like these types"—he waves dismissively at his own thugs—"and then she winds up with you? What the fuck?"

"What are you talking about?" I said.

"You look familiar."

I tell him we've never met before.

He says, "Not that kind of familiar. Like, line of work familiar. You ever do collection?"

I could tell by his gruff manner, the way he talked, the goons who worked for him, what kind of work he was in. He made sure construction projects got done on time. He made sure the trash got hauled. He made sure the bankers and stockbrokers and boat owners whose wives didn't give them what they needed at home could find young, firm-bodied relief in the local motels. He rerouted truckloads of goods from the retailers who had purchased them to his associates who sold merchandise at a discount. He maybe sometimes delivered South American pharmaceuticals to the hungry markets in New York.

"Answer me," he commanded.

"Yeah. I did collections." I was ashamed of that. Deeply ashamed. But that was in another life, when I was young and still seeking the humility that only a failed career and a failed marriage and a few well-aimed bullets could drive into me.

"Come in."

He ushered the three of us into his office. Me, Donuts, and Slim.

35

The first thing the guy said when we were all situated—him standing behind his desk, me sitting in front, Donuts standing at the wall to my left, and Slim standing with his gun to my right—the first thing the guy said was, "You may call me Anthony."

Very formal. Very strange.

"You can call me Freddy."

He gave a little bow, just the slightest nod to say he got it.

He looked at me quietly for a few seconds, then he said, "You're not a cop."

My wallet and phone were on his desk. Slim had put them there.

"I'm a detective. Private." I nodded toward the wallet. He picked it up and checked my investigator's license. Checked my driver's license too.

He put them back inside and handed me the wallet. I looked to Slim to make sure he wasn't going to shoot me if I made a move to put my wallet in my pocket. He nodded okay.

My phone was still on the desk.

"Want to tell me what's on those hard drives?" Anthony asked.

"What hard drives?"

"What hard drives? In the bag, you stupid fuck. What's on them?"

"I don't know."

"You don't know?"

I shook my head. "I have no idea what's in that bag."

"How did you know to come here?"

"I got the key from a woman in Virginia."

"My daughter's name is Virginia, but she lives in Seattle. Goes by Ginny. What did this woman look like?"

I got a bad feeling. A very bad feeling.

"I asked you what she looked like. Why do you look scared all of a sudden? You afraid to meet your girlfriend's daddy, Romeo?"

He had a good radar for fear, just like me. I wasn't going to bullshit him. I admitted I was scared. Then I asked him to describe his daughter.

"Why don't you start?" he said. "Describe the woman who gave you that key."

"About five foot five," I said. "Dyed blond hair, dark at the roots. Like your color dark. Light brown eyes, with a thick black ring around the iris."

He nodded. "What else?"

"She uh..." I didn't want to say it.

"She had a figure. Like her mother."

"She had a figure. Yeah."

He stared at me hard for a few seconds, and I got even more uncomfortable. Angry people don't scare me. The hotheads who have no discipline, who have to respond to every slight because they feel threatened—those people don't scare me. The ones who scare me are the ones like him, who can stand there thinking very unpleasant thoughts without getting upset. They process it all coolly, figure out what they want to do, and how and when. And when they do decide to strike, they're effective and cruel because they've checkmated you before they even make their move.

"Tell me about my daughter," he said.

I didn't want to.

"Just say it plainly."

I said, "A body matching the description I just gave you was found in the James River in Richmond, Virginia." And then I held my breath.

He just nodded. As far as I could tell, his breathing didn't even change.

"And did you talk to this body? When it gave you the key, what did this body say to you?"

"I didn't talk to her."

"Then how did you get the key?"

I took a deep breath. How do you tell a man a story like this about his own daughter?

He walked around the front of the desk, sat on the corner, and looked me in the eye.

"Just say it, Freddy."

I told him everything. The dog, the shoe, her lying there with no pulse. The storm, the dam, her washing away.

He took it in quietly. I could see him picturing it, scene by scene. When I got to the dam break, I got upset. I couldn't help it. Then he got upset. His type, the most they'll show is the breathing. Heavy, irregular breathing, a frown, and a flash of anger in the eyes.

Me and Donuts and Slim were all watching him. I think all three of us were afraid of what he might do because a man who controls his emotions so tightly has to let them out sometime, and if he's running a show like this, if the goons are reporting to *him*, he's probably pretty damn violent.

"When did you find her?"

He shut his mouth, breathed through his nose. Deep, slow, shaking breaths.

"August nineteenth."

"And when did they find her in Richmond?"

His eyes were like lasers burning through me.

"August thirty-first." I remembered, because the news story appeared the following day, September first.

He nodded slowly, eyes boring in. Two deep breaths. Exhaled loudly through his nostrils. His breath was shaking.

"Where was she in between?"

"In the Tye River. And then in the James."

Finally, he exploded. "And no one pulled her out? Twelve days in a fucking river and no one pulls her out? What kind of fucking people live up there?"

"It might not be your daughter," I offered.

"The woman you described is my daughter. The key you brought in here was on her wrist. Give me your wallet."

I gave it to him. He pulled out the licenses again and picked up the phone.

"Yeah, it's Anthony. I want a background check. You ready? Frederick Ferguson." He read my date of birth, address, and driver's license number. Then he read the number on my investigator's license.

"Pull his credit records too. Let me know if he had any charges in Seattle. If he flew into or out of Seattle in the past year... What?... What the hell do I care how you get the info, just fucking get it... No, not tomorrow. Now, you stupid piece of shit!"

He hung up.

Then he said to Donuts, "Hey Manny, go in the club and get us some lemonade."

"Why do I gotta do it?"

Anthony didn't even respond. Just turned his laser glare on him, and Manny obeyed.

36

The four of us sat there for what seemed like hours.

During that time, I told Anthony about the letter in his daughter's room at the Olympic and the note she'd left.

Anthony's friend eventually called back and told him what I knew my background check would say. Both licenses were legit. I'd lived in DC for years.

The credit report would show nothing from Seattle. I hadn't set foot in that town in five years. He said his daughter had lived there. I think he wanted to make sure I wasn't connected to her, wasn't her boyfriend pretending to be someone else. He listened for a long time, asked a few questions, and finally seemed satisfied.

He pushed my wallet across the desk, then folded his hands and looked at me. I could see the wheels going in his mind.

"Whatever happened," he said, "it wasn't you. It was Romeo."

"Who's Romeo?"

"No idea. From the story you told me, my daughter dies leaving two notes. A love-gone-wrong to Romeo, and another that says she didn't bring the stuff. That stuff." He pointed to the bag. "Encrypted hard drives. My guys couldn't get any data off of them. You know anyone who can?"

Leon had told me that strong encryption was unbreakable and would remain that way until quantum computers came along.

"I don't think so."

"How good a detective are you?"

"I do well enough."

"Does that mean you're humble or does that mean you suck?"

"A humble person would never say they're humble."

"And people who suck don't know they suck. Look, you found this place somehow. Think you can find Romeo?"

I probably could, if I had a few leads, but I wasn't sure it was the right thing to do. So far, Anthony had shown enough restraint to refrain from killing the messenger—me. I didn't think he'd extend that restraint to the man he was blaming for his daughter's death.

"Let me put the question to you another way," he said. "Do you want to walk out of here and do a job—for which I will pay you—or do you want to not walk out of here and not do any more jobs?"

I chose option number one.

37

Anthony and I had a pleasant dinner that evening, all things considered. It was just the two of us in a restaurant on Atlantic Avenue, near the Intracoastal Waterway. Donuts and Slim had to wait in the car, like dogs whose owner was on an errand.

Virginia Villarosa was twenty-eight years old. She graduated from Rutgers University with a degree in biology, then added some courses in data science. She had been working for some tech company in Seattle.

"*Some* tech company? You don't know the name?"

"I don't know." Anthony Villarosa seemed annoyed. "They all have meaningless names. Someplace where everyone drinks lattes and thinks they're woke."

She had a stormy relationship with her father. They'd get in fights and go months without talking.

"She didn't approve of the way I make a living. The way I put a roof over her fucking head and paid her college tuition. Okay, great. Find a new dad. That's the kind of fights we had."

Her mother had died of breast cancer a few years ago.

"A very aggressive kind. It happened fast," Villarosa said. "Shocked us both, Ginny and me. In a normal family, that kind of thing can bring a father and daughter together. We're not a normal family."

Ginny didn't like her father's associates. That was what she wanted to get away from when she "left Del." Hence his surprise when I walked in. Not the Romeo he was expecting.

"The kind she likes, they're book smart. They're talkers. They can blab about art and music and literature, they're full of ideas, but they can't *do* anything. The exact opposite of the kind of people I work with. You don't sit there talking about what you're going to do, much less about what some dead

145

writer said four hundred years ago. You go out and *do* shit. That's how things get done. By doing, not talking. But her..." He shook his head.

"She had her fucking head in the clouds. A romantic. Clueless about how the world works, because she *wanted* to be clueless. Because she didn't want to believe that what gets things done is labor and money, greasing palms, cutting deals, making sure everyone gets paid. She wanted fucking Romeo and Juliet.

"A girl like that is easy to con. You see she's got her head in the clouds, you go up to the clouds and sweet talk her. Some guy's gonna come along and figure that out. He's gonna sweet talk her and get her to do something for him, because *he* knows how the world works. He knows the value of whatever the hell is on those encrypted hard drives, and he's probably put in the legwork to find a buyer. If he doesn't already work for the buyer.

"I want you to find this fucker and bring him to me so I can wring his fucking neck."

"I can't bring you a person to kill."

"Excuse me? Do we not have a deal? If you don't want to do this, I'll find someone else who will, and you won't be walking home. You won't be doing any more work, ever."

What could I do? I said okay. I figured it would buy me some time.

"I know that kind of okay," he said. "That's okay, I'll get started. Okay, I'll get the fuck away from this Anthony guy and figure a way out of this. Let me tell you what that okay really means. It means you're gonna find Romeo. If you don't want to bring him to me, don't. Just find him, let me know where he is. Then you can walk. Wash your hands of this."

I'm not the kind of guy who can set someone up and just "walk." I'm not the kind of guy who can wash my hands of anything in which I've played a part. Anything I do, good or bad, I own. All responsibility for my own actions starts and ends with me.

When I used to box and I got hurt, I wouldn't show it. When the doubt crept in about whether I could win, or even make it to the end of the round, I wouldn't show it. My trainer always counted that among my strengths. A good opponent, he said, would go in for the kill when he sensed weakness. If he couldn't sense it, he wouldn't know. He'd miss his opportunity.

I told Anthony Villarosa I'd find his Romeo, and then I dug into my steak.

However much this was bothering me, I didn't show it, and he didn't press me again. We had a nice meal. We talked about boxing, and his passion, fishing.

The next morning, he sent a couple of friends to drive me to the airport in Fort Lauderdale. Not Donuts and Slim. Two fresh new friends. So he'd have two more who knew what I looked like.

38

September 22
Seattle, WA

Anthony Villarosa had given me a lead, two friends in Seattle his daughter Ginny hung out with. A couple that lived in Ballard, just north of the drawbridge.

I drove up there in a rental. My escorts—the two who had taken me to the Fort Lauderdale airport—tagged along in a second car. The couple I was looking for lived in a craftsman just west of 15th Avenue. Villarosa gave me their names, Zenobia and Steve, and when I asked for background, all he could tell me was "He's a pussy and she's a bitch."

Not helpful, though I'm sure that reducing people to those kinds of descriptions makes it easier for a guy like him to do the things he does.

The guy, Steve, greeted me at the door. He looked to be about thirty. He was skinny, five foot ten, straight brown hair, a professionally sculpted goatee, with the smooth pale skin of a schoolgirl. He wore khaki pants and a short-sleeve button-down shirt. The boldly colored tattoos on his milk-white arms made him look like a choirboy who'd fallen asleep on the subway and been vandalized.

We chatted at the door for a few minutes, me standing outside, him in the doorframe. We both agreed that the weather was fine for this time of year, and he told me how global warming was extending the summers in the Pacific Northwest.

I don't know what that had to do with anything. He knew I was there to ask about Ginny because I had called ahead and told them to expect me. He went on rambling about how the longer dry season led to more forest fires and I was wondering why he didn't notice that Villarosa's escorts had circled the block five times.

People in rich, low-crime areas just aren't tuned in to that kind of thing. They think about long-term threats like climate change because they don't have imminent threats like muggers and robbers.

This guy's cluelessness bothered me almost as much as the stupidity of Villarosa's goons. Park the fucking car already! You drive one more time around the block and *someone's* going to notice, I guarantee you. Even here!

If this went on another minute, I'd lose my temper, so I just said point-blank to Steve, "You mind if I come in?"

"Oh, yeah, sure."

I followed him to the kitchen in back, where his girlfriend Zenobia was chopping carrots, her dyed black hair pulled back in a ponytail. She had dark eyes and fair skin. She wore a black tank top and she was tatted up just like him.

I introduced myself and asked her about Ginny's boyfriend, Romeo.

"Romeo?" She wiped her nose on the back of her hand. "You mean Carlo?"

Good start. Carlo was the name on the letter Sheriff Kessler had found in the room at the Olympic Inn.

"You know him?"

"I've met him a few times."

I could tell from her tone she didn't care for him.

"What's he like?"

She turned back to the cutting board and took out her dislike of Carlo on a big fat carrot.

"Okay, so like, when a woman's, like, *always* talking about her guy..." She turned so I could see her roll her eyes. "Like, *always*. Like, you ask her if she wants to go out for Thai food and she says, Carlo doesn't really do Thai food. Okay, well Carlo's not even here, so who gives a shit what he likes? I'm asking *you!*"

149

She brought the knife down with a thwack, and the end of the carrot rolled onto the floor. Steve picked it up and put it in a compost bin under the sink.

"Seriously," she said, "it was fucking annoying. Like, why do these smart, capable women who can totally manage their own lives fall for guys like him?"

Steve cut in. "She had a bad relationship with her dad." *She* being Ginny Villarosa. Her dad had told me as much.

"Don't give me that Freudian bullshit," Zenobia said. Thwack. Another piece of carrot went flying. "No one believes that patriarchal dick-think anymore. Like if daddy didn't teach her how to deal with men, she'd never figure it out on her own because women are just too stupid. Give me a fucking break!"

Thwack!

Steve gave me a sheepish look, an admission like, yeah, I shouldn't have said that.

"The guy was a cult," Zenobia said. "A one-man cult."

"What do you mean?"

"My mother was in a cult," she said, and Steve gave me another look. A funny kind of look, full of admiration, like, See how special she is?

"The first thing they do is separate you from your friends," Zenobia said. "It's easier for them to control you when you have no one else to turn to. Then they start working their charm. Their black magic. They start probing your psychological weak points, don't they, Steve?"

Steve nodded. "They do."

"How would you know?" she snapped.

"I've read about it."

"So, what? That makes you an expert? Don't talk about things you don't know about. That's the root of mansplaining right there. You say one thing you don't know about, and what's to stop you from saying another? These bad habits start with a lack of awareness. Listen to yourself, Steve!"

Then to me, she added, "They figure out what you want to hear, the cult leaders and the narcissists, and they start laying it on thick."

Where did the narcissist come from? I couldn't keep up with her shit list, but it had to be a mile long. And now Villarosa's goons were in the alley with the windows rolled down, smoking cigarettes. Those idiots!

"The big thing they want to get across," Zenobia said, "and it's subtle how they do it, is that *they* have all the answers. *They* have the power to fix everything in you. They and only they. And it's not a one-shot deal either. They're not going to give you the fix and then let you move on and continue growing on your own. No, ma'am."

Ma'am?

Who did she think she was talking to?

Thwack!

"They're the sun," she said. Thwack! "They're the rain and the soil and the stars. You need them twenty-four-seven, like a plant needs the earth."

Steve nodded gravely, like an acolyte testifying to the guru's deep truth.

"I've had enough of guys like that," Zenobia said. "They— seriously—they have no power over me. I can smell them a mile away, which is why Carlo didn't like me. He knew I could see through him, and I think he was afraid I would expose him. Because I'm the kind who calls out fakes. I don't let that stuff slide."

"It's true," Steve said. "She would totally take him down."

"You know, I'm right here," Zenobia said. "You don't have to talk about me in the third person."

"Sorry." Steve turned to me and added, "I'm trying to root out my male privilege, but it's so ingrained."

"Carlo was an asshole," Zenobia said. "But not an obvious one. A wolf in sheep's clothing. Comes on all charming to a woman and then takes over her life. I'll tell you, when a woman talks about a man all the time, but you never see him? When she can't tell anymore what she likes versus what he likes? When she stops having her own opinions and starts spouting his? When you get all that, plus you never see the guy, like, he won't hang out with her friends? Then she's in a cult. She's in the cult of patriarchal narcissism, lost in the Temple of Asshole."

"It's the total supplanting of feminine power with male oppression," Steve said. "And it's been going on for thousands of years. But I think we're at a turning point in human history, where for the first time, we're finally becoming aware of this dynamic. We're calling it out and moving to quash it, we're moving toward a more enlightened place. And Zenobia is right at the vanguard of this movement."

"Shut up, Steve. Nobody asked you." She turned to me. "Why are you so interested in Ginny?"

"She seems to have disappeared."

"Well, duh!"

I didn't want to tell her Ginny was dead. God knows what kind of lecture that would unleash. All of Western society would be to blame. The political parties, capitalism, the church. Even Elmo and Sesame Street would have blood on their hands. Besides, it wasn't official because her dad hadn't identified the body yet, though he probably would do so in the next few days.

"Her father hired me."

"Oh?" said Zenobia. "Mister tough guy? Mister I don't have feelings? He hired you? Maybe he shouldn't have fucked her up in the first place."

I don't usually lose my patience with people I'm interviewing, but this woman really rubbed me the wrong way. I couldn't resist throwing in a little barb.

"I thought you said fathers couldn't mess up their daughters."

"Oh my God! That is *not* what I said! I didn't say that at all! How dare you come in here and put words in my mouth!"

Steve was up on his feet, waving his hands at me like, No, no, no! Don't go there.

He hustled me outside, which turned out to be a good thing, because then I could get his take on Carlo, without the politics and anger. If he even had his own take...

"You can't come in here and say things like that to my partner," Steve told me.

We were out on the front stoop. The sky had clouded over and a cold grey mist was blowing in from the west.

"You have to understand," he pleaded. "Zenobia is very aware. When someone has that level of awareness, every little touch registers. Every little thing."

My grandfather used to call that being thin-skinned. But I don't know... Maybe he just wasn't enlightened.

"Did you meet this guy?" I asked. "What did you think of him?"

"I met him a few times. I saw him at parties with Ginny. Zenobia didn't go."

"She let you go out by yourself?"

Oops. That slipped.

"She was working."

"Where's she work?"

"She's a stripper."

That knocked me for a loop. "She— What?"

Steve nodded. "It's very empowering for her to turn the oppression of the male gaze against the perpetrator, because when she's up there on that stage, those poor men who think they control the world are just slaves to their own desire. She says it's like leading a bull by the nose."

"Well that's great," I said. "I'm glad she's reclaiming her power."

That was the first time I saw Steve smile. I think it was because I got the words right. "Reclaiming her power." I saw that on a poster at SeaTac Airport after my plane landed. It was an ad for deodorant.

"What was your impression of him? Of this Carlo guy?"

"He's smart."

"Like how? Like book smart?"

"Yeah. Very cultured. Can talk about art, music, literature. I think that's part of what hooked Ginny. He was also very controlling."

"In what way?"

"Like, he held her arm a lot. Guided her when they walked. She went where he wanted her to go. At parties, he always kept an eye on her. He always knew where she was, and how engaged she was with whoever she was talking to. If she got too engaged, he'd come over, lead her away, cut off the contact. It was subtle, the way he did it. I wouldn't have noticed it myself if Zenobia hadn't enlightened me. And he did it every time. Literally *every* time. There's another thing too."

"What?"

"He didn't really talk to guys. Only women, the really good-looking ones, whether they were single or not."

"At the parties? What about the ones who weren't good looking?"

Steve shook his head. "Nope. But he had a knack for catching women alone. Like, he'd watch them head toward the bathroom, and then he'd drift over there and catch them on the way out. He'd strike up a quick conversation, get them to laugh. And he always touched them too. Just a little innocuous touch, like on the elbow, while they're laughing. Zenobia calls that the feeler. If a guy can get away with that one, the next time, he'll touch her again, try to get her accustomed to it, so that after a while, she can't really say no to the touch because it's part of how they interact.

"It's a plan. Zenobia calls it boiling the lobster. You know the story of the lobster in the pot of water? At first the water is cool, but then it gets hotter and hotter, and by the time the lobster realizes what's going on, it's too late. He's cooked.

"Zenobia says it's a classic strategy, and it can be so subtle even the guy doesn't realize he's doing it. But it reinforces the patriarchy. It reinforces oppression."

I thought about what Bethany had told me about her TA in grad school. It was the same thing. Zenobia was right.

"What's this guy look like?" I asked. "Carlo."

Steve wrinkled his nose. "Average. Like if you took a composite of every thirty-five-year-old white man in America and averaged them all out, you'd get him. Brown hair, brown eyes, average height, average build. He dresses pretty well though. I'll give him that. And he's a smooth talker. That's his grift, as Zenobia would put it."

"You know Carlo's last name?"

"No."

"You know where he works?"

Steve shook his head. "I'm not even sure he does work."

"Was he sponging off her? Off Ginny?"

"I don't know."

"What about Ginny? You know where she worked? Some tech company?"

"Not tech," he said. "Biotech. A company called Mitogenic."

"What!"

Boy, that set off the alarm bells. That's how she erased her DNA record without the administrative records. *She* was the insider.

Steve was taken aback by my reaction.

"Yeah. Down in South Lake Union. Why?"

"What did she do there?"

He shrugged. "I don't know. Something with data."

"Do you know if when she left, do you know if she was planning on being away a long time?"

"She didn't say so."

"Did she say she was going out of the country?"

"No. She didn't really say anything. Just that she'd quit her job and was taking a trip. She left her apartment keys with Zenobia. Asked her to bring in the mail once a week."

"Think she'd let me borrow the keys?"

He shook his head. "I think you burned your bridges with her when you made that comment about fathers and daughters. Zenobia is very enlightened. She doesn't forgive. Besides, the whole idea of a man entering a woman's apartment without consent, the symbolism of the key sliding into the lock, she'd be totally against that."

"How 'bout you just swipe the keys and give them to me? I'll bring them back tomorrow."

He looked petrified.

"Look, I'm working for her dad," I said. "I'm trying to find her. She might be in trouble. Any bit of information I can get brings me a step closer to finding her." I almost said "finding her killer," but my words would have more weight if there was some hope of saving a young woman in trouble.

"I don't know..."

I felt like I was asking a kid to swipe cigarettes from his mom's purse. There was no way this milquetoast was going to stand up to his domineering girlfriend, so I tried another tack. "You think if Ginny's father calls, he can get Zenobia to give me the keys?"

He sucked in a breath through clenched teeth.

"She hates that guy."

I figured.

"Have you ever talked to him?" Steve asked. "He's, like, the incarnation of male evil."

"I'll have him give her a call," I said.

I turned to leave, knowing Villarosa would set Zenobia off, and she'd turn around and take it out on Steve.

He grabbed my arm. "Wait! This will be a lot easier if I just sneak the keyring out of the kitchen. She doesn't have to know it's gone. But you have to bring it back as soon as you're done. Like, that minute."

"Fine."

"I'll be right back."

A few minutes later, I walked into the blowing mist with the keys to Virginia Villarosa's apartment in my pocket. I had Steve's number too, in case I had more questions.

I didn't see my chaperones around. Maybe they got distracted. Or lost. After seeing the caliber of Anthony Villarosa's associates, I stopped wondering why he wanted to hire *me* for this job.

39

I didn't start the car right away. I was thinking about the deletion of Ginny's DNA records and what might be on those encrypted hard drives.

I texted my contact at Mitogenic, Vivek Parmar, asked if the company had suffered any data breaches. I also wanted to know if he could get in touch with human resources, find out when Ginny Villarosa quit the company's Seattle office.

When she went to Virginia to meet Carlo, her Romeo, she was supposed to have a payload with her, the hard drives she left in a locker in Florida. But she didn't bring them.

Why did she bring her passport? Natasha said she had seen it on the desk in Ginny's room. Who needs a passport in rural Virginia?

Maybe Carlo, the sweet-talker, promised to take her overseas. He gets his hard drives, gets paid, tells her they can walk away from it all and live in hotels in France or Bali or the Maldives. Whatever sounds good to the ears of a woman in love.

But why meet in such an out-of-the-way place?

Maybe he never intended to take her overseas. Maybe the point was to get rid of her all along. If she had reached this point of doubt with him, if she was wavering or beginning to sour on their love, she might expose him, either through weakness or on purpose, for revenge. If she's no longer on board with the plan, she's a liability.

Why not get rid of her in a place where no one knew her? Where no one would think to look for her? He could get a big head start toward wherever he was going before anyone even noticed she was gone.

Did he instruct her not to tell her friends where she was going? Did he instruct her to not give her full name when she checked in to the Olympic Inn? Did he tell her to use a prepaid credit card? She had told Philip Nikander her name was Rachel. Was that part of *his* plan, or *their* plan?

I got a text from Vivek Parmar.

In a meeting right now. We did have a breach. Major APT, super sophisticated. State actors for sure. Took us months to clean up. Will call in a few.

I puzzled over that for a while. APT?

I looked it up. Google gave me a stock price for a company called APT, and then there was Alabama Public Television, a manufacturing company, and lots of apartments for rent.

I forwarded the text to Leon, asked if he could make sense of it. Thirty seconds later, he called.

"Advanced Persistent Threat."

"What's that?" I asked.

He gave me the lowdown. A hacker gets someone at a company to open an email, click on a link, maybe even plug in a USB drive they found in the parking lot. That causes a hidden program to be installed on the employee's computer. That's step one.

Step two, the program searches for other computers on the corporate network, starts copying itself. Now more than one machine is infected, so this thing is harder for the IT guys to root out.

Step three, the program starts scanning the hard drives of all the computers it's infected. By now, that may include the desktops and laptops of a few dozen workers, plus some of the company's servers, where the valuable data is stored.

Step four, the program connects to C&C servers, "command and control" machines on the public internet, where it asks the hackers, What do you want us to do while we're in here? The C&C servers send instructions back.

The objective is to steal as much data as possible. The C&C servers might tell the malicious programs to look for financial databases and spreadsheets, design documents containing trade secrets. The malicious program runs its searches and uploads data to C&C servers. The hackers retrieve it from there. Investigators never know where the hackers came from, because they never actually touched the machines they looted. Their bots did the work and left all the goods at a neutral drop point.

Leon started geeking out on the technology. He said the really sophisticated APTs knew how to hide from virus scanners. Some of them actually replaced the virus scanners with new ones that would permit them to run. Some lived only in memory, never on disk. That meant anyone scanning their hard drive in search of an APT program would always come up empty.

When a computer was shutting down, the APT knew it was going to get wiped out of memory, so it copied itself into the memory of another computer on the same network.

"How can a program *know* it's going to get wiped out?" I asked.

"You ever notice how when you click shutdown, the computer doesn't turn right off?" Leon said. "That's because some programs are still doing work. The operating system sends two signals to every running program. The first is an interrupt. When a program gets that, it wraps up what it's doing and waits for the next signal, which is a kill. These APTs get the interrupt and they copy themselves to another machine before the kill comes through."

"Where the hell do you learn this stuff?"

"Reddit. Hacker News. Brian Kreb's blog. What do you think I read in the bathroom?"

"Too much information, Leon."

"APTs aren't the work of average hackers. They're made by governments. China, Israel, Russia, the US. That's how we keep tabs on each other. It's virtual spying."

He sent me links to further reading. One of the recurring themes in all the articles was the difficulty of rooting out an APT. It often required wiping out the hard drives of every computer in the organization—every desktop, every laptop, every server in the data center—and then rebuilding them all from scratch—the operating system, all the programs, every user account. Think how much work that would be for an organization that had thousands of computers.

They couldn't even restore the systems from backups, because the backups might be infected too.

Vivek Parmar called and confirmed all of this while I was still digging through Leon's articles. This was exactly what Mitogenic went through. It took months to clean it all up, and they had to set up special systems to monitor outgoing traffic. Those systems, he said, were looking for large streams of data headed for China. Any sign of that and a built-in kill switch would shut down their whole network.

"You think it was China?" I asked.

"We're pretty sure. So is the security company we hired. And the FBI, and some other agencies of the Federal government."

Other agencies he declined to name. If China was involved, "other agencies" would include the CIA.

"This was a big breach, huh?"

"It was a big attempted breach. We actually caught it before too much data went out. The losses weren't that bad."

I asked him what the hackers were after.

"Genetic info. We have the DNA of millions of Americans."

"Why would they want that?"

"Genetics is the future of medicine. Customized, genetically engineered treatments, mRNA vaccines, gene splicing, CRISPR. You heard of that?"

He told me CRISPR lets scientists edit an organism's DNA the way a programmer edits code. You change the code, you can fix how the system works. One day they might be able to edit the cancer out of your lungs. How much did I think that was worth?

"They say data is the oil of the twenty-first century," he told me. "Whoever has the data has the power. If you want to cure an incurable disease, if you want to provide better treatments for chronic illnesses like diabetes, you need to know what's in people's DNA. You need lots of samples. Millions, if not billions of records.

"The US is an incredibly diverse country. The DNA samples in our database come from Americans descended from every corner of the earth. That's gold to the researchers in China. You think American pharmaceuticals extort you with their drug prices? Wait ten, twenty years. Wait till China holds all the patents on all the gene treatments you need to stay alive, or to keep your kids alive.

"By then the central party office in Beijing will have all your financial information, if they don't already. Their APTs have been swiping American data for over a decade. They'll know how much your house is worth, what stocks you own, how much you have in the bank. They'll be able to set a custom price based on the upper limit of what you can afford for that lifesaving medical treatment.

"If that doesn't chill you, I don't know what will. The public doesn't understand this new arms race. The data race. The governments get it. That's why they pour so much time and money into cyber weapons like APTs.

"The Chinese know exactly where they want to go in the fields of science and medicine, but they can't get there without the kind of data we have. America's rich tapestry of DNA. They'll do anything to get it."

He told me again that the APT didn't net the intruders much data. For all the trouble it caused Mitogenic, it was a bust as far as the hackers were concerned.

"Then something else happened," Parmar told me. "Something really perplexing. Have you ever heard of a mapmaker's wife's island?"

He explained it to me. In the fifteen and sixteen hundreds, when Europe was sending ships all over the globe, maps were among the most valuable pieces of information in the world. How do you get a ship from point A to point B? Where are the dangerous places you need to avoid? Where are the harbors, the rivers you can pull into when you arrive?

All that data was stored on paper and parchment, with everything carefully drawn and labelled. Kings were jealous of their maps, and of each other's. Maps were trade secrets, objects spies risked their lives to steal.

The mapmakers used to throw in features here and there that didn't really exist. Like a tiny island named after their wife.

When a copy of a map turned up in enemy hands, the king would look for those telltale signs, the made-up features. A mountain, an island, or a river that didn't really exist. The mapmaker's wife's island would tell him which map the enemy had copied, and from there, he could trace who had access to it and maybe catch the spy in his court.

"We still use that technique," Vivek told me. "All of our datasets include some made-up sequences. DNA of people who don't really exist. Internally, we know to weed those out of our research, but if anyone steals our data..."

He didn't finish the sentence. I got where he was going.

"Now here's the weird thing," he said. "A few months ago, this Chinese medical journal published a paper claiming a breakthrough in genetic treatment for a rare disease. The online version of the article linked to a dataset they used in their research. The data contained one of our fake DNA sequences. Our mapmaker's wife's island.

"The disturbing thing is that that specific data didn't exist until *after* we had cleared out the APT. When we saw the Chinese article, we did a full audit of our systems, brought in this really expensive security firm and confirmed there was no more APT, no data leaking out.

"So how did China get our mapmaker's wife? It wasn't through a hack. Someone must have given it to them some other way."

I saw Ginny Villarosa and her hard drives. I didn't like how this was adding up.

40

Ginny Villarosa's apartment was in a new-looking building on Dexter Avenue North, walking distance from her office in South Lake Union. I walked a block from my parking spot through blowing mist to the building entrance.

The ring I got from Steve had two keys. One for the mailbox, which was in the lobby. I scanned the names on the boxes. Villarosa was 424. I opened up her box to see what was there.

A big wad of bills. It looked like Zenobia hadn't been by in a while.

I took the elevator up, slide the key into the lock of 424, gave it a twist, and the door swung open.

The place was a mess. Someone had taken all the books off the built-in bookcase in the living room, then put a few of them back. Not upright, the way you see books on library shelves, but stacked. The rest were on the floor.

The cabinets under the bookcase were open, with papers spilling out. The kitchen drawers were open. The cabinets above the counter and under the sink, the pantry—it had all been searched. I checked the fridge. She had cleaned it before she left. Wiped down the glass shelves and everything. That told me she was planning on being away for a while.

The bedroom was especially bad. Clothes pulled out of drawers and strewn across the floor. The mattress and box spring were leaning against the wall so whoever was here could get a look underneath. And inside too. They cut them both open.

In the bathroom, stuff was everywhere. They even left the lid off the toilet tank.

Someone really wanted those hard drives.

I called Steve, asked if Zenobia had been checking on Ginny's apartment or just collecting the mail.

"She just gets the mail."

Yeah. She would have said something about a mess like this.

I poked through the clothes on the bedroom floor, but there wasn't much point. Whoever went through this place was pretty thorough. If what they wanted was here, they took it.

There was one thing though. A small card with a red valentine heart. It had a hole in the top right corner with a loop of red ribbon running through it. The kind of card you attach to a gift.

I turned it over. Her handwriting was familiar to me now. All that time I spent reading the notes that Sheriff Kessler passed along...

How lucky am I to find someone who means so much? How many people even get this chance in life?

She drew a heart and signed her name.

Whoever ransacked this place left their shoeprint on her love.

I was guessing she gave Carlo his Valentine's gift here in her apartment. He kept the present and left the card.

Idiot.

She was right, I thought. Maybe not about you, Carlo, but— how many people *do* get the chance? And how many are aware enough to express that kind of gratitude?

I was sorry for Ginny Villarosa. I told myself I'd do my best to get to the bottom of this, to salvage whatever justice we could find.

I slipped the card into my pocket, went back to the living room and stood there for a while, thinking.

What was missing here?

There were books, knickknacks, posters all over the place. But no photographs. The framed photos people keep on tables and bookshelves. There weren't any.

I did another check of the place, room by room. I could understand Ginny not having photos from Florida. Her father said she didn't approve of his line of work. Maybe she wanted to forget that part of her life.

After a few minutes, I found some college photos from New York City on the floor in the closet. Ginny's father said she went to Rutgers. The photos showed she had taken a trip into the city with her friends. I found three shots of her and her girlfriends in Soho, in Washington Square, on a rooftop overlooking the Hudson.

She was smiling in all three. Her face was puffier than when I found her. Maybe that was baby fat. She might have been eighteen in those pictures.

But there was nothing from Seattle. No pictures of her and Carlo. Maybe he took them. Tried to erase himself from her past.

When I left, I checked the hall for security cameras. There was one at each end. Her apartment was the last in the hall, just a few feet from one of the cameras.

In the lobby, I looked around. There was no desk, no concierge. Just the grid of mailboxes, an elevator, and some big potted plants by the door.

The sign by the mailboxes said, "See something suspicious? Report it." I called the number for the security firm, asked them where they're located.

"SoDo," the guy told me.

"Where's that?"

"South of the Dome."

"What dome? Never mind."

When I left the building, I checked the street. No signs of Anthony Villarosa's goons. Maybe they backed off, or maybe they left. Maybe Villarosa just wanted them to watch me walk into Steve and Zenobia's house, to confirm I was starting the job he wanted me to start.

I hope to God he called them back home. Those ham-handed fools would be on my nerves from morning to night.

I looked up the security company on my phone, then pulled up the address on the map. It wasn't far.

I wondered how many days of security footage they kept from those cameras in Ginny's hallway.

41

I misjudged what "nearby" meant in terms of driving time in Seattle. It took over an hour to get from South Lake Union to the Industrial District south of the stadiums.

I did stop along the way though. When I left DC, it was hot, and I was going to Florida. I didn't pack anything for this cool, wet weather. I picked up a jacket and a couple of shirts at Nordstrom Rack. That set me back thirty minutes.

The security company that monitored Ginny's apartment was in a one-story building next to an auto repair shop.

It was a bare office: linoleum floors, fluorescent lights, nothing to decorate the fresh-painted drywall. Two desks were empty. One was manned. A short dark-haired guy in a swivel chair talked into a handheld radio, telling whoever was on the other end to head up to an office on Capitol Hill.

He had an accent. Wasn't born here.

I introduced myself when he put the radio down, showed him my investigator's license, and without missing a beat he said, "Freddy Ferguson. Thirty-two and three. You were a top twenty heavyweight."

If the guy had heard of me, he must have been way into the sport. Some of my fights were on cable back East. I didn't know anyone on this side of the country was watching.

His name was Julio. He was from Nicaragua.

We talked about some of the guys who are fighting now. Terrence Crawford, the kid out of Omaha, is superb. Canelo Alvarez, Vasiliy Lomachenko, both top notch. Almost without a weakness. And then the heavies, Tyson Fury and Anthony Joshua. What a time for the Brits, to be able to claim both those guys as their own.

"And Chocolatito," I said. "Don't sell your countryman short."

He smiled. "Chocolatito can beat anyone except Sor Rungvisai. Qué lástima."

"I watched both those fights. Sor Rungvisai was a terror, but I thought Chocolatito won the first one. Bad decision from the judges that night."

Julio asked what I was investigating. I told him a woman in one of the buildings they serve over on Dexter had disappeared, but someone had visited her apartment.

"You guys have cameras in the building. How long do you keep the footage?"

"Eh... S'pose to be ninety days, but sometimes longer. Like a year."

"That's long enough," I said.

I couldn't compel him to show me anything. But I figured I might be able to get Sheriff Kessler to get a warrant. Except that, so far, there was officially no crime. And Kessler's office didn't have the time.

"Which building?" Julio asked.

I gave him Ginny's address.

"Which floor?"

He was already pulling something up on his computer.

"Four. But I need time to get a warrant."

"For what?"

"To look at the video. You have a legal officer I can contact?"

He waved off the idea. "Freddy Ferguson don't need no warrant with me. Why you stop boxing? You were beating everyone."

"That's a long story."

"El crimen?"

"Sí. Organized fucking crimen."

"You said fourth floor?"

"Yeah. Her apartment's at the end of the hall, away from the elevator. You sure you want to do this?"

"You see anyone here to stop me? I don't like el crimen. You trying to find a girl, I help."

He brought up a screen full of thumbnails, each one dated. He had months of video from every camera in Ginny's building.

A voice came over his handheld. One of their guards didn't know where he was supposed to be going. Julio picked up the radio. "No, man. Spring Street. Past Boylston. You gotta check the alarm."

He put the radio down, shook his head. "Guy never know where he going 'cause he always eh-stoned."

"How the hell do you search through this much footage?" I asked.

He showed me.

They have this software now where, if nothing is moving in the video, it just skips over it. So, in twenty-four hours of surveillance, if there's only ten minutes where people and things are moving, you only have to watch ten minutes. Less than that, because you can speed it all up.

I told him I wanted to see anyone going into or out of that apartment from August 1 on.

"It could take a while," I said. "What if your boss walks in?"

"Take less time than you think. And the boss is in Palm Springs."

I picked August 1 because I wanted to see if I could get a glimpse of Ginny Villarosa alive. If possible, I wanted to see what she looked like the day she left, which was sometime before the nineteenth. Was she tense? Excited? What?

We saw her a few times. She went out in the morning, came back in the evening. Carried a purse and a shoulder bag just big enough to hold a laptop.

We raced through two weeks of video in ten minutes. Not much happening on her floor.

August 15 was the day she left. She went out of the apartment with a big shoulder bag and a suitcase on wheels. And the black bag I found in the locker in Florida. The camera showed a brief clip of her face. She didn't look stressed. She turned and made sure the door was locked, then walked to the elevator. Casual stride, body at ease.

"You want me to switch to the camera at the other end? So you can see her face?"

"No. I feel like I'm stalking her already. Let's stick with this camera. Fast forward. See if we can catch a glimpse of who went in later."

It didn't take long to find out. August 21, two days after she died, this guy came down the hall twirling a set of keys. Her keys. He must have taken them from her room at the inn in Virginia.

Steve was right. Everything about the guy was average. Height, build, looks. Julio froze the picture just as he looked into the camera. It was eerie seeing him again after all those weeks.

Unfreeze. He slid the key into the lock and went into the apartment.

Fast forward three hours and he was back out. Three hours he searched that place.

We skimmed through the rest of the footage. No one else went in or out of that apartment except me.

Julio said, "Check this out."

He raced through a video feed from the underground parking, got to the day our friend appeared. There he was, walking off the elevator, then right out of the picture.

Julio found another angle, caught the guy getting into a dark red Porsche SUV. The car pulled forward and Julio froze the picture.

"There you go," he said.

A nice clear shot of the Washington state license plate. I wrote down the number.

I thanked Julio, picked up lunch, and checked into the Westin on Fifth Avenue, a pricey hotel in the middle of downtown. We usually stuck to the cheaper places to keep expenses down, but Anthony Villarosa was kind of a dick, and he didn't give me a choice about taking this assignment, so he didn't get to choose where I stayed. I didn't think he was hurting for money either.

I thought about calling Bethany to check in. I had left her a message the night before, after my dinner with Villarosa, told her I was in Florida heading for Seattle. The office needed to know where I was. Sometimes we let the local cops know too, depending on the case. Not this time though. Villarosa wouldn't stand for that.

I had texted Bethany when I landed at SeaTac, told her I'd call later.

But I didn't want to talk to her.

From my hotel room, I dialed Claire instead, told her the dead woman's boyfriend ransacked her apartment after her death. I told her I had a good lead. A license plate. She congratulated me.

"You know what else?" I said. "Besides this guy being in her apartment?"

"What?"

"He was in Virginia. In Nelson County the day of the murder."

"You're calling it a murder now? You're no longer undecided?"

"This was a murder," I said. "And he was there."

"How do you know?"

"Because I ran into him on the road. I helped him change his tire. Guy wouldn't even shake my hand."

I thought about what Steve said. How this guy liked to talk to women.

He sure as hell wasn't going to talk to me. He'd remember me, wonder how the hell I followed him from Nelson County to Seattle. He'd clam right up.

But he would talk to her. A thousand to one, if he liked an attractive woman who could carry a conversation, he'd like Claire.

"Come out here," I said. "I need your help."

42

The red Porsche, a $130,000 Cayenne Turbo, was registered to Carlo Ivanov of Mercer Island. That was just east of Seattle. To get there, you crossed a floating bridge over Lake Washington. Mercer Island was one of the wealthier suburbs of this wealthy city.

According to his LinkedIn profile, Carlo was either an entrepreneur or a tech evangelist, or a CEO coach with CTO-level expertise who could consult on all aspects of data intelligence. I didn't know what that was supposed to mean. He talked a lot, I guess, and made a boatload of money doing it.

I texted his info back to Bethany and Leon for a background check. I also asked them to check with Hertz, find out who returned a dark blue Mazda 3 with a bent steering rod in Virginia on August 19.

Leon called. "How am I supposed to get Hertz to give me the guy's name?"

"They know the car was in a collision. Tell them he hit something on your property and took off. You need the info for an insurance claim."

"Right, Champ."

I crossed the I-90 bridge and got off at Island Crest Way. The vibe here was mellower than in the city, but the weather was just as bad. Still that cold, sideways-blowing mist.

I found his house, a tan and cream three-bedroom on a normal-looking suburban street. If it was outside of St. Louis or Jacksonville, it might run $300,000. Zillow said he bought it for 1.2 million six years ago, and it was now worth over 2 million.

The yard had a few nice touches, including sculpted bushes that looked like they came out of the Dr. Seuss books I used to read to Lenny. There was a birdbath and a couple of birdhouses. Other than that, it was just wet, like everything else around here.

The Cayenne was in the driveway. I saw Carlo, or a man anyway, cross the living room behind the big bay window. I was too far away to get a good look. I wasn't going to hang out there either. Carlo didn't need to know anyone was looking for him.

Claire texted and said her plane would land at 11:50 the next morning. I told her I'd pick her up.

But first I wanted to talk to Steve again. I wanted to get an idea of how to approach this guy. What would make him want to talk to Claire? I mean, besides the obvious. What would keep him engaged?

I called Steve, asked when's a good time to talk.

"Tonight," he said. "Zenobia is working, and I need those keys back. She was looking for them earlier. I told her I must have moved them when I was cleaning. You have them, right?"

"I'll bring them by this evening."

43

I went back to the hotel, showered, called Claire. I wanted to get her up to speed on the case.

"Hey, Freddy."

I told her what happened in Florida. The locker, the hard drives, Anthony Villarosa, his daughter Virginia, and this guy Carlo, aka Romeo.

The only part I left out was how Villarosa forced the case on me.

She interrupted me a dozen times, wanted to know more about the father, the daughter. How could they go months without talking?

"I don't know. People do that."

"If I had a father, I'd talk to him every day."

"What? What happened to your— Never mind."

We didn't need to talk about that because if we did, she might ask about my dad, and there was no need to get into *that* subject. He was a violent bastard. Heavy drinker. Didn't give a shit about anyone because he wasn't capable of it. Died in prison.

We're not going there. You need to stay on point with her, Freddy, I told myself. Just like you do with everyone else.

"Look," I said, "this girl, Virginia—"

"Woman," Claire said. "What about her?"

"She falls for this guy Carlo. Like, an intellectual type, a smooth talker."

"Sure."

"What do you mean, sure?"

"Well, if he's smart and he's interested in her, that's a compliment. I mean, it's a lot better than dad, who's a thug and ignores her."

Wait a minute. I couldn't say I liked Villarosa, but I was a lot more like him than I was like Carlo. Anthony Villarosa took care of business. Bad business, but it was business all the same, and he got it done. If he didn't, he wouldn't be where he was.

Carlo, from what I'd heard so far, was a poseur, a seducer, a fake. I fixed his tire and the guy wouldn't even shake my hand.

What the hell's so attractive about that? Would she seriously be flattered by *his* attention?

I was starting to hate the guy.

Okay, calm down, Freddy. You're getting off track here. This is why you don't mix business and... Claire. Put your unruly feelings behind the dam with the rest of them. Focus on what needs to get done.

I told Claire that Ginny worked for the biotech company. She had her DNA analyzed, then deleted all her records. Why?

Claire didn't miss a beat. "You said her mom died of breast cancer. She'd want to be tested to see if her genes made her susceptible. And her dad is in a violent line of work. He might have killed some people to get to the top."

She was right on board with what I was thinking.

She said, "You know how they caught the Golden State Killer?"

Right on board.

"Tell me," I said, even though I already knew.

"They found his relatives' DNA in online databases. They were able to identify his family. Then they started asking which family members were in the towns where the murders occurred back in the seventies and eighties. Only one guy fit the bill, and they caught him."

"Exactly," I said.

"So, if there's a body out there with her dad's DNA on it, a cold case that was never solved, the police may have no idea who they're looking for, until they find a match in his daughter's DNA. She only has one father, and he happens to be in a line of work where killings happen. So, bingo. Her dad probably made her delete the data."

I told her I would be talking to a guy named Steve that evening. A guy who had met Carlo and watched him operate. I'd try to get info on how Claire could approach him.

"What makes you think this Carlo guy will talk to me?"

"He likes pretty women. Can't help but strike up a conversation."

There was a pause on the other end of the line as she digested that I just told her she was pretty. Dammit! I couldn't keep this stuff from slipping out.

My first instinct was to cover my ass. "It's just a fact, Claire. You're fucking lovely! Ask Bethany if you want an objective opinion."

But I bit my tongue to keep from making it worse.

She said, "So you want me to be bait?"

"He'll talk to you. That's all I'm saying. I want you to strike up a conversation, see if you can draw him out."

Another pause. Then she said, "You trust me to do this?"

"Of course, I do."

"Okay, Freddy. Eleven-fifty tomorrow morning."

"See you at SeaTac."

I hung up, lay back on the bed.

Was it bad that I was excited for her to come out there? Or was it worse that I was willing to put her in front of a guy I thought might have killed someone?

I didn't know. I never used to second-guess myself.

44

Steve and I were in the kitchen of his Ballard house. Zenobia was out at the strip club, poking her enlightened politics into the eyes of the male gaze.

Steve told me he was an analyst for Amazon. His job was to figure out which products they should manufacture under their own brand.

"Some of it is a no-brainer," he said. "Like computer cables, undershirts, stuff everyone buys. If we can offer decent quality at a good price, why not? It's another revenue stream for us.

"Other stuff takes a little more research. You think of a backpack or something like that. What do the top sellers have in common? What kind of materials? What kind of zippers? How are the pockets laid out? My team looks into all that. We come up with a composite that sort of looks like all of them. We find a manufacturer in Asia. Then we can sell essentially the same product for cheaper, because we have no real marketing costs, we don't have to pay for branding or ad campaigns. We already know which of our customers will buy it, so all we have to do is make sure they see it when they come to the site."

"How can other companies compete with that?" I asked.

"They can't. They just don't have the data that we have. Data is king. Whoever owns it owns the world."

Same thing Vivek Parmar told me.

I showed him Carlo Ivanov's LinkedIn profile. He sipped his beer, nodded and said, "Yeah! That's him!"

"Read his profile."

Steve took a minute to skim through it. A look of annoyance clouded his face. Finally, he shook his head.

"I don't know what this guy does," he said. "But I've heard lots of people who talk like him. They're usually consultants. They come in, interview people, write up a report saying you need to do X, Y and Z, and then they leave a hefty bill. It's kind of pointless. It's like having an athletic coach who tells you you need to be faster and stronger, and then he walks away and leaves it to you to figure out how to do the work."

"What about the specifics?" I pointed to some of the consulting work listed in his profile. "Like, what does this mean? *Advised a major Seattle-area storage provider on media cost optimization.* What does that mean?"

"He's talking about data storage. There are only two major Seattle-based providers. Amazon and Microsoft. And neither one of them needs outside advice. They have teams of people dedicated to this stuff. People with masters degrees and PhDs."

"Well the guy's doing something right," I said. "He lives on Mercer Island."

"Oh, that's right!" He said it like he suddenly remembered. "Ginny used to like to go out there. She said she could fall asleep without having to hear all the traffic noise. That section of Dexter she's on is like a canyon, and the buses run through there. They're loud."

"What kind of stuff did Carlo and Ginny talk about?"

"He's into the arts. He and Ginny would have long discussions. I think that was his go-to. I heard him talking about art and literature with women at the parties we attended."

Then his eyes lit up with a sudden realization. "Actually! Actually, now that I think about it, I think that was kind of his entree. If he overheard a woman talking about a writer or a musician, he'd butt into the conversation, or he'd circle back to her and catch her alone and start talking about the artist or the book."

I asked if he could remember any specific artists or musicians, any book titles, anything he talked about with Ginny.

He had to think for a while.

"Yeah. Okay. She told me he collects records. Old vinyl records, and he has this high-end stereo system. She said she was amazed at how good some of the old jazz records sounded through a good set of speakers. Miles Davis, John Coltrane, Dave Brubeck and... What's the other guy?"

"I have no idea." I was writing down all the names. I've heard them before, but I know nothing about jazz.

"You know who I'm talking about?" Steve asked. "He had a style all his own. He didn't sound like anyone else at all. You know, 'Better Get Hit in Yo Soul'?"

I shook my head.

"He punched that trombonist in the mouth. Um... Mingus! Charles Mingus!"

I wrote that down.

"He liked orchestral music too. Stravinsky and Dvořák. And painters. De Chirico. Carlo had the same print in his house that Ginny had in her apartment. *The Disquieting Muses*. I remember her saying that specifically. She thought it was a sign they were meant for each other."

After the painters came the writers. Graham Greene, Joseph Conrad.

"Especially Conrad. Ginny liked the book he wrote about a man and a woman on an island in Indonesia. I can't remember the title, but she was blown away that Carlo had actually read it. He liked the one about the spy. What's it called?"

"You're asking me? I've never read anything by Joseph Conrad."

"*The Secret Agent.*"

I added that to the list. I would give it to Claire and hope she knew one of those guys. It could be a conversation starter. The list might also give her a sense of his tastes and how his mind works. None of it meant anything to me.

I asked Steve for one last favor before I left.

"You mind if I look at Ginny's mail?"

He panicked. "Oh God, Zenobia would not be cool with that. That's like, stalking."

"It is, but I'm like, a detective, so it's what I do. I can't ignore anything that might help locate her."

I still couldn't bring myself to tell him Ginny was dead.

"Okay, you have to wash your hands before you touch the mail. Because if you, like, leave any grease stains or fingerprints on the envelopes, she'll be like, What the fuck, Steve? Why are you touching this when I told you not to touch it? I really don't want to have that fight again."

I wondered if "that fight again" was about him touching the mail or just generally about him not doing what she said.

Whatever. I washed my hands and dried them carefully and went through the stack. Bills, advertisements, a letter from a doctor, and a couple from her old employer, Mitogenic. Nothing personal, nothing to raise a red flag. I put it all back exactly as I'd found it, in case Zenobia's eagle eyes had memorized the order of the letters.

I thanked Steve, returned Ginny's keys, and went back to my hotel, where I spent most of the evening combing through the Work Experience section of Carlo's LinkedIn profile, making a list of places to call in the morning.

45

September 23
Mercer Island, WA

I started watching Carlo's house around 5:30 in the morning, in case he was an early riser. With his impressive résumé, all those companies he'd advised, you'd think he'd be a bundle of energy just raring to go. He wasn't.

There was no sign of life in the house until about 8:30 when the lights came on behind a frosted window, which I took to be a bathroom. He must have showered, because when he came outside fifteen minutes later, his hair was wet.

Steve was right. The guy dressed well. Dark grey slacks, a white button-down with the collar open, dark grey jacket. Designer work, custom tailored. Suits don't fit like that off the rack.

He drove the Cayenne half a mile to a coffee shop. Got some coffee and a scone, or maybe a bagel, I was too far away to see, then he parked himself on a stool at the counter behind the window, facing out toward the street. He set up his tablet and started reading.

I was in the car across the street and one shop down. At nine, I started calling places I had looked up the night before, companies his LinkedIn profile said he'd worked for or advised. None of them had ever heard of him. If a few had forgotten his name, that was understandable. Consultants come and go. But when none of his references pan out, that's a problem.

Finally, I found one woman who remembered him. She had worked with him years earlier at a tech company in San Diego that made software to monitor databases. Carlo was a cofounder. His smooth talking brought in investment money. The other cofounder ran the day-to-day operations.

This woman didn't have warm feelings for Ginny's Romeo. She said if the company succeeded, it was in spite of Carlo, not because of him. The other cofounder put in the sweat and blood.

They sold out to a bigger company. Carlo walked away with over a million dollars, probably close to two million, by her estimate. Maybe that's how he could afford the house on Mercer Island.

But he cashed out of the San Diego company more than seven years ago. How did he make money after that?

I asked the woman if she thought Carlo could be a successful consultant.

"Anyone can be a consultant," she said. "All you have to do is tell people what they want to hear. Now, being a worthy consultant is a whole different story. Those exist too."

"Do you think he's capable of advising companies on..." I read off a list from his LinkedIn page. "Storage optimization, network security, data security, and regulatory compliance?"

"Stop," she said. "No. In fact, those are all different specialties. Most consultants specialize in one area. There may be some people out there who can advise you in all those areas, but not many. With that much valuable knowledge, I imagine they'd be very busy."

Carlo sat in the coffee shop for almost two hours looking anything but busy. A number of people said hello and stopped to chat. Apparently, he was a regular. He also had an eye for the ladies, as Steve had mentioned. Of the six people he talked to, five were women. All young, as far as I could tell from across the street. He didn't waste his breath on the older crowd.

When he wasn't talking to people, he was drinking coffee— three cups—reading on his tablet, or people-watching. At one point he pulled what I thought was a phone from the inside pocket of his jacket. Then he found a pen and starting writing.

It was a notebook, the little pocket kind that detectives and news reporters used to carry in the old black and white films. When he was done, he closed it up and slid it back into his jacket.

I still had time to burn before Claire's plane arrived, so I scanned through Wikipedia articles on some of the names I'd gotten from Steve: Miles Davis, Igor Stravinsky, Antonín Dvořák. I had never felt so ignorant. Each of these guys had thousands of articles written about them. Dozens of books. Where was I when all that was going on?

I read the summary of the Joseph Conrad book Steve mentioned, *The Secret Agent*. It was about this sort of nothing guy, this guy going nowhere in life. His day-to-day was boring, so he created this fantasy life where he was a spy. He was on a secret mission to undermine the government. Only, after a while, it stopped being just fantasy. He met with others and they talked about blowing something up. The cops knew about him. They knew he plotted with a group of like-minded losers, but they also knew he wasn't competent, didn't have it together enough to carry out a grand plan to change the course of history.

But he tried, and it didn't end well.

Why would that particular story appeal to Carlo Ivanov?

46

Carlo was still sitting there. No coffee, just swiping at his tablet.

I drove around the block, where he couldn't see me, and started a video call with Bethany and Leon. Their background report turned up the same information as mine. Except for the San Diego gig, Carlo's work history was unverifiable.

His credit report showed six active credit cards, including an American Express Platinum. Most people who have an Amex use it for work, or for the travel perks. They do a good job sorting out headaches with hotels, airlines, and the like.

He still owed a million on the house. That was a hefty monthly mortgage. Why keep it if he lived by himself? At least, I thought he lived by himself. He had had a girlfriend until a month ago. I doubted he had replaced her already. The monthly payment on the Cayenne had to be pricey too. And he was paying all of it? With no job?

"Forget the house and car, there's another thing," Bethany said.

"His girlfriend," Leon cut in.

"Ginny?"

"No," said Bethany. "A girlfriend from years ago, when he was in San Diego."

"What about her?" I asked.

"She spent four years in prison," Leon said.

"For what?"

Leon: "Stealing design secrets."

Bethany: "From an aerospace company. Lockheed Martin."

"Did you guys talk to her?"

Leon: "Nope. She's in China."

"China?" I thought about that for a minute. "Was Carlo implicated? In any way?"

Bethany shrugged.

"All right. You get any info from Hertz, Leon?"

"Yeah, your boy Carlo picked up the Mazda at the airport in Baltimore, August eighteenth. Dropped it off the nineteenth in Harrisonburg, Virginia, 'cause the steering was whack. They gave him a Chevy Malibu and he drove to BWI. You been to the Rock and Roll Museum?"

"No."

"Is it true the monorail goes right through it?"

"I just told you I haven't been there."

"You gotta take a picture," Leon said. "Who runs public transit through a building?"

"Okay, Leon. Is Ed there?"

"He's here."

"Tell him this guy Carlo is stealing data, probably for someone who's paying him big bucks. Enough to keep that house and Porsche Cayenne. I want to know if the FBI or any other agency has him on their radar."

"Yeah, all right."

Bethany tried to elbow him out of the picture. He shoved her right back, got into the middle of the screen, and said, "Is Claire with you?"

"She hasn't landed yet."

Bethany shoved him out of the picture. She had this big playful smile on her face. "Leon hacked into my phone."

He popped back in. "She got pictures of you, Freddy! I think she's stalking you!"

She gave him a shove but couldn't get him off screen.

"Hacking my phone is not cool!"

"Stalking Freddy ain't cool."

"I'm not stalking him!"

"Then why do you have that picture?"

"We were at lunch. He was feeding a bird on the ground. Jesus, Leon, it's right there in the photo!"

"All right," I said. "Remember what I told you. Pass this one up to Ed. You have to nag him, Bethany, so he can nag his friends in the Bureau. An answer won't do us any good if it takes six weeks. The sooner we know, the better."

"I like your use of the royal we."

"We're a team," I said.

"The Royal We?" Leon asked. "What's that? Like the Royal PlayStation?"

"We," Bethany said. "Not Wii."

"Hey, sorry to bail," I said, "but I gotta go."

I hung up knowing those two would keep goofing off like this for the next twenty minutes, whether the camera was on or not. When they got excited, that's just how they were.

When we first hired her, Bethany was formal and tentative, didn't express her opinions. Maybe that came from being the only woman in the office. Maybe from being the youngest, or from working with a six foot three former boxer and a six foot five retired Special Agent.

Leon was even more stilted. He didn't understand nuance or sarcasm. Still doesn't, for the most part.

If you had asked me what would happen when we put those two together, I never would have pictured this.

But that's how they are sometimes. Like brother and sister. She has this protective attitude toward him, correcting him when he's socially tone deaf. And in return, he tells her when she's being a dumbass.

The clock on the dash said 11:00 a.m. Time to go to the airport.

47

Low dark clouds were blowing fast over the city all morning, over Lake Washington and Mercer Island. Same thing going down I-5 toward the airport. A wet blanket of gloom. If I lived here, my mornings would be like Carlo's. Three cups of coffee before I could get in gear.

On the exit to SeaTac, the radio weatherman said the high would be fifty-two and the low forty-five. "And we can expect a few sunbreaks today."

I didn't know what a sunbreak was. In DC, we have sunny days and cloudy days and rainy days, sometimes all three in one day. But sunbreaks?

Claire texted as I approached the terminal, said to pick her up outside baggage claim. Rolling along in the crowd of cars, I could see her standing on the sidewalk in a dark blue suit. She always dressed like that for work.

She looked cold, arms folded across her chest, bouncing up and down. She wasn't dressed for this weather.

At least the mist had stopped. She wasn't getting wet.

I forgot to tell her what kind of car I was driving. A grey Ford Fusion. I pulled up right in front of her, but she looked past me, scanning the cars as they rolled in. I sat there for a second because... Well, I just wanted to look at her. I could admire her for a second without hurting anyone.

The clouds parted and the sun brought out the rich dark brown of her hair as the wind whipped it around her face.

Some people look okay in a restaurant or an office, but shine too bright a light on them and their flaws start to show.

I'm one of those people. She's not. The more you see of her...

Put that behind the dam, Freddy. She just got off a long flight and she's cold.

I rolled down the passenger window, said her name.

She leaned down, put her hand to her brow to shield the sun.

"Hey, Freddy."

The way she squinted in the light, her smile when she said my name...

That's a sunbreak.

48

We were driving up I-5 in heavy traffic toward downtown Seattle.

"Check this out." She held up a corporate ID card with her photo on it.

I gave it a quick glance. "What's that?"

"Leon made it for me. He copied the Amazon design."

"You work for Amazon?"

"Amazon Web Services. Infosec."

"What's that?"

"Information security. I thought it might appeal to your friend Carlo. A pretty woman with access to corporate systems filled with valuable data."

She was razzing me about the "pretty" part. I could see the smile she was trying to suppress.

I told her Carlo was not my friend.

She asked where we were going.

"To the hotel."

"I mean, which hotel?"

"The Westin."

"Ooh!"

Half an hour later, we were eating in the hotel restaurant. Claire was a light eater. A Caesar salad with grilled salmon, and that's it. For me, halibut, potatoes, asparagus.

She told me she spent last night and the whole of the five-hour flight reading technology white papers. She told me thousands of companies stored data on AWS—Amazon Web Services. To get that business, AWS had to prove they comply with data security standards. They published papers describing how they do it.

"How much of that stuff did you understand?"

"Most of it. I used to evaluate companies, remember? For corporate takeovers. Data and systems security was one of the things we looked at, so I'm familiar with the basic principles.

"These papers read like a best practices manual. I'm really impressed with what Amazon has built here. If I do strike up a conversation with Carlo and I'm supposed to work in AWS InfoSec, I should at least be able to drop a few comments that make me sound legitimate."

"What if he asks you something specific?"

"I'll tell him I can't discuss details. That's par for the course at most companies. No one discloses trade secrets."

I told her what I learned from Steve. Carlo liked to talk about art, music, and literature.

She scanned my notes, said, "Well that's a lot more interesting than databases and security."

"You know any of these people? The musicians? The painters and writers?"

"Sure."

"Which ones?"

"All of them."

"Seriously?"

"Why wouldn't I?"

That was a blow, straight to the solar plexus of my ego.

She went to college. I didn't. She had the natural curiosity and interest to keep up an intellectual life. I had seen the inside of her apartment: neat, clean, tasteful, well composed. Like she had a clear vision of what her home would look like even as she was collecting the pieces. The couch, the chairs, the rug. Vases on the tables, artwork on the walls.

My apartment was functional, utilitarian. The kitchen junk drawer had just about every tool you'd ever need.

"Well yeah," I said. "Some of the guys on that list are household names. Miles Davis, sure. But Dvořák? Stravinsky?"

"I love Dvořák. And Stravinsky's *Rite of Spring*, but not his tonal stuff."

How did this conversation keep getting worse?

"Did you read that book?" I asked. *"The Secret Agent* by Conrad?"

"No."

For a half second, I felt like I'd scored a point. Like, at least in this matter, she was closer to me than to Carlo.

"But I did read *Victory.*"

Why did there have to be a but?

I took the notes back from her, scanned for *Victory,* but I didn't see it.

"That one's not in the notes."

"That's the book about the man and woman on the island."

How did she know that? Steve couldn't even remember the title.

I could see she was pretty confident about talking to Carlo. She asked what we wanted to get out of him.

"First, we want a general sense of the guy. Ask if he has a girlfriend."

"Didn't he just kill her?"

"That's not the point."

"What's the point then? Women don't just walk up to men and ask if they have a girlfriend."

"Okay, take a step back here."

"Do you have a girlfriend, Freddy?"

"Is it any of your business?"

"Exactly," she said.

"Okay, you're starting to get on my nerves. Just shut up for a second and let me explain. 'Ask' wasn't the right word. You just draw whatever information you can out of him. If he even thinks you're fishing around the girlfriend question, he gets the sense you're interested."

"I know how it works, Freddy."

Good God! Miriam, Bethany, and now her. They could all piss me off without even trying.

"I know you know, Claire. The point of this conversation is to make sure we're on the same page. Also, I want you to gauge his reaction once he gets the clue that you're interested. His girlfriend has been missing for weeks and he hasn't reported it.

She's dead, and he knows it. I want to know if he shows any emotion when he talks about her, or when you mention her. Sadness? Remorse? Is he nervous? Evasive? Or just cold-blooded and indifferent. How good are you at reading people's feelings?"

She looked away.

"Huh?" I tapped her knee under the table. I don't like people tuning out on me, especially when it's work and we need to coordinate.

"Pretty good," she said.

"Like, Bethany good?"

"I'm not blind, Freddy."

"Okay. So— Look at me, will you?" She turned back, looked at me, like I asked. "I want us to get this all straight before you approach him. This guy might have killed a woman. I want to get as much info as we can with the least possible risk."

"Where am I supposed to meet him?"

"At a coffee shop. I'll be watching. But back to the point: See how far he starts probing into your job. Does he ask you what kind of data you have access to? Do you get any sense at all he's trying to feel you out as a source? Someone he can exploit to get at data he wants to steal? Let me ask you something. Can you tell when someone is measuring you, or probing for weaknesses?"

I gave her the same cold, direct stare I gave my opponents in the ring. It didn't faze her.

"Always," she said. "I'm hyperaware of that kind of thing. I had to be, in the world I came from."

"You can tell when someone is feeling you out?"

"You're doing it right now."

"And if he's interested in you? If he's attracted, you can tell?"

"Guys can never hide it."

"Okay, so that's an angle you can work. But you don't have to touch him. Don't feel compelled to do anything like that."

"I thought that went without saying."

"And if it gets uncomfortable—"

"Goddammit, Freddy, stop talking to me like I'm a child. What do you think a woman deals with, day in and day out, every fucking day of her life? Do you think I don't know how to handle myself?"

"Look, I'm not trying to belittle you. I'm just nervous about putting you in an uncomfortable situation."

"Life is an uncomfortable situation." Her tone was sharp and hot.

I tried to calm her down. "I'm only saying it because I feel like I'm asking a lot of you."

"Which is exactly what I want you to do, because I want to deliver. What else, Freddy? What else am I looking for?"

"See if you can get him to talk about his work history. Because what I see on LinkedIn doesn't add up. He's got money coming from somewhere that lets him keep up this lifestyle, but it's not coming from that bullshit consulting. You know more about the business world than I do. You can tell if he's faking it."

"Okay."

"Now, the meeting place. He seems to be a regular at the neighborhood coffee shop. Sits for hours and chats with the other customers. We'll start there. You bump into him, strike up a conversation. See how interested he is in what *you* do, that big juicy treasure trove of data *you* might have access to."

"Okay."

"From there we get the subject matter for our next conversation."

"You mean my next conversation with him."

"Yes. That's what I mean."

The waiter cleared the plates and asked if we wanted dessert.

We both answered at the same time. I said no, Claire said yes.

She ordered tiramisu. Before it came, she asked why I was still pursuing this case. If it looked like a murder, why not just turn it over to the police?

"Well... I have my reasons."

"Give me a straight answer, Freddy. Anthony Villarosa doesn't seem like the kind of guy you'd work for."

There it was again. Her uncompromising directness, her ability to see through all the bullshit to the heart of the matter. I felt another surge of admiration for this sharp-minded woman, and I put it behind the dam with all the other feelings I didn't want.

I told her Ginny's father made me an offer I couldn't refuse. Find Romeo. I had to say yes to get out of Florida.

I knew what Villarosa would do to this guy when I found him. I wasn't going to lead a guy to his own murder, even if I did think he was a killer. But that was just one problem with this case.

The hard drives were another problem. Why was Carlo stealing DNA data? Who was he working for? Vivek Parmar's words stuck with me. What if we did get to the point where millions of Americans had to rely on Beijing for genetic treatments, vaccinations, life-saving medical technologies?

I understood that bringing down one guy wasn't going to stop that, one smooth-talking guy who convinced a woman he loved her and then got her to steal twenty-one hard drives full of data from her employer. A guy like him could be replaced in a matter of months. Whoever he was working for probably had twenty other agents just like him, spread all over the country.

But if I let Anthony Villarosa kill the guy, the cops or the feds or whoever was interested in these massive data thefts would never get a chance to interview him. He might have info that led to the next guy up the chain. He might be the missing puzzle piece whose arrest leads to the disruption of a major network. If Villarosa just offed the guy, we'd never know.

In my mind, the national security considerations trumped the murder. This also gave me an out. If I could convince the feds that this guy was of interest to them, then Villarosa couldn't kill him. The FBI or whoever would bring him in for questioning, and if he really was a player in this data theft game, they'd either bust him, which would save his life, or they'd watch him like a hawk until he led them to the big boys.

Villarosa wasn't going to kill a guy who was under surveillance. That would mean killing him in front of federal agents. He wasn't going to insult the FBI like that and risk a takedown by the feds over what was essentially a personal affair.

I explained all this to Claire. She was an excellent listener. I liked that about her.

When I was done explaining the big picture, she said, "This is what I like about you, Freddy. You're not playing checkers. You're playing chess. You're playing the long game."

I hadn't thought of it that way. For me, there was no other way of looking at it. You want the best outcome for everyone, the closest you can get to justice, and that has to take into account the big picture and all the players.

She said, "A lot of people wouldn't even recognize who all the players were. You want a bite of this?"

She pushed her tiramisu toward me. "Try it," she said. "It's really good."

She was right. It was.

When I paid the check, she said she was going to her room to shower and rest. She asked what about me?

"I'm going to surf the 'net. Maybe learn more about Stravinsky and Joseph Conrad, so I can catch up with you."

In the elevator, I pressed eight for me, twelve for her.

As we passed three, she asked what was on my mind.

"Nothing," I said.

"No. It's something."

I was thinking about how hard it was to look at her sometimes, how much energy it took to hide my admiration. I wanted to ask if I'd ever done anything to make her uncomfortable. If there was anything I could do to be a better mentor.

But I couldn't ask those questions without making everything awkward and uncomfortable.

We had had a good lunch, an excellent conversation even if we both got a little touchy now and then. She listened. She understood. I was grateful for her intelligence, her professionalism, the dimension her perspective and understanding brought to our work and to my life.

I couldn't tell her any of that without the feelings slipping out. There was too much behind the dam already. And even if I could keep the feelings hidden, she'd wonder why I picked up on so many details about her, why I observed her so closely and considered her words and actions so deeply.

Close attention and deep consideration are the hallmarks of affection. And of detective work. And of stalkers.

When I got out on eight, she said bye.

I couldn't work with this woman, and I couldn't work without her.

Alone in my room, I looked out over the cloudy harbor and thought of how the code of professionalism turned the natural world upside down. After all these years in the wilderness, I finally knew exactly what I thought and what I felt and what I wanted. For once, it was all crystal clear. But I couldn't express it. I kept to myself feelings whose whole purpose was to be shared. The world was backwards, like a photo in negative. Black was white and white was black. Right was wrong and wrong was right.

The feelings on which the survival of our species depends, the feelings of a man for a woman, of me for her, were forbidden in this context.

I got that. No woman wants to be hounded. No one wants a mess at work. But where did all this go if I couldn't let it out?

My phone chimed. A text from Ginny's dad. He just touched down in Richmond. Did I have time to talk?

I called, we exchanged hellos and then he got to the point.

"You found him yet?"

"I'm close."

I didn't want Villarosa to send any more goons out here to follow me or Carlo. I was glad the two he did send disappeared.

"Close. Like how close?"

"Maybe a couple of days."

"I'll call you tomorrow."

He hung up. Not very civil.

I thought about all the things that Anthony Villarosa and I had in common. We both worked on the wrong side of the law, though I went straight and he climbed the ladder. We were both upset about what happened to his daughter. We both wanted to kill Romeo. Only he wanted to kill Ginny's Romeo and I wanted to kill Claire's. So far, I was doing a pretty good job on both counts. I mean, we had Carlo in our sights. And Romeo Ferguson was dying a little each day.

I swear, this was killing me.

49

September 24
Seattle, WA

Claire and I met at 6:30 a.m. in the hotel restaurant. Eggs, bacon, and hash browns for me; oatmeal, yogurt, and blackberries for her. She skipped coffee, said if she had to drink a cup with Romeo, she'd get overwound.

Seven thirty, we were on Mercer Island, watching Carlo's house. The blowing clouds began to clear, and the DJ on KEXP predicted sun by midmorning.

Eight fifteen, Carlo was up and showering.

Eight thirty, out to his car. Dressed in a dark suit jacket and pants, white shirt, no tie.

"That's him?" Claire asked.

"That's the one."

We left as he got into his car, went around the corner and waited. When he passed, we followed, keeping a block behind. I knew where he was going, so I wasn't worried about losing him.

I parked a block and a half from the coffee shop. I watched him park and go inside as Claire clipped her fake Amazon ID to her jacket pocket. Then she dialed my number from a burner phone. I picked up, tested the connection. Nice and clear. She put the burner in the inside pocket of her jacket, her real phone in her purse. If I needed to get in touch with her, I'd text her on the real one. The rest of the time, I'd listen to her talk with Carlo.

Claire grabbed her bag and her prop, a paperback she picked up at Elliott Bay yesterday afternoon. Not Joseph Conrad. Graham Greene. *Our Man in Havana.*

I asked her why she picked that one.

"Because I want to read it."

"But if you know he likes Joe Conrad—"

"Then he probably likes Greene too. Wish me luck."

"Good luck."

She got out. As she walked down the street, I heard the muffled swishing of her jacket.

I could hang back, sit in the car and listen, but I wanted to see how she worked. I walked to the coffee shop across the street from the one she was going to. It's true what they say about Seattle. Coffee everywhere. They need it to stay awake through the dripping permagloom.

In a minute, I was in. Cup of coffee, headphones on, I got a table by the window. Carlo sat in the window across the street, left hand on his coffee, right hand swiping a tablet. I could hear Claire order. Double soy latte and a croissant. Then the screech of the milk steamer made me take the headphones off.

I took a look around the shop I was in. Only three other customers. No line. The place across the street was full. I waited till Claire moved away from the steamer, put the headphones back on, and listened to the chatter coming from the popular side of the street.

She grabbed her coffee from the pickup area, turned, looked at Carlo by the window, hesitated a second, then made a beeline for the stool right next to him. The place was crowded enough that that wouldn't seem weird. There weren't many open seats.

She put her coffee down, set her bag on the counter, then slid her book across, hit his coffee, and knocked it over. He jumped up off his stool.

"Oh, God! I'm so sorry," she said.

Very convincing. In my mind, I added acting to her list of talents.

Carlo righted the cup. "No harm, no foul," he said. "It's empty."

He checked her out.

She dresses pretty well, doesn't she, Carlo? Just like you. Now which part interests you the most? The clothes? The face? Or the Amazon badge?

I couldn't see his eyes from where I sat.

"Graham Greene?" he said.

"Yeah." That was Claire.

"Vacuum cleaner."

"Excuse me?"

"How far are you in the book?" he asked.

"Chapter one."

"Ah. You haven't got to the vacuum cleaner yet. Have you read any of his other books?"

"*The Power and the Glory*," Claire said. "*The Ministry of Fear. The Heart of the Matter*." She named three more.

Where did she find the time to read all that?

"This one's on the lighter side. I'm Carlo."

"Claire."

They shook hands. Till then, they'd been standing. She sat first, then him. They were already pretty close, not a lot of room between the stools, and then this big guy took the stool to her left. She scooted away from him, closer to Carlo.

I didn't like it when she sat that close to me. Her nearness put my nerves on edge. I liked it even less when she sat close to him. Mister I-Read-Ten-Graham-Greene books and now I'll sing you some Dvořák in my fancy-ass Porsche Cayenne. Asshole.

"You work in Infosec?"

He must have read her badge. He said it casually, an opener to get her talking.

"Yeah."

"Amazon or AWS? The store or the cloud platform?"

"The cloud," she said.

That's what would interest him. The AWS cloud full of corporate data.

"You must be pretty sharp."

Yeah, smartass, she is. You have no idea how condescending you sound. *You must be pretty sharp.* What's the presumption there? *To do a man's job.* That's exactly the wrong thing to say to her. She doesn't put up with that kind of shit.

"Oh, it's not that hard."

Wait, what? She shrugged that off like it was nothing. She sounded almost bashful. That wasn't the person I knew. Maybe it was the person he wanted her to be, but I liked the real Claire better.

I reminded myself to calm down. She's playing him, I told myself. Acting interested, maybe a little coy, maybe not like the strongest person in the world, because he's looking for a woman he can manipulate, like Ginny.

He asked her something about her job, but I couldn't hear the question because my phone beeped. Ed was calling.

Claire said something about data access and regulatory compliance. I couldn't hear it because the beep cut in again.

I texted Ed. *On a job. Can it wait?*

Ed: *Where's Claire?*

Me: *With Carlo.*

Ed: *Safe?*

Me: *Yeah. I'm watching from across the street.*

Ed: *Ease her out.*

Me: *What's up?*

Ed: *Call me. Now.*

I couldn't figure out how to start a second call while I already had one going. I didn't know if my phone even allowed that. I cut the call with Claire and called Ed.

"What time is it there, Ed?"

"Almost noon. I got a response from the Bureau a while ago. They told me they were watching Carlo Ivanov a few years ago in San Diego. His girlfriend stole data from Lockheed Martin. Design data for a Pentagon contract. She refused to talk about anything. Kept a strict silence and went to prison. She was a dual citizen, US and Taiwan. But after prison, she went to mainland China. That's a red flag."

"Did the Bureau talk to Carlo on that case?"

"They did. And the CIA too. Neither of them liked the guy, but they didn't have anything on him, so they let him go. Then, about three years ago, the CIA was watching a woman in San Francisco who worked for a big-data company, the kind that uses artificial intelligence and machine learning to analyze hundreds of billions of records. They were ahead of the game with their technology, and their source code became a target for other governments who wanted to analyze data at that scale.

"The company thought this woman had walked out the door with their code. The Bureau interviewed her twice and was starting to build a case. Then she turned up dead in her apartment. Overdosed on sleeping pills."

"Like Ginny Villarosa," I said. "I mean, Ginny was barbiturates and Rohypnol. But the same thing. An overdose. Was the woman in San Francisco connected to Carlo?"

"Only tangentially," Ed said. "During surveillance, the Bureau saw them meet up a couple times at a coffee shop on Divisadero. They kissed. I spoke to one of the agents on that case, and a few things bothered him. First, the San Diego thing. The fact that Carlo Ivanov was involved with the woman down there who had been convicted, who for sure was stealing.

"Second, they did a trace to try to connect Ivanov to the woman stealing the source code in San Fran. They checked his cell phone location history and compared it to hers. Their phones were never in the same place at the same time. What bothered the agent about that was that he saw the two of them together. Her phone location for that meeting showed up in the data the Bureau got from Verizon. Her phone was with her, at the coffee shop. His phone was still in his apartment, both times.

"Foreign governments train agents like Carlo to do that. Don't bring your phone to a meeting because it leaves a digital trail."

Ed asked if Ginny's hard drives were still in Florida.

"As far as I know."

"The Bureau will be paying Anthony Villarosa a visit. You might want to warn him."

"He's not going to like that," I said.

"I don't care if he likes it. Tell him the Bureau is coming for the drives and he better not tamper with them."

"They're encrypted," I reminded him. "There's no way to tell what's on them."

"Until we find the encryption key. How's Claire doing?"

I looked out across the street. She was so close to him, they were practically touching. They were smiling like a couple of high school kids on a date.

"She's doing great."

"Ease her out. Get her back to the hotel. Someone from the Bureau will meet you there. And possibly someone from the CIA."

"You serious?"

"I'm serious. If a foreign government is involved, and this guy's been in their sights before, the CIA is going to want to keep tabs."

"All right, Ed."

I waited a few minutes after I hung up, my jealousy rising as I watched Claire flirt.

Finally, I sent her a text.

Ed says it's time to blow.

I saw her check her phone. She said something to Carlo but didn't leave.

They talked a few more minutes. Actually, six minutes. I timed it. I wish I hadn't cut the line when I got on the call with Ed. I wanted to know what they were saying.

Before she left, they swapped phones. She typed something into his. Her number. I knew she was giving him her number. And he was typing his into her phone.

They could have swapped numbers like normal people, but no! They had to go through this flirty high school crush routine.

I was burning with jealousy. What else of hers was she going to let him touch?

I had to calm down. She'd be next to me in the car in a minute. I couldn't get mad at her. This wasn't about me. This was work.

Come back to reason, Freddy. I reminded myself it was faster if each person types in their own info. Better than taking turns talking, typing, repeating your words in a loud public place. The phone swap was just Claire being sensible and efficient.

On the drive back to Seattle, she told me he wanted to take her out to dinner.

"Perfect."

My heart was in my throat and my ego was circling the drain.

"You did good work, Claire. A friggin' phenomenal job."

50

When we reached the Seattle side of the I-90 tunnel, I called Anthony Villarosa. It was half past noon on the East Coast. The sooner I could warn him, the better.

He picked up on the second ring, and he sounded angry.

The woman in the morgue was Ginny all right, though after all that time in the water, she didn't look like what he was used to seeing.

"She was distorted," he said. "Like, warped."

He said they had warned him. They didn't like showing a body in that condition to family members. Usually, if she had a birthmark or some distinguishing tattoo, they'd have him identify that.

But he had to look at her face, and I know it was hard on him. He practically broke down right there on the phone.

"Hey," I said. "I hate to talk business at a time like this, but—"

"No," he said. "Tell me some good news. Tell me you found Romeo."

I looked at Claire. "Yeah. We found Romeo."

"We?"

"I have a partner."

"Romeo's gonna pay for what I had to look at yesterday. Where is that fucker?"

"Hold on," I said. "Are you in Richmond or Delray?"

"Delray. Where's Romeo?"

I told him we had a complication.

"What? I don't like complications. I don't pay you or anyone else to bring me problems. I pay to make problems go away."

"You still have that bag that Ginny left? The one with the hard drives?"

"It's back in the locker. I've been holding on to it in case Romeo shows up. But it sounds like he's with you."

"You're gonna get a visit from the feds later today."

"Come again?"

"The FBI is coming by to pick up those drives."

He went ballistic. The guy was cursing so much I had to pull the phone from my ear. Somewhere in the stream of obscenities, I thought I heard him say he was going to kill me.

"Listen," I said. "All they want is the hard drives, that's it. They're not going to turn your club upside down."

"How do you know what they're going to do? They're fucking cops. You think I trust those bastards? Shit! I gotta do some cleaning in here."

I could hear him walking as he talked. It sounded like he went outside.

"I don't think you have to do that," I said. "Just give them the hard drives and they'll leave."

He got into his car. I heard the engine start, the seatbelt warning chime. He was still cursing.

"Do you get me, Anthony? This isn't about you."

"It's never *not* about me," he said angrily. "It's fucking *always* about me. Goddamn cops! Goddamn fucking cops!"

He hung up.

A minute later, I got a call from Sheriff Kessler in Nelson County, Virginia.

"You seem to have stumbled into something," he said.

"What makes you say that?"

"The FBI doesn't call me often. You know who that girl was? Your woman in the woods?"

"Virginia Villarosa."

"Maybe I asked the wrong question," Kessler said. "Do you know who her father is?"

"I know now," I said. "In fact, I just talked to him. But this isn't about him."

"You sure?"

206

"I'm pretty sure. He's a businessman who doesn't like attention. This isn't the kind of thing he'd get mixed up in."

"What kind of thing is it then?"

"You'll have to ask the Bureau."

"All right," he said. "They have a guy in mind in connection with the girl's death. The coroner in Richmond still has the cause as undetermined, but the FBI read the handwritten report you left in the Lovingston station the day of the storm. They're asking about a guy named Carlo Ivanov. They're up in Afton now, talking to Phil Nikander and Natasha, going from restaurant to restaurant, trying to find a waiter or someone who saw the two together. I'll tell you something, Freddy, even if this is a murder, it's tied into something bigger. A run-of-the-mill murder doesn't get this kind of response."

"Yeah, I know."

"You have any sense of what's going on?"

"I do, but I'm going to have to get back to you on that."

As we pulled into the hotel's underground lot, I got a text from Ed.

They're waiting for you in the restaurant. Ned Charles, Bureau SAC. Maria Koh, CIA. Charles needs info for a warrant. Whatever Koh asks, tell her.

As we stepped off the elevator, I got a text from Vivek Parmar. The FBI called his personal cell. Agents were interviewing his coworkers in his office in Austin and in Ginny's old office here in Seattle.

"Boy, they don't waste time," I said to Claire. "They come from every direction at once."

51

They were waiting by the elevators. Ned Charles, clean cut, freshly shaved, nice gray suit. Bureau, one hundred percent. He looked maybe thirty-five.

Maria Koh looked ten years older. Long dark hair, dark eyes, tan skirt suit. I would have pegged her as a legal secretary.

Koh hustled us onto the elevator and took us to a room on the thirty-second floor. On the table by the window, a pot of coffee and a tray of pastries and fruit. On the bed, two laptops. His and hers. They'd brought in a couple extra chairs for us, but we didn't use them.

I stood by the TV, Claire by the window. They asked if they could record us.

Sure.

Each had their own recorder.

Ned Charles sat on the edge of the bed, Koh in the desk chair, facing us. Charles opened his laptop and asked for my account of what happened.

"Start at the beginning," he said. "You were in the woods with a dog."

I told him everything I had told Sheriff Kessler, except I hadn't told Kessler about the key.

"Why didn't you tell Kessler about the key?"

"Sometimes I hold on to things."

Charles typed a lot of notes. Koh was more of a watcher. I could see her making mental notes on my posture, body language, facial expressions. She could listen to the recordings later. Right then, she wanted to get a sense of who she was working with.

"You shouldn't omit things like that when you make a statement," Charles said. "The defense will pick at it when they get you on the stand. They'll try to paint you as unreliable. Anyhoo, what happened next?"

I told him about Villarosa's gym, Ship Shape, the locker, the hard drives, the goons. Koh piped in with her first question.

"How did you find the place?"

The seahorse on the key, a woman jogging in Delray Beach, the tedious block-by-block digital walkthrough Leon and I spent so many hours on. She said she admired us for the grunt work. The least exciting part of the job is the most essential.

Ned Charles put us back on track.

"So, two guys came after you and hauled you around back to the boss?"

"Yeah."

"What was your sense of him? You think he had any interest in the drives?"

"No. He's got a pretty good thing going down there. He doesn't need this kind of trouble. Plus, I don't think he knew his daughter was mixed up in anything like this. All he knew was she was with a guy he didn't like. He was waiting for this guy to come open the locker. When I showed up, he didn't even know his daughter was dead. I had to tell him that."

"How'd he take it?"

"He kept his emotions in check, for the most part. The guy's pretty cold-blooded when he needs to be."

"And in the bag," Charles said, "how many hard drives would you estimate?"

"Twenty-one."

"You counted? How did you have time to count if one guy was hitting you and another had you under the gun?"

"I didn't count. I had dinner with Anthony Villarosa that night. He said there were twenty-one drives. From the size and weight of the bag, I'd say that's about right."

"You know how big they were? How many terabytes?"

"Villarosa said eight each. A hundred and sixty-eight terabytes total. He tried to get some tech guys to read them, but they're all encrypted."

Charles looked at Koh. "That's a pretty big haul."

He finished typing his notes, then read it all back to me.

These weren't notes. What he read was a statement. An official statement by yours truly.

"Sound good?" he asked.

"No," I said. "There's one more thing."

"What's that?"

"I saw Carlo Ivanov in Virginia the day of the murder. Less than a mile from the body. I helped him change a tire."

Koh, the CIA agent, gave Charles a look. "That's what we want," she said.

Charles wrote that into the statement, explaining as he typed that what I said about the key and the locker and the hard drives was enough to get a warrant to recover the drives from Anthony Villarosa's gym.

"I thought you already had a warrant," I said.

"We'll have it within the hour if you sign this statement."

He printed it on a portable printer and handed me a pen. Before the ink was dry, he called the Bureau and told them it was a go.

So far, only Ginny was implicated in the data theft.

The fact that I could place Carlo near the body tied him in. Maybe not to the theft, but to a potential murder. Charles told me that was enough to get a second warrant—to search Carlo's house on Mercer Island.

This is where Koh perked up. The CIA didn't care about the murder. They did care about an agent stealing valuable data to advance the interests of a foreign government. They'd jump at a chance to comb through Carlo's house, find out what secrets he was hiding there. Communications with handlers or other agents on his laptop? A notebook with the names of leads he was cultivating? Info about jobs he'd pulled off that they hadn't even heard about yet?

Charles and Koh seemed to have a cordial professional attitude toward one another, but the tension between the agencies they represented had already seeped into the room. I knew what that was about because Ed had told me stories from his years in the Bureau.

The Bureau has to take the long view in all its work. They're not really "solving" a case. They're gathering evidence for a prosecutor to argue a case, and everything they do has to be by the book, or the evidence gets chucked, the prosecutor gets screwed, and the criminal walks free. The Bureau is cautious and methodical because everything they do is going to get picked apart in court by attorneys.

The problems the CIA deals with almost never wind up in court. The nature of their cases forces them to take a more pragmatic view. Every second a guy like Carlo is at large, the country is bleeding information. The enemy is getting stronger and we're getting weaker. They want to stop this guy before he makes his next move. Doesn't matter how. Just stop him. If we have to play dirty, so what? His team is just as bad.

You can see how this causes problems. The Agency wants any info it can get, any way it can get it. To them, the Bureau's caution is a frustrating restraint. The Bureau wants evidence that's lawyer-proof. Searching without a warrant, contaminating evidence, neglecting to document chain of custody—that's recklessness.

Ed summed up the FBI's frustration when he told me about a case he'd worked for two hard years, only to have the judge throw out key evidence on a technicality. "We scored a ninety-yard touchdown run, and it got called back on a holding penalty."

Ned Charles and Maria Koh would have to work out how they were going to share their pie.

By now, it was almost noon. We hadn't touched the coffee or pastries, but we were hungry. Charles offered to treat, so we went down to the restaurant.

52

Claire gave us a full rundown of her coffee with Carlo.

"He is a smooth talker, but kind of a poseur. I think he's the kind who reads books just so he can say he read them. He wants people to think he's smart, but he's not as smart as he tries to appear, and I think he knows it. He definitely flirts. He lets you know he's interested."

I had to remind myself to unclench my fists. The thought of that guy letting her "know he's interested"...

Claire ate light again. Caesar salad with chicken. Ned Charles and Maria Koh and I got sandwiches.

Koh gave us some background on what happens to guys like Carlo when they get caught.

"He won't have a good lawyer if he gets indicted," Koh said. "Because he won't be able to afford one. The government will seize his assets. If the Bureau can't make that happen, we will. We can play the national security card. Whoever recruited and groomed Carlo—and we have a pretty good idea who did— they'll abandon him. He'll be on his own with a crappy lawyer, and he'll be looking at a long prison term. He'll plea. He won't go to trial."

"That's for the espionage," Charles added. "On top of that, there's the murder. And we do think it's a murder. Ginny Villarosa's death is too much like the woman Carlo knew in San Francisco. I mean, the sleeping pills."

As we finished our sandwiches, Claire was still picking through her salad. Koh told us that the software stolen from the company in San Francisco, the data mining technology that could process huge mountains of information, seemed to have wound up in the hands of a Chinese company with close ties to the Communist Party.

"Think about it," she said. "They're a totalitarian government that has over a billion people under surveillance twenty-four-seven. The ability to sift through that volume of data is gold to them. This guy, Ivanov, has done way more harm than any one man should be allowed to do. Ginny Villarosa is just collateral damage."

I asked her what motivates a guy like that. Is it hatred of America? Devotion to some other country's political ideology?

She said no, not necessarily. If you're sending someone behind enemy lines to do risky work, ideological motivation helps. Irrational love of ideas can motivate people to take huge risks. But if you just need a thief, look for someone motivated by money.

"Ideologies change," she said. "A person could be in love with a regime one day, and then the regime crosses some line and the person feels betrayed. Not only will they stop working for you, they might start working against you. You don't want an ideologically motivated agent if you can find a greedy one, because greed is consistent. If you want your agent to be fifty percent more motivated, pay him fifty percent more. A greedy person doesn't care what you're doing, or what your regime is doing. If he gets caught, what can he tell his captors? They paid me. That's as much as he knows. That's as much as he cares about."

Ned Charles asked us to stick around the hotel. He wanted us nearby and on call.

I knew why.

53

Three o'clock that afternoon, Ned Charles called Claire and me to his room. The Bureau had their warrants.

Charles asked Claire if she thought she could get a dinner date with Carlo tonight.

"We've been texting for the past hour," she said.

My blood pressure went up. Doesn't this guy know she has a job? Just because he's a bum who doesn't work doesn't mean she's sitting around on her ass all day too. She could be in meetings, for Christ's sake!

Claire showed the messages to Ned Charles. He grinned and made a motion like a fisherman reeling in a catch.

"Right, but he thinks *he's* reeling *me* in," Claire said with a smile. "Want to see?"

She offered me the phone but I declined. No need to whip up my emotions.

Ned Charles told her to keep stringing him along. Definitely do dinner tonight.

The Bureau had warrants for a property search and electronic surveillance. That meant the search wasn't just about the murder. The electronic surveillance warrant must have been granted based on Carlo's prior association with data theft suspects in California.

The Bureau—and probably the CIA as well—wanted to get into his house ASAP, do a preliminary search, and set some bugs. I assumed they'd mic his house and try to get something on his computer to monitor communications.

"We want him out of the house for at least three hours," Charles said. "Think you'll have any trouble entertaining him that long?"

"He entertains himself," Claire said. "Some people like nothing better than to hear their own voice."

"You mind wearing a wire? He might drop a name or some detail in conversation that means nothing to you, but it could mean a lot to us."

"I don't mind."

I knew this was why they wanted to keep us close. I had called Ed after our lunch conversation. He told me that when things move this quickly, it meant the Bureau was already deep into an investigation. Carlo had showed up on their radar once in San Diego and then again in San Francisco, and whatever organization he was a part of was obviously still active. The fact that the Bureau had talked to Sheriff Kessler in Virginia and Vivek Parmar in Texas, Ed in DC, and us in Seattle told me the stakes were high and the Bureau was hungry.

I think Claire understood it too, but it didn't seem to faze her.

Sure, she'd wear a wire. Her voice was smooth and cool.

Her phone chimed. Carlo again. Whatever he said made her smile.

"Call him now," Charles said. "Ask him out."

"Where?" she asked.

"Make him come to this side of the lake. It'll give us more time to search his house."

"Okay, but I'm not from here. Where do I want to go?"

"Canlis. You can have a long slow meal. And it'll show him you have class."

Like he couldn't tell that by looking at her? The thick-headed bastard.

She made the call.

"Hey!" Big smile on her face. "Yeah, I've been thinking about you too."

Wait, really? I couldn't tell when she was acting and when she was serious. And was she thinking about him the way an investigator is supposed to think about a suspect, or some other way?

"Yeah," she said. "It was a great conversation."

I bet it was. How refreshing it must have been to talk with someone so intelligent and cultured.

He said something. She tried to agree, but he kept going. She tried to cut in again, but he just kept blabbing away.

"No, no," she said. "I don't want to go to the east side. How about something in Seattle?"

She gave Charles a quick glance as she repeated Romeo's suggestion. "Serafina?"

Ned Charles shook his head, mouthed "Canlis."

"Canlis," she said. Again, there was that directness I liked. Not "How about Canlis?" She just said what she meant.

"Alright then." She covered the phone, mouthed to Charles a silent "What time?"

He flashed seven fingers, then three, then made an O with his thumb and index finger.

"Seven thirty," Claire said.

Romeo blabbed again. All he had to say was okay, but instead he yakked on for a solid minute. I got so frustrated I just about hung up the phone for her.

When the call ended, Ned Charles was pleased. The Bureau would have a team in place to execute the warrant as soon as Romeo drove off in his hundred-thousand-dollar Porsche. If they had to bail early, they'd get plenty of warning from the team monitoring Claire's wire.

Claire looked happy too. Excited, almost.

She said some things to Carlo on that nine-minute call that she would never in a million years say to me.

Ned Charles asked if I was alright.

"I'm fine," I growled.

54

By six thirty, a woman from the Bureau had Claire miked up. She'd be sending high-quality audio to a car in the Canlis parking lot. If the connection dropped, it would all be recorded.

The wire was basically just a phone slipped into the pocket of the coat she'd wear. They didn't want to put anything on her body because this was a date and if Carlo's hands started wandering... Well, I didn't need to go there.

They told Claire to wear her coat to the table, say she was cold, drape it over the chair. They showed her where the tiny mics were stitched in. Point any of those his way. The guy in the van can remotely control the phone to use the best mic.

Ned Charles and Maria Koh coached her on how to lead him in conversation. Mention a couple of financial services firms that ran their infrastructure on AWS. Also mention a company that was designing a quantum computer. They actually did the designs for those on traditional computers. Mention also the company that was working on a guidance system for NASA.

If Carlo was working for China, all of those targets would be of interest to him. They'd want to see which ones piqued his interest most.

"You're working in Infosec," Koh reminded her. "So you don't need to know what's actually in these systems. Just that they're there, running on infrastructure that you can access."

"Got it," Claire said.

"If he starts getting into details that are over your head, deflect. Talk about the meal. Ask him about himself. Flirt."

I saw her making mental notes, tucking away details. That was part of what made her a good detective.

"You ready?" Koh asked.

She said she was.

Ned Charles chimed in. The team over on Mercer Island was pretty thorough. They had already established that Carlo Ivanov had no alarm system, no dog, and no housemates. His house was shielded from the neighbors on both sides by bushes. The house across the street had a direct view of his property, but the owners were away. The search team wasn't worried about being noticed.

Carlo would have to leave by seven to make the restaurant in time. Sunset was at 7:16, and the cloudy sky meant it would be dark enough for the team to move in soon after.

At seven, Ned Charles and the woman who had put the mic on Claire were getting ready to take her down to the lobby. They had a car waiting out on Fifth Avenue with a glowing Lyft sign in the window. It was their car, their driver, but to anyone looking, it was a Lyft.

Claire was wearing a fitted black dress. I had never seen her in a dress.

I was about to pull her aside to give her some final words of encouragement, but Koh grabbed her first and said something I couldn't hear. She waved Claire into the bathroom. Whatever they talked about in there took about a minute and a half. When they came out, I couldn't read Claire's face, but I told her I wanted a word.

"What's up, Freddy?"

"Come here."

I pulled her into the bathroom, shut the door.

"What's the matter?"

"Did you pee?"

"What?" She scowled at me like I was wasting her time with a stupid question.

"This guy poisoned at least one woman, maybe two. What happens if you have to pee? You leave the table for a minute, you have no idea if he put something in your drink."

"He's not going to poison me before he gets anything out of me. That would be like throwing away the key before you robbed the vault. Are you worried, Freddy?"

"Yeah."

"You don't have to worry about me. I'm fine. I got this."

I wanted to remind her again that she didn't have to put up with any unwanted touch, but she got mad last time I brought that up.

"Remember, you have a wire in that coat. If you feel like you're in danger, just give the word and you'll get help."

"We've already been through that, Freddy."

Ned Charles had given her a safe word, even though she probably wouldn't need it.

I really didn't have anything important to say. I just wanted to reassure her, so she knew she had a team behind her. It wasn't all on her. No need to stress out.

But I was the one stressing out, and I could see she thought it was funny. You know that trying-not-to-smile look that people get when they're watching you act stupid? They're too polite to call you out and too amused to look away.

She squeezed my hand and smiled like a girl on her way to prom. "Relax, will you? Go to the bar and have a beer."

Relax, she told me. When the Bureau said I couldn't be in the surveillance car, couldn't listen in because this is *their* case, I was supposed to relax. When Mr. Smooth was about to bowl her over with his knowledge of music and painting and literature, lighting up that quick, sharp mind of hers, I was supposed to relax.

I wished this jerk was a boxing fan. I'd go on the stupid date myself, show him a thing or two about conversation.

55

The windows behind the bar in the Westin lobby looked out on Fifth Avenue, where pedestrians hustled head-down through blowing mist and taxis plowed furrows through puddles beneath the haloed streetlamps. Inside, fireplaces warmed travelers coming in from the cold. The cushioned chairs and couches were filled with men and women warming into conversation over martinis, wine, and beer.

I stuck to club soda in a chair by the window.

My adrenaline always rose when a case approached a turning point. I was alert, energetic, on edge with expectation. This was the proper response, the body and mind mustering resources for an important event. This was how I used to feel in the dressing room before a fight.

But tonight, that energy had nowhere to go. For once, it wasn't my mission to complete. When Claire came on as a contractor, she said, "Give me the hard work. The tough jobs. Challenge me."

I had tried, but I didn't think anything had truly challenged her so far. If anything, this was more challenging for me, sitting here doing nothing at what I sensed was a key moment in a case that was much bigger than I had initially thought.

I couldn't sit in my room, so I came down here to people-watch, to play detective with the hotel guests. Who's here on business? Who's having an affair? Not the middle-aged German couple sitting on the couch over there. They hardly talked to each other.

Every now and then, Ned Charles called or texted some tidbit of information from his surveillance team outside the restaurant. I think he could sense my unease. I think he interpreted it as a veteran worrying about his rookie investigator walking into a high-stakes setup.

Claire and Carlo met at 7:35 and got a secluded table away from the chatter and the noise. Of course, someone set that up so they could get a clear audio feed, but all I could see was Romeo's hand on her thigh.

The main course didn't arrive till after 8:30. Ned said they ate slowly and talked a lot.

"She's doing fine," he told me. "She leads him when she needs to, and she backs off whenever she's out of her depth. She'll talk about the food, the wine, and the view."

View?

This place has a view?

Nine sixteen, I got a call from Ned Charles. They were waiting for dessert. Carlo was most interested in the quantum computing company and the company designing a guidance system for NASA.

"Those are targets a nation-state would be interested in," Ned said. "Particularly nations with space programs and those looking for a technological edge. China fits both categories."

The team on Mercer Island was wrapping up their search of Carlo's house. Ned got a preliminary report that surprised everyone. Carlo's MacBook Pro was set to automatic login, meaning anyone could get in without a password, and none of his data was encrypted. The technicians plugged in a USB drive and copied his files. They installed monitoring software so they could watch his communications.

"But if he's not taking basic precautions like password protection and encryption," Charles said, "we're not going to get much off that machine. He isn't using it for communications."

They found a wall safe in his bedroom and were able to open it. Inside was $1800 in cash, Carlo's passport—which was legit—and two old Swiss watches. Maybe family heirlooms. Nothing incriminating.

Carlo's minimalist style made the place easy to search. Not a lot of furniture or knickknacks. No boxes of papers to sort through. No overstuffed drawers or extra hard drives, no basement, no trapdoors. A peek into the attic showed the loose insulation hadn't been disturbed. He didn't go up there.

"Of course, this is just a preliminary search," Ned said. "We weren't expecting to find a smoking gun."

He let me in on another little tidbit. The Bureau sent a request to Apple through some formal channel—maybe it included a warrant, I don't know—but they wanted to know what software he was running on his phone.

No Signal, no Telegram, none of the encrypted communication apps that hackers and spies use to hide their chats from prying cops. His phone was as wide open as his MacBook.

"That," Ned told me, sounding perplexed, "was not what we were expecting. If Carlo is stealing data, who's telling him what to go after? And how are they telling him? And how does he get the data to them?"

Nine thirty-one, the Mercer Island team was out. They were heading back across the bridge to Seattle. Ned sent Claire a text, a prearranged message about preparing slides for a 9 a.m. client meeting. That told her all was clear. She could end the date at any time.

She texted back. *Slides not ready.*

That meant she couldn't leave just yet.

Why not?

Maybe it would seem unnatural to break off the date too soon. Maybe they were heavy into conversation about de Chirico or Stravinsky, or whatever the hell that asshole talks about.

I couldn't stand sitting in that damn lobby with those wine-sipping dullards staring at their phones. I had to get up off my ass and do something.

I had the rental car. I decided to get out of there.

56

Nine forty-eight, I was pulling into the lot at Canlis. It was a straight shot up Aurora Avenue.

The lot was smaller than I expected. Too small for me not to be noticed. This was a bad idea. Ned and his surveillance team must be somewhere else. They'd be noticed too, hanging around this tiny lot.

I looped around, headed back toward the exit.

Nine forty-nine, text from Ned. *They're leaving.*

I sat there idling, letting traffic pass by on Aurora. I needed to turn left to get back to the hotel, which is where I should have been when Ned and Claire returned, but there was a divider in the middle of the road. I could only go right, away from downtown.

In the rearview, a man and woman, lit in the red of my brake lights, made their way from the exit to a row of parked cars. His hand was on her shoulder. I couldn't tell if it was them. I turned to look behind. The lights flashed on the red Cayenne. Carlo unlocking his car.

Ned relayed a text from Claire. *They're going for a nightcap.*

Why? Was she falling for this guy or what? For the guy Ginny Villarosa insisted "really did love her." Was he that convincing?

I pulled out onto Aurora. The Bureau's surveillance team would have to follow them, and I didn't want to be in the way.

I shouldn't have been touching my phone on the bridge, but I needed to know how to get back to the Westin. I drove slowly in the right lane, slow enough to annoy the drivers who pulled around me.

Halfway across, I got directions. Take the next exit, Bridge Way, then go left.

Coming up on the exit, still going ten miles under the speed limit, a pair of headlights came up fast in the rearview. The car whipped around me then cut back into my lane. Carlo in his stupid Porsche. Guy drove like a teenager. He took the exit way too fast.

If Ned's team was following, I was between them and their mark and I needed to get out of the way. Google maps said to go left on 38th, under the bridge, then left again to get onto the bridge's southbound lanes.

Carlo turned left on 38th and I got another text from Ned. *Lost them, but we can track her phone. We'll catch up.*

How did he lose them? How far away from the restaurant did he park? Did he have trouble cutting into traffic on Aurora?

Why did Carlo have to leave one restaurant and drive somewhere else for a nightcap? Didn't they serve drinks at Canlis?

Carlo went straight on 38th. I followed. That way, we'd have eyes on them until Ned's crew caught up.

Down Fremont Way, to 39th, to Leary and into Ballard.

Carlo parked in front of a place on Ballard Avenue. I circled the block, looking for parking. As I pulled into a spot a few minutes later, Ned's text told me his crew was on the scene.

She's competent, I told myself. She's not in danger. The problem is you, Freddy. You need to calm down.

I wondered if this was what Miriam used to feel when I was away on a job. Did she just sit there worrying, unable to act?

I needed to call her to apologize when I got back. I didn't get it back then. I just didn't understand.

I got out of the car, took a walk, tried to burn off some of my nervous energy.

57

I walked two loops of the neighborhood. Down Ballard Avenue, up Leary to Market Street and back down Ballard. Romeo took my protégé into a restaurant at the north end of the street, near Ballard and 22nd. I passed without looking in.

And I thought I found Ned's car on Leary. A dark blue Volvo XC 90 with a Nathan Hale High School sticker on the back. They wanted to blend in, right? No white van, no black Chevy Suburban. Drive what mom and dad would drive here in the Emerald City.

The tipoff was two adults in the front seat looking at screens. I walked a ten-minute loop and they didn't move. You're out near a strip of bars and restaurants, you should have either gotten out of the car or driven away. Every other car on the street was empty, so it had to be you.

On lap three, the mist was starting to soak through my clothes. A wet fifty degrees felt a lot colder there than in DC.

No word from Ned.

This was it, I told myself. Go back to the car and call it a night. Change into something dry at the hotel, maybe shower, then wait for the call when Claire and Ned are ready to debrief.

My car was two blocks down, past the restaurant. What was taking them so long anyway? How many drinks were they having? Was he going to slip her a roofie, like he did to Ginny? The toxicology report showed Rohypnol in her system. No one gives that to themselves.

This was what I was thinking when they walked out less than half a block in front of me. I should have crossed, used the other sidewalk. They were stopped in front of the restaurant door, talking. Her back was to me. They stood close enough to kiss. I could hear his voice. What was he saying?

I put my head down, looked at my feet as I continued toward them. It wouldn't look strange—just a man trying to keep his face dry in the cold drizzle of a city night.

I heard the kiss. I looked up. His hand slid down the small of her back—down, and then past.

My blood was boiling and my head was going to explode. Who the hell did that stupid bastard think he was? You don't touch a woman's ass when she's working. If that doesn't qualify as harassment, I don't know what does.

All these months, I'd held myself back, kept on my best behavior, done everything to help her grow in this job, and you treat her like a crude piece of meat, you fucking—

They separated as I reached them. A foot and a half between them, and it was just instinct, it was just a raw animal response to take that swing.

Have you ever regretted something even as you're doing it? Have you ever had the blinding realization of what a stupid mistake you're making right in the middle of making it?

I did my best to pull that punch, because if I had hit him like I used to hit guys in the ring, I would have really hurt him. I pulled the punch, not in time to stop it from landing, but in time to take the power off of it. It landed like a tap, but the guy was soft in the belly, and he doubled over.

Claire yelled, "What the fuck!" Fierce, hot anger, right from the gut.

She threw a swing with her curse. Punched me in the back of the shoulder. A good solid one too. The girl can hit.

I kept going, head down the whole way, burning with shame and humiliation.

What happened to me? When did I stop being sane?

58

Eleven thirty-seven p.m. We were in Claire's room on the twelfth floor of the Westin. Charles and Koh congratulated her on a job well done. Both mentioned Carlo's interest in the quantum computing company, the NASA navigation contractor. He, or whoever he was working for, was after something bigger than money.

"The fact that he didn't care about financial data," Koh said, "means he's probably not working for organized crime. The Russian mob and the Eastern Europeans go for quick cash. China goes after the big stuff. They can jump a decade ahead on technology if they get their hands on the right work."

I kept quiet. I had already made a fool of myself, and I knew Claire was still mad, because she wouldn't look at me. Charles and Koh didn't sense the tension, because we were both good at putting aside feelings that got in the way of work. At least, I usually was. The only chink in my armor was her.

I leaned against the wall by the window overlooking Pike Place and the Puget Sound. Charles sat in the desk chair, Claire on the end of the bed. Koh stood beside the bed, a little fidgety, pacing now and then.

Charles asked Claire, "What's your sense of him?"

It wasn't an official question. Everyone was just chatting at that point.

"I think he overestimates his intelligence."

"What makes you say that?" Koh asked.

"I've worked with guys like him before. When you name drop as much as he does and you make it a point to show how well read you are, it often means you don't have much original thought. You're just trading on other people's ideas. I've seen a lot of seemingly smart people fall down on the job because real life isn't a book with the answers all spelled out."

I liked that perspective. I liked it a lot.

"You didn't have to go out with him after the restaurant," Charles said.

"I know."

"But you wanted it to feel natural? You didn't want to bail on him, in case we needed you to meet up with him again?"

Claire shook her head, no.

"What?" asked Ned.

"I thought it was funny that he didn't use a passcode on his phone. No fingerprint either."

"We noticed that about his computer too," said Ned.

"When I walked into the restaurant, he gave me a little hug. Just a half-second, happy-to-see-you hug. I noticed something hard in his jacket when he hugged me. In the inside breast pocket. I thought it might be another phone. I wondered why he would have two."

She went on. Between the main course and dessert, she had gone to the bathroom. On the way back, she saw him jot down a note—in a notebook, with a pen. Then he put the notebook back in his jacket.

This was the same notebook I saw him take out at the coffee shop on Mercer Island.

"Who writes notes when they have a phone?" she asked. Ned and the other agent looked at each other.

"Unless they're noting things they don't want to appear in a digital record, things they don't want hackers to steal or law enforcement to intercept."

She pulled a small blue notebook from her purse and tossed it on the bed.

"I took that from his jacket when we kissed outside the restaurant in Ballard. He was holding the jacket over his shoulder, so it was behind him. I had my arms around him and I slid it right out."

And then I walked up and punched the guy. What the hell? This is how far I had slipped. My super-sharp protégé swipes what might turn out to be a valuable piece of evidence. And all I can think about is her kissing a guy I want to kill.

The way my mind was working now, I needed to turn in my resignation. I needed to tell Ed I wasn't up to the job anymore because I just couldn't think straight. She did this job as well as me, or better. And she thought she was a beginner. She thought she needed a mentor.

"I flipped through it in the Lyft on the way back to the hotel," she said.

That would be the fake Lyft. The one the Bureau set up with their own driver to take her from the hotel to the restaurant. It brought her back too.

"Most of the notes seem innocuous enough," she continued. "But look at page sixteen."

Charles counted through the pages and stopped on sixteen. Koh bent over his shoulder to read.

"He has phone numbers, email addresses, notes about what to pick up at the store, the names of at least a dozen women, and then there's that. Thirty-two random letters and numbers printed in neat block letters. What do you think that is?"

Koh seemed to get it right away, Charles a second later. They exchanged a glance and a few low words I couldn't hear. Their body language told me they were going to move on this. This was going back to headquarters.

Koh and Charles thanked Claire for her work, told her they'd be in touch tomorrow. They excused themselves and left.

I didn't want to be alone in the room with her. I was ashamed of myself and she was beautiful in her fitted black dress.

I told her goodnight, made a move for the door, and she looked hurt.

"That's all you have to say? Goodnight?"

"Well yeah. And you did great work. I mean, phenomenal, once again."

To get from the window to the door, I had to cross the room. She stood from the bed and intercepted me halfway.

"*What* is the matter with you?" Her tone was sharp, angry. "Seriously, Freddy, what the fuck? I look up to you, do you know that? I asked you for coaching and advice, show me the ropes, and you come out here and act like a child! Is that how you solve problems? Go beat up the bad guy? Get a grip, will you?"

"I'm sorry. I lost my head."

"I can handle him, Freddy."

"Obviously."

"What's that supposed to mean?"

"It means you can handle him. And you did. You did well."

"No. There's something else in your tone. Be open with me, please. I want to trust you."

"Look," I said, "you can't go stealing stuff from people you're investigating."

"The notebook?"

"Yeah. If it's a private investigation, that's one thing. When law enforcement is involved, you have to go by the book or the evidence gets thrown out of court."

She gave me an angry look, eyes narrowing. "Do you think I'm stupid, Freddy? Do you honestly think I don't know that?"

"Well you took it, didn't you?"

She paused a second, got her anger in check, then said, "Maria Koh pulled me aside before I went to the restaurant. She told me to get whatever information I could by whatever means I could. If the FBI had a problem with that, she and her agency would work it out. I got the sense she knew more than Ned Charles about what Carlo was up to.

"So, yeah, Freddy. I know what I did wasn't by the book. But it was expedient. My instinct told me it was the right move at the right time. I trusted Maria and I did what I did. The FBI and the CIA can take it from here."

I felt like an asshole. My point about evidence gathering might have been valid in any other case, but tonight was the wrong time to bring it up. Why diminish her triumph? Let her bask in all she'd done right.

I could have talked about the notebook over breakfast. I could have couched it in a by-the-way, could have softened the impact with an explanation of how the Bureau can work around things like this. That if there turned out to be evidence in that notebook, then on balance it was a good thing she got it. If there was no evidence, no harm done.

But I couldn't take back my words. I couldn't put back the smile that should have been on her face after a job well done. The smile she had earned and deserved.

And that wasn't even the worst of it. The worst thing was that she had asked me outright to be honest with her about what was wrong, about what made me lose my cool and punch a guy when she had the situation all wrapped up.

How could I tell her? How could I tell her *that?*

So, what did I do instead? I made it her fault. I told her I was mad because *she* did something wrong.

As bad as I felt outside that restaurant in Ballard, I felt worse now.

I didn't know what to do, so I just said sorry and left.

She put a knife in my back on the way out. I mean, her words did, and her tone.

"That punch wasn't about the notebook, Freddy. You didn't even know I had it till we got back to the hotel."

I went back to my room on the eighth floor and asked myself what the hell was wrong with me. If I had thought for one second before I opened my mouth, if I had considered all she had done that night, instead of how miserable and insecure I had been, I would have given her nothing but praise.

But the thought of her kissing another guy really hurt. And the way she did everything so effortlessly, the way I imagined her holding these conversations with Carlo that were over my head, that I couldn't even be a part of—all of that made me feel like crap.

I sat there on the bed hating myself, wanting to kill that stupid Romeo, that jealous, petty fool inside that kept getting the better of me.

59

Twenty minutes later, I was at the desk in my room, composing my resignation letter. Not that I was going to send it. I just needed a threat to hold over myself to remind me to behave.

How do you tell your business partner that you have to quit the company because there's a conflict of interest between your head and your heart? Microsoft Word doesn't have a template for that kind of letter.

I tried composing a professional-sounding memo that talked around the problem, but it came out stilted and unintelligible, like something a lawyer would write for a client accepting punishment without admitting guilt. I closed my laptop, picked up a pen, and wrote the letter on the Westin notepad. The small size of the paper forced me to get to the point.

> Ed,
> You know I go off the deep end every now and then. Well, I've really lost it this time.
> I'm no longer fit for this job.
> Sorry.
> —Freddy

That about covered it.

There was a knock at the door just as I was tearing the page from the pad. I jammed the paper in my pocket and got up to answer the door. On my way across the room, I told myself that every time my feelings started flaring up, I'd pull out my resignation letter and read it. If that wasn't enough to keep me in line, then I truly wasn't fit for the job anymore.

I opened the door, and there was the source of my mental and emotional instability in that damn black dress.

You know what she said? She said, "You're right, Freddy. About the notebook. And you told me in the right way, at the right time. I was still high on how the whole evening had unfolded. I was congratulating myself for doing a great job. Instead, I left the FBI in a bad position."

Can you believe this? What kind of person thanks another person for being an asshole?

She didn't ask to come in, she just pushed past me and said, "Thank you for teaching me."

What?

I saw this in her when I offered her the contract. The desire to learn, to always be improving. Few people are willing to look at their successes and say to themselves, This is where I fell short. This is where I could do better.

She was one of those few—even with a bad teacher like me. In a stupid, poorly executed exchange like the one that we just had, she found a lesson and she took it to heart.

She thought for a second, and then a smile lit her face.

"After you hit him, he said, Why do guys always punch me?"

"Is that funny?" I asked.

"Kind of, yeah." Her smile grew wider. "I had the sense during dinner that he had to project this big intellectual presence to make up for some deeper insecurity. I could totally see him getting picked on in school."

"That's not funny," I said. I got picked on on the streets. I learned to fight to make it stop. By high school, I made sure anyone who fought me once never wanted to do it again.

We chatted for a few minutes, me standing by the desk, her pacing by the window. I told her about the search of Carlo's house. We speculated about what may come of the bugs the FBI planted in his home and on his computer. The conversation didn't ease the tension between us. We both knew it.

"How was dinner? What'd you guys talk about?"

"Just stuff." She waved it off.

"For two hours? I haven't had a date in years that could talk that long. Except you, and that wasn't a date."

"I had to keep him engaged." She said it like it took no effort at all.

"I have nothing to say about Miles Davis or that Stravinsky guy," I told her. "I've never read Graham Greene or Joseph Conrad."

"And I don't care."

"Well I do."

"Freddy, that guy was a fraud. There's a kind of person who appreciates art, who truly gets something out of it, and then there's the kind that name drops. The most important thing to them is that you think they're smart."

"Did you enjoy the conversation?"

"Parts of it. But in the end, it doesn't matter to me. Why are you so glum?"

Why? Because inside I was a thirteen-year-old boy with a hopeless crush on a girl who was out of his league. I'd just spent a whole evening imagining her talking with a guy who could meet her on her own ground. I wouldn't have understood half of what Carlo talked about, but she was right there with him, stride for stride the entire evening. At least, that's how I pictured it.

She walked toward me, looked right at me, and I had this sudden flash, a memory of what makes marriage so terrifying. The fact of being known, the fact that someone knows you, inside and out.

"I like art," Claire said, "and literature, and music too."

She was too close. With her, I need at least a few feet.

"But all of that comes from life," she said. "Whatever meaning you see in the words or hear in the notes comes from real life, and real life is flesh and bone. Life isn't what's heard or read or spoken about. It's what's lived firsthand. It's *you*, Freddy. You're not the words. You're the story. At the end of your life, if someone could take your brain from your head and extract from it the story of *you*, it would be a hell of a work.

Guys like Carlo can talk all they want about the secondhand life they find in art. But they can never *be* that. That's you, Freddy. That's the real deal, and at the end of the day, that's what I respect."

"Well that's a hell of a thing to say."

"Isn't it?"

And then she did the craziest thing. She stepped forward, gave me a little peck on the cheek, squeezed my hand, and said goodnight.

"What was that for?"

"I hate to see you so down."

She let herself out, said she'd see me tomorrow.

How was I supposed to go to sleep after that?

Was she just being nice to me? Was that pity? Because I'm illiterate? I mean, I'm not, until you start comparing me to people in her league. Until you get to someone who knows about HIPAA and Stravinsky and de Chirico and business contracts and corporate accounting.

And what am I? Flesh and bone, she said. Like, a brute? Is that what she meant?

How could she be so trusting? Giving me that little peck when I've been burning for her all these weeks? I'm on fire for her, body and soul, and she tells me she respects me and gives me a friend-zone kiss.

You know what's even worse than the friend zone? The respected coworker zone. That's where she put me.

Fuck!

I called Miriam. So what if she was in bed with her husband? He's used to it. Every twelve months, like clockwork, I freak out about something and her phone rings in the middle of the night. It's gotten so regular, she can use it as a reminder to change the smoke alarm batteries.

"Goddammit, Freddy, what is it this time?"

That's how Miriam answers the phone.

"I don't know."

"Yes, you do. I told you you were in love. Who is she?"

"A coworker."

"In that little company you work for? There's like three of you. You can't do romance in a company that size."

"There's five of us, and I know."

"Well, which one is it? Bethany or Leon?"

"Claire."

"Who?"

"She's new."

"What is it?" she asked. I heard the sheets rustle as she turned. "Is she pretty?"

"It's more than that," I said.

"It always is with you. Come on, give me the lowdown."

By the time I got done describing her, Miriam was in love with her too.

"How can a woman like that not be taken?" she asked.

"She was. Engaged almost, but she panicked and screwed it up."

"Okay, I sense issues."

"I think she's worked through them."

"Then why is she with you?"

"She's not," I said.

"She's not into you?"

"She said I was respectable flesh and bone."

"What kind of woman describes a man that way? That's the kind of thing your promotor used to say about his fighters."

"Don't remind me of that guy. All my life, I've been trying to rise above that, to rise above being flesh and bone."

"Well, from what you described, she sounds like she's got you outclassed. Plus, don't hit on your coworkers. Especially ones who report to you. That's just gross."

"How's Lenny?"

"Both his front teeth are out. The two on top."

"How much is the Tooth Fairy paying these days?"

"Five bucks a pop."

"Seriously?"

60

September 25
Seattle, WA

I knew from the beginning that I wouldn't get to see this case through. I didn't know it would turn into this, but I did know that it would ultimately wind up in the hands of law enforcement, or some government agency that would muscle me out.

My interest was personal. Seeing what happened to the woman in the woods, watching her wash away—how could I not have a stake in the outcome of this investigation? Maybe that's another case of my head and my heart not being in accord. Ed and I are running a business, and if we want to survive, we have to stick to paying work.

But, still... I'm human, right? I suspected from the beginning this was a murder—though I wouldn't encourage nosy Mrs. Jackson by saying so—because I knew the woman in white didn't get into the woods under her own power. Murder cases, even if they start with private investigators, ultimately go to the police.

Then Anthony Villarosa came into the picture, and I knew the case was slipping further from my grasp. He's running a criminal operation down there in Florida, and maybe he's two steps ahead of the cops, but that means the cops are just two steps behind. And the feds probably know about him, because guys like him can't confine their work to one state. So, at this point, I was already out of my depth.

Then the case kicked up another notch because Carlo was stealing high-stakes data, possibly for another country. Now the FBI was in on it, and the CIA as well.

Even though I wouldn't be satisfied until Ginny's killer was brought to justice, I was happy to walk away from this one, because I didn't want to lead Anthony Villarosa to his prey. Let the justice system handle Carlo. He deserved the same due process we give to everyone else.

I called Villarosa from my room. It was 6:30 a.m. in Seattle, 9:30 in Florida. He told me two gentlemen and a lady had come by the day before to pick up the hard drives. They didn't harass him, didn't look around the place any more than a prospective new gym member would. The only questions they asked were about the drives, where Ginny may have gotten them, what might be on them, who had accessed them, when Ginny left them. And they wanted to know if anyone else had been by to try to pick them up.

"No, no one else has been by," he told them.

"Are you sure? No one lingered by the locker? No one looked like they might have been here to pick up and then lost their nerve?"

"What do you mean, am I sure? Of course I'm sure. I got guys out there watching the thing. This is my fucking daughter we're talking about."

I told him Carlo Ivanov was under federal surveillance. The FBI would know where he was at all times.

"Don't even try to go after him," I said. "Anything you do, you'll be doing in front of the feds, and there's a good chance they'll get it on camera."

I didn't really know how closely the feds would watch Carlo, but I wanted to dissuade Villarosa from killing his hated Romeo.

He didn't seem too put out by what I told him.

"I'm not worried about the feds," he said. "There's only two sides a coin can land on, and I got 'em both covered."

He didn't have to explain what that meant. Heads: Carlo walks free for one reason or another and Villarosa hunts him down. Tails: Carlo is convicted and goes to prison. Villarosa finds a friend inside to get rid of him.

"The important thing," he said, "is that all accounts are settled. I got people watching me all the time, looking for signs of weakness. Someone kills my daughter and he's still breathing? Then I'm weak. I'm dead. Not that I wouldn't take care of this anyway. Even if no one is watching, this is a score that gets settled."

I was glad to have that problem off my plate. And I was looking forward to getting back to DC. Things were still slow there, but in an investigation like this, with the feds running the show, I'd have nothing to do. In DC, I'd give Claire the run-through on how we break down expense reports, which things we itemize, which get lumped into "daily expenses." And then I'd go home to my own bed. No more hotels.

There was still *that* issue to deal with though. Claire herself. I'd still have to see her in the office every day. She'd probably sit too close when I ran through the expenses with her. For her, it wouldn't be too close. For her it would be just close enough to read the things I was pointing to on my computer screen. But for me—anything inside of three feet and her force field runs right through me.

I'd have to talk with Ed about this at some point. My feelings were affecting my work, and that wasn't fair to him or anyone else in the office.

I told myself I'd talk with Ed, but really, I needed to talk with me.

What was *I* going to do? How was *I* going to resolve this?

Not by sitting on my ass watching the whirlpool spin in my head. Ultimately, action is the only way anything gets resolved.

I went down to the hotel restaurant at 7:00 for breakfast. I didn't ask anyone to meet me because I wanted to eat alone.

When I got there, the host asked me to wait while they cleared a table. I waited, and when I turned around, there was Claire, freshly showered and dressed for work. She caught me when my guard was down.

The waiter waved us over to a table for two. He assumed we were together.

What is that old saying about the best laid plans of mice and men? I do everything I can to make my morning easy, to avoid unnecessary tension, and then the universe decides that's not how it's going to go. The universe decides it's going to be two against one—Claire and the waiter against me—though neither of them knows they're in on the plan to ruin Freddy's peaceful breakfast with the problem he can't seem to work out.

Claire asked how long I thought we had left on this case.

"Me? Zero. I have nothing more to contribute. You? Depends. Maria Koh might find something in that notebook she wants you to follow up on. Maybe she sends you on another date. Back to his house. Maybe she decides Carlo needs a girlfriend for a while."

Her posture stiffened. Not enough for others to notice, but I notice everything about her.

The girlfriend comment was mean. I didn't need to say that. And it wasn't the words she reacted to, it was the tone.

"Sorry," I said.

The waiter came with coffee. Claire ordered oatmeal again, with fruit and yogurt. I was starting to be able to predict her. I got eggs, bacon, hash browns. I was hungry.

I told her we'd walk through expense reports when we got back to DC. She said okay, she was looking forward to that. She had billed meals before, and incidentals, but not travel.

"We don't usually stay in this kind of place," I told her. "We try to keep the known expenses down because the unknown ones can add up fast. Clients argue about that. Even the ones who can afford it. But this client, I don't care what he thinks."

"Do we have a contract with him? With Villarosa?"

I shook my head. "Guy like that isn't going to sign a contract. If Carlo gets murdered, the contract will tie Villarosa to the case."

"How do you know he'll pay us then?"

"When a guy like him looks you in the eye and says he's going to pay you, he's going to pay you. Besides, it's his daughter. He's not going to skimp."

"What's the point of doing expenses," she asked, "if we're not going to present them to him?"

"Who says we won't present them? I just said there's no contract. Nothing official on the books. He's a businessman. He'll want to know as a matter of course how much we spent. Besides, I want to rub it in. I don't like criminals."

When the food came, we ate in silence. To tell the truth, I didn't want her there.

The waiter brought the check and I signed it to my room.

As we got up to leave, she said they might not need her. The feds might have enough with the notebook and the bugs they planted.

She asked about booking flights back to DC. I told her to choose any flight she wanted. It didn't have to be the discount red-eye. She could fly in the middle of the day. Don't worry about the cost.

On the way to the elevators, I told her I was taking the day off to tour the town. I'd fly out on the red-eye. I said it so she'd know which plane not to book. I didn't want her sitting next to me for five hours.

I figured if she got the all clear from Ned Charles and Maria Koh, she'd leave that afternoon. Maybe even before lunch. She was efficient. She didn't waste time.

But no. She wanted to see the town too. The market, the art museum, the Rock and Roll Museum.

"Take some photos for Leon," I said.

"Don't you want to go?"

I did, but, "No. I need a day to myself."

"Okay," she said. "I get that. It's good you can say it. You're not one of those people who feels pressured into doing something just to please someone else, are you?"

"No."

That question stung, but I didn't know where or why. I just knew I needed some alone time. I was done talking with her.

Of course, there was no elevator. Of course, we had to stand there in silence, waiting, waiting, waiting... Finally, the bell rang, like it used to at the end of a round where nothing was going my way.

In the elevator, she asked if something was bothering me.

I said, "You kissed me last night."

That was the first time I saw her blush. She was always so cool and collected, I had never imagined her blushing. I didn't think it was in her repertoire.

"I felt bad for you," she said.

"It wasn't very professional."

God, that came out wrong. Completely wrong. I wished I could take it back.

"You just seemed so down and out of sorts," she said. "I didn't even know I was going to do it until it happened. It's a natural human response to seeing another person in distress. You want to reassure them. But you're right. It wasn't professional. It was human. And I'm human, and so are you. I'm sorry if I made you feel awkward, but I wouldn't take it back."

The doors opened on eight, and she got out.

What was I supposed to make of that answer? Did I want her to regret it? Did I want her to take that kiss back?

I stood there looking at the lighted button as the elevator ascended.

Twelve was *her* floor. I was supposed to get off on eight.

61

October 1
Washington, DC

I flew back on the red-eye. Claire stayed in Seattle a few extra days, not because Koh and the CIA needed her. The FBI did.

Claire's hunch about Carlo's notebook turned out to be right. He wrote things in there that he didn't want government snoops to find on his phone or computer. Interspersed with his personal notes—women's names and phone numbers, shopping and to-do lists—were coded messages that the feds would have to study and decipher.

Who was Parakeet? Who was Budgie? What did the dates mean?

Ginny Villarosa was Canary. His book showed a date with her on August 19, as well as a sequence of dates before. But none after.

The big revelation though, the smoking gun, was the item Claire pointed out to Charles and Koh that night in her hotel room. That neatly printed block of thirty-two letters and numbers. Ned Charles passed it along to the team in South Florida that had seized the hard drives from Anthony Villarosa's gym. They plugged in that code, and bingo! All the drives decrypted. A hundred and sixty-eight terabytes of DNA data.

Vivek Parmar confirmed it came from Mitogenic. Ginny had worked in the Seattle lab as a data technician. Parmar had told me earlier, and told the FBI now, that some of Mitogenic's researchers downloaded subsets of data to analyze on local workstations. The company was trying to stop the practice, but until they did, it wasn't unusual to see big streams of data flowing out of their cloud servers into their labs. Their information security team was too focused on external threats, another APT, to worry about data that only seemed to move on their internal network.

Ginny had free access. To Carlo, she was a gold mine. He probably instructed her to encrypt the drives. If she ever got caught with them, no one could prove what was on them. And he would have given her the encryption key, a key he possessed himself, to be sure that once he got the drives, he could access the data.

I asked Leon what were the chances that Carlo just happened to write thirty-two nonsense characters that coincidentally matched the encryption key for those hard drives.

He looked at me like I was an idiot.

"I'm just playing devil's advocate here," I said. "And by devil, I mean Carlo. And by advocate, I mean his defense lawyer. He'll throw something out there like, My client jotted down the serial number from his Wi-Fi router because he was going to file a warrantee claim."

Leon broke down the probability. "There's twenty-six letters in the alphabet. Times two is fifty-two."

"Why times two?" I asked.

"Upper case and lower case. And there are ten digits, zero through nine. Fifty-two letters plus ten digits equals sixty-two unique characters."

"Okay."

"If the key was just two characters long, there are sixty-two times sixty-two possible combinations. That's three thousand eight hundred and forty-four total possibilities. For three characters, it's sixty-two times sixty-two times sixty-two, which is over two hundred thousand possibilities. This key had thirty-two characters. Sixty-two to the thirty-second power is an astronomically large number."

He said the chances of Carlo's notes accidentally matching the encryption key were slimmer than the odds of someone winning the Powerball and the MegaMillions on the same day they got struck by lightning while watching the Detroit Lions win the Super Bowl.

"In other words," he said, "impossible."

The notebook was a boon for the CIA, who now knew Carlo was part of a larger network. He could lead them to others.

The FBI, however, had a problem. If they wanted to prosecute Carlo for conspiracy, for hatching the plan to steal the data, their key piece of evidence would be thrown out, because Claire had stolen the notebook.

So, what's the solution? Three simple steps.

One: Photograph every page of the notebook for further study.

Two: Wipe Claire's prints off the cover.

Three: Set up another date with Carlo.

This time, he would pick her up outside Amazon headquarters in South Lake Union in his fancy-ass Porsche. They go to a restaurant. He gets out of the car first. She drops the notebook in the gap between the driver's seat and the center console. Ned Charles told her to try to place it so it would slide forward when he braked. Then he'd find it, pick it up.

The Bureau waited a day, then got a warrant to search his car. They waited till he was in it. Sure enough, the notebook was back in his pocket. His fingerprints were all over it, and now, unless Carlo's attorneys knew better—and they wouldn't—the notebook was legitimately obtained evidence.

That was on the twenty-seventh. Four days ago. The Bureau executed the warrant, held Carlo on suspicion until they could go through the motions of confirming the already confirmed encryption key, then they arrested him.

I asked Ed what the Bureau did with a suspect in cases like this.

"They'll isolate him, question him as many hours a day as they can, to try to wear him down."

"What about the CIA?"

"They'll get their crack at him too."

Sheriff Kessler called from Nelson County. Someone had put pressure on the medical examiner in Richmond. The manner of death on Ginny Villarosa's death certificate changed from "undetermined" to "homicide."

"We have the written statement you left at the station on August nineteenth," he said. "We're getting official statements from Phil and Natasha Nikander, so we can tie this all together. The physical descriptions all match. Nikander's guest, the woman in the woods, and the one who washed up on Belle Isle. Your guy Ed passed along the info about Carlo returning a damaged vehicle to Hertz in Harrisonburg on the day of the murder. I'm going to need another statement from you about seeing him near the scene. Ed says you helped him change a tire?"

"That's right."

"Okay. Sherri will talk to you about that. You want to do me a favor and call Mrs. Jackson? Ever since I let slip that you'd found a suspect, she's been hounding me for details."

"Yeah, I'll talk to her."

I had been ignoring her texts, and she was getting impatient. I called her after Kessler hung up.

The first thing she wanted to know was what Carlo looked like. Then, what kind of personality did he have?

"Oh, cultured? Well they're always interesting."

What was Ginny's apartment like? What was Carlo's house like? I told her.

"He must have had *some* job to afford a house and a car like that! Why would a man who had it made kill someone?"

Guys like Carlo never had it made. They know everything can be taken from them in a second, if not by the law, by the people they work for.

I didn't tell Mrs. Jackson that. I just told her I couldn't speculate. I didn't want to mention the feds being involved. The Bureau doesn't discuss ongoing investigations. The CIA doesn't discuss anything. I wasn't going to leak info they were trying to keep under wraps. All I told her was that Carlo was in custody in Seattle and the investigators out there would figure out the story. If the case came to trial, she could follow it in the news.

I had been back in DC for five days. Claire would be flying back from Seattle that night, and I wouldn't have to see her again until Monday. The office was a different place without her. Peaceful. Easy to focus.

62

Three p.m., I was ready to leave. Call it an early Friday, maybe see if I could get some time with my son, Lenny. I was about to call Miriam when Ed came in from the hallway with a guest.

One look at the guy and I knew who sent him. This was one of Anthony Villarosa's losers. I'm sure he felt confident and tough on his way in. A guy like him, representing who he represents, is used to calling the shots. But he looked sheepish next to Ed. Ed is the image of the commanding lawman: six foot five, arrow-straight posture, clean shaven, fresh pressed suit. You know at a glance he's FBI. Or in his case, ex-FBI. Ed's the kind of guy a crook in Villarosa's organization crosses the street to avoid.

"What's up?" I asked.

Ed said, "You're taking a trip to Florida."

"For what?"

The loser, a skinny guy in jeans and grey bomber jacket, said, "Anthony wants to talk to you." He handed me a plane ticket. Reagan National to West Palm Beach, first class, leaving Sunday morning at eight, returning that night at ten.

After he left, Ed told me it was time to collect. The firm lost money in August and September. Bethany, Leon, and Claire needed to get paid. Ed was angry about me taking on a job without a contract and then racking up expenses in Seattle. He didn't say so, because that wasn't his way. His way was to make me take the plane ticket and fix the problem. Which happened to be my way too. This is why we got along.

63

October 2
Bethesda, MD

When I got to Miriam's house, Lenny was running around the yard with a lollipop in his mouth. I could tell by his energy he was all sugared up. His hair was cut short, like a Marine. Why didn't Miriam tell me?

"What difference does it make?" she asked.

"I come over here with a picture of him in my mind and he looks completely different."

"He doesn't look different. He's Lenny with shorter hair. Is something wrong with you?"

"Why does something have to be wrong with me?"

"Just take him, will you? I don't want to stand here and argue."

Lenny and I walked to Leland Park with a pair of tennis rackets and a bag of balls. We played for an hour. No score, just batting the ball around. The kid is surprisingly coordinated for a seven-year-old. Determined too. He went after every shot, even the ones he had no chance of returning.

We walked to Panera afterwards, got some lunch. He had trouble with the firm bread of his sandwich. Two missing teeth will do that to a kid. I took the meat out, told him to eat that.

He asked why I didn't come over as often.

I told him I was in Seattle.

He screwed up his face, trying to place it in his mind. "Where?"

"Russell Wilson," I said. He got that. His hero.

"The Seahawks? Did you go to a game?"

"No."

"What's Russell Wilson like?"

"I don't know. I didn't actually see him."

He couldn't believe I went all the way out there and neglected to get together with Russ. What was I thinking?

We walked back to Miriam's, and my interlude was over. The good part of life.

The next day, Sunday, would be two plane rides and a business meeting with someone I'd rather not see.

64

October 3
Reagan National Airport
Washington, DC

Seven thirty-nine a.m., walking down the jetway onto the plane, my phone chimed with a text from Sheriff Kessler.

Is it too early to call?

On board, I found my seat. A window in the second row. Nice and wide. First class.

I didn't bring a bag because I'd be flying back out of West Palm twelve hours after I arrived.

I called Kessler.

"What's up, Earl?"

"We're dropping the case against Carlo."

"What? Why?"

"He's dead."

"How?"

Kessler told me the Bureau called him twenty minutes ago with the news. A bunch of high school kids partying in Seward Park on the south end of Lake Washington found a body around 1 a.m. Pacific time. That's 4 a.m. Eastern, just over three hours ago.

"The man had been beaten and then shot eight times," Kessler said. "His wallet was still in his pants. The Seattle police checked his driver's license. They knew the FBI was out there talking to the guy, so they called in an agent to identify the body. It's Carlo."

"That's crazy."

"I don't get it," Kessler said. "Why'd they let him out when they had him in custody? They should have waited for a bail hearing, and they should have requested a bail he couldn't post. The agents who interviewed me here a few days ago let on he was involved in something big. So why let him out? And if they did let him out, how did he end up murdered? You'd think they'd be watching his every move."

"I don't know, Earl. Look, I'm on a plane. I have to go into airplane mode in a minute. You mind passing the news to Mrs. Jackson, so I don't have to?"

"I already had it on my list. Where you headed?"

"Florida."

"A little R and R?"

"I wish."

65

October 3
Palm Beach, FL

A blond-haired woman called my name as I left the secure area of Palm Beach International. She was in her mid to late forties, wearing a dark blazer and slacks. A limo driver's outfit. She was on the heavy side, with most of the weight in her back and shoulders, like a linebacker.

She smiled. "No bag?"

"No."

In a black Mercedes with the air conditioning cranked, we went east instead of south. Not to Delray, but to a marina.

The driver pointed to a fishing charter, told me Anthony was waiting.

I stepped into the blazing sun and put on a pair of dark Aviators. Villarosa was leaning off the back deck of a thirty-footer, untying rope from a cleat on the dock. He wore a white polo shirt, khaki Bermuda shorts, and brown leather topsiders. He looked like he could have stepped out of a minivan at a kids' soccer game.

"You ever go for tarpon?" he asked.

"No."

"They put up a fight. I figured you'd like it."

As we motored out of the Intracoastal into open water, he told me there was no guarantee of hooking anything around here.

"Better luck in the Keys," he said. "But there are a few around here now and then. What kind of beer you like?"

"Before lunch? None."

"Alright then." He opened the cooler. "I got Corona and Corona Light. It's practically not even beer, so drink all you want."

As the coastline faded behind us, he explained the gear. Nine-foot rods and fifty-pound line. He was after the big fish.

"How often you come out here?" I asked.

"Once a week. Sometimes twice."

"I'm surprised you don't own your own boat if you come out that often," I said, remembering that we were on a charter.

"Who says I don't own it?"

He grinned, like the charter company was a favorite gem in his crooked empire.

When the coast was far behind us, the captain, who I sensed had been given instructions not to talk to us, cut the engine. Villarosa baited the hooks as we drifted in the balmy breeze.

"Cast straight back," he said, pointing off the bow of the boat.

I cast my line rear right, he cast his rear left.

"Now what am I supposed to do?"

"Put your rod in the holder, have a seat, and crack a beer."

"That's it?"

He dropped his rod into a holder on the rear rail. "What do you mean, that's it?" He pulled a tube from his pocket, popped the top, and slid out a cigar. "You know what my fucking life is like, managing all these cocky shitheads? You send a guy out to take something from someone else, he starts thinking he can take things from you too. I'm watching these bastards all the time. I get a couple hours to sit on my ass, you're damn right I'm gonna take it. Especially out here, where no one can barge in. Want a cigar?"

"No thanks."

"What fun are you? Don't drink, don't smoke. Fucking teacher's pet."

He grinned, took a little guillotine device from his pocket, chopped off the tip of the cigar and lit it.

I told him I came here to get paid.

He nodded toward a briefcase beside the captain.

"What's that?" I asked.

"What do you mean, what's that? You just told me you wanted to get paid."

"Cash?"

"You think I'm going to write you a fucking check? With my name on it? After what happened to Carlo?"

That put me on alert. "What happened to Carlo?" I asked.

He couldn't have known. Even if the story of the body in Seward Park had made it into the news, it wouldn't have included his name. Not until after he'd been formally identified and his relatives notified.

"That's a good question," he said, leaning back in his chair and blowing a puff of thick white smoke into the salt air. "From the looks of him, I'd say someone beat the living shit out of him. And then the poor fucker must have wandered onto a shooting range."

I stood there staring at him. I couldn't hide my anger, but I couldn't do anything about it either.

"Have a seat, will you? You make me nervous standing there."

"I think I will have a beer," I said. I pulled a Corona Light from the cooler and took the seat next to him. We were about four feet apart.

The breeze died down and the sun came on strong. I should have worn shorts.

"I dug up videos of some of your old fights," Villarosa said. "Three you won by knockout. You know what I like? The way you approach your opponent. Like Chavez and Mike McCallum. Laser focus on the body. Keep hitting that body and eventually the guy will fold. Six, seven, eight rounds, they've had enough. You can see it in their eyes. They lose their will, and once the will goes, there's nothing left to hold them up."

"I always thought that was the saddest part of the sport," I said. "Beating the will out of a guy."

Villarosa, cigar clenched between his teeth, blew a cloud of smoke as he leapt from his seat toward his bending rod.

"You think?"

He pulled the rod from the holder and the line went slack.

"False alarm," he said. He put the rod back and added, "It's only sad when it happens to you. The way I see it, when you're on top, you gotta enjoy it. We're all gonna fall someday. We're all gonna be that guy who goes down. God's plan, right? But till then, why make yourself suffer? You got a clear blue sky, a clear blue sea, a boat to take you wherever you want. If you're still suffering with all that"—he tapped two fingers against his temple—"then the problem's up here. You gotta change the way you think. You like your job, Freddy?"

"For the most part."

"Ever think about coming back to the other side?"

"No chance."

"That's a shame. We could use a guy like you. You see some of the guys that work for me? It's not crème de la crème. These days, guys can go to a coding boot camp, learn some computer shit, and start pulling a six-figure salary. They don't have to worry about the law catching up with them. The guys I get, either their English isn't good enough for the cush jobs, or they're stupid. I'm a bottom feeder." He shook his head. "It sucks."

"How'd you know about Carlo?" I asked.

He looked me dead in the eye. "How do you think I knew?"

"How the hell did you get to him when he's under surveillance by both the FBI and the CIA?"

"You mean how would someone theoretically get to him? I'm assuming that's what you mean, because I don't think any private dick would have the balls to step onto my boat and accuse me of such a heinous act."

"Cut the shit, Anthony."

"All right, let's ask the question a different way. Let's ask how long it would take the FBI to build an airtight case on these data theft charges. A year? Maybe two? And how many agents and prosecutors does that tie up? Then they go to trial. How much does that cost?

"And then there's the murder charge. Guy kills a young woman for no fucking reason. No fucking reason at all. That's a whole other investigation, a whole other trial. And there's no guarantee the government wins either one of them, but let's say for the sake of argument they convict him.

"How long is he going to be in prison? For murder, espionage, data theft at that scale? He'll be locked up fifty years.

"You know how much it costs to keep a guy in federal prison for a year? It's like fucking college tuition.

"Run the numbers, Freddy. Two investigations, two trials, fifty years of college tuition. Who the hell wants to shell out for that? For a loser like Carlo? A little pawn in someone else's game? You think China's going to miss him?"

"I still don't see how you got close to him," I said. I took a sip of the beer, and then another. The cold beer was a good antidote to the sun's heat.

"That Corona Light is good for day drinking, isn't it?"

"It hits the spot," I said, reluctantly. "How'd you get close enough to Carlo to get him?"

Villarosa rubbed his chin and thought for a moment. I could see he was choosing his words.

"Some of the work I do and some of the work the government does, it overlaps."

"You're not talking about the FBI," I said.

"No, I'm not. I'm talking about sometimes somebody needs to borrow fifty kilos of cocaine—"

"Why?"

"Is it my business to ask? Or there's a foreigner wandering around South Florida. A shady kind of guy that the not-FBI keeps losing track of. Do any of my guys know where he is? Well, sometimes they do. Every once in a while, someone comes along that neither one of us likes. If I get the right signals, he's fair game."

Villarosa studied me for a second then asked, "Why do you look so disillusioned, Freddy? You know how the world works."

"I'm not disillusioned," I said. "It's just that part of me keeps thinking that somewhere in this world, everything is honest and aboveboard. Even if it's just a tiny island in the sea. Somewhere, people are actually decent enough to live up to their own ideals."

Villarosa shook his head. "Why trouble yourself with thoughts like that? The world is what it is. Work with it. And put some sunscreen on. You're gonna burn."

He got up, dug a bottle of SPF 50 from a bag beside the cooler, and tossed it to me.

* * *

I didn't count the money till I got home.

Fifty-five thousand in cash. That was more than double what we would have charged a normal client for that amount of work.

66

October 4
Washington, DC

"What do you expect me to do with that?" Ed asked.

He was angry about the cash.

"We can't walk into a bank with that. Why couldn't you get a check? Or a contract?"

"I told you, Ed. I didn't have a choice."

"You should have called me before you left Florida the first time. Before you flew to Seattle. That kind of threat Villarosa made against you—"

"And then we never would have cracked the case," I reminded him.

"And Carlo Ivanov wouldn't have been murdered," he said.

"What makes you think Carlo's murder—" I stopped short. Ed had spent decades in law enforcement. He'd seen everything. "Never mind."

"I'll let you in on a little secret," he said. "Carlo was a low piece in a Jenga tower that's been wobbling for months. Both the Bureau and the Agency got enough info from him to move on a ring they've been wanting to take down for years. That's why they released him. They didn't need him anymore."

He looked again at the cash. "I don't want this."

"What am I supposed to do with it?"

"Hand out bonuses. Cash, off the books."

"To who? How much?"

"You, Claire, Leon, Bethany. You decide the amount. But nothing over ten thousand to any one person at once. The banks have to report that level of cash."

I ran the numbers in my head. I'd spread it evenly. One payment now, one at Christmas.

"We're good on money now anyway," Ed said.

"How's that?"

"That company out near Dulles. It's a big job. Their lawyers are reviewing the contract I sent. They might change a clause or two, lock down the nondisclosure terms, but that's just a formality. I expect to have the contract signed by Wednesday."

"How'd you sell them?"

I didn't have to ask. I already knew.

"Claire and I met with them yesterday, while you were down in Florida."

That meant he was keeping her. Her three-month contract ended this week, and he was bringing her on full time.

"What's the matter, Freddy?"

I shook my head silently.

"Words, Freddy. What is it?"

"I don't know, Ed. I got a lot to think about."

"All right. Take a long lunch if you have to. I sent you a draft of Claire's offer letter. It's in your inbox. Take some time to review it. You're going to present it at dinner."

"I'm going to present it? Tonight?" The alarm in my voice caught him off guard.

"Yeah, tonight, Freddy. I'd go with you, but my daughter is being induced this afternoon. She wants me to be there for the birth. You're taking Claire to Farmers, Fishers, Bakers, on the waterfront in Georgetown."

"Yeah, but—you decided without me?"

Again, he looked surprised. "You've had nothing but good things to say about her work. What's your objection?"

My mind went blank.

"If you have a problem with her, out with it, before we commit."

He looked at me, waiting. I could say nothing against the woman. Nothing at all.

Neither could I see myself walking into this office day after day, suppressing that attraction that kept getting stronger.

I had never failed to tell Ed anything relevant to company business. I had never withheld a thing.

I reached into my pocket, felt the note I'd written at the Westin. My resignation letter. I froze.

Ed couldn't seem to read my distress. He looked at me like he wanted to get back to his to-do list, like I was wasting his time over a decision that had already been made.

"Why don't you go to the gym?" he said. "Work your mind back into focus."

I left his office in a zombie state, not really seeing where I was going, not knowing what I was doing, until I walked smack into Leon.

He chuckled. "You drunk, Champ?"

Bethany shot Claire a worried look.

She followed me into the hall. Claire did.

"What's the matter, Freddy?"

"Nothing."

I didn't look at her. Just got in the elevator and left.

67

The gym was a good call. I lifted for an hour, then spent forty minutes on the treadmill. I didn't resolve my dilemma, but it made me stop thinking about it for a while, and it took off the nervous edge.

I called Bethany in between to tell her to tell Claire we were having dinner in Georgetown.

"Why are you calling me?" Bethany asked. "Why don't you call her?"

"Just tell her," I said.

"She already knows. Ed put it on her calendar. And yours. Do you know what time you're meeting her?"

"No."

"Seven, Freddy. And don't dress like a dick." She hung up.

A dick? When do I dress like a dick? What the hell does a dick even wear?

I wasn't going back to the office, because I couldn't face her. Claire, I mean. I still didn't know what I was going to tell her. Technically, Ed and I were both supposed to agree on hiring decisions. He just assumed I was on board, but I never told him I was.

Our next case, whatever this Dulles thing was, depended on her, so if we got rid of her, the firm might lose the gig. That meant I had to go. My resignation letter, folded and well worn, was in the pocket of my pants back in the gym locker room.

I didn't need to read it again. No one needed to tell me I was nuts. It was the only thing I knew for sure now.

I waited till six thirty to go back to the office. I wanted to be sure Claire was gone.

She was, but wouldn't you know it? Who was still there? The next worst thing to Claire.

"Dammit, Freddy, I told you not to dress like a dick!"

Bethany has a way of channeling Miriam sometimes. When we were married, Miriam used to lie in wait for me behind the front door. I'd get home late from work, and she'd unload on me with comments like that.

I looked down at my clothes. Apparently, dicks wear jeans, a long-sleeve button-down shirt, and hiking boots.

"Shut up, Bethany."

I walked past her to my desk. I had to find Ed's offer letter in my email, print it out, and sign it. Bethany followed close on my heels.

"Jesus, Freddy, you sweat right through your shirt."

"Leave me alone."

"You need to put on some deodorant."

"Go away, will you?"

She went away.

And then she came back. Because that's what Bethany does. She came back with the suit I kept in Ed's office for days I had to testify in court. And the black dress shoes.

"Put this on."

"No!"

"Freddy, you stink and your armpits are soaked. You're not going to a restaurant like that. Go in Ed's office and change. Now!"

I tell you, that's wife material right there. Commands me like a dog. It's her way or the highway.

I went in and changed because it was easier than arguing. She came in a minute later. Didn't even knock. Caught me with my shirt off, tossed me a stick of deodorant with a pink and white label, and told me to rub it on good.

"This is gonna make me smell like a woman."

"You act like a woman!"

"What the hell is that supposed to mean?"

"It means put your pants on and be a fucking man! The suit pants, Freddy. You're not going to wear that shirt and jacket with jeans."

"Get out of here!"

She had this little smirk on her face when she shut the door. Like she was pleased with herself. Like pushing me around was funny.

I pulled everything out of my jeans pockets, transferred it all to the suit pants.

When I came out, she said, "Call a Lyft."

"What's the rush?"

"You don't want to be late."

"Who says?"

"I say."

Now she was really getting under my skin.

I said, "What the hell is wrong with you?"

"What the hell is wrong with *you*?" Fire and fury lit her eyes. "I'm not the one who's bent out of shape."

Actually, that wasn't true. Internally, I was a mess. But at the moment, she had me so mad, I forgot.

"Okay, sorry, Freddy. You're right." She grabbed my lapel, turned it out the right way.

"What are you doing?"

"Why don't men look in the mirror when they dress?"

"What mirror? There is no mirror."

"When you put on clothes, you have to put them on right." She had this urgency in her voice that I wasn't used to hearing. She was usually pretty even-tempered.

"Boy, you really are bent out of shape." I said it in a joking way, trying to make light of the situation.

She kicked me hard on the shin.

"Ow! What was that for?"

"Wake up, Freddy! Wake up!" Her whole face was red. That surprised me. She never got that upset. Ever.

She was so rattled, she couldn't think straight. The next words out of her mouth had nothing to do with anything.

"Claire didn't leave her phone."

I looked over at Claire's desk. There was no phone.

"Why would you bother telling me about something Claire *didn't* do?"

"I took it out of her bag," she said.

I looked again. There was no bag. No phone. I felt like I was fighting with Miriam again, with a crazy person.

"What bag?" I said. "What the hell does that have to do with anything?"

"So *you* would have to return it." She shoved me when she said *you*.

Again, I looked. No phone, no bag, nothing. "How am I supposed to return it if she didn't leave it?"

She rolled her eyes and groaned. It was an angry, frustrated groan from deep inside.

I asked her if she was losing her mind.

"I will if you screw this up," she said.

"Screw what up?"

Another roiling groan. I knew to walk away before she blew her top. We both needed time to cool off. I mean, I've been married. I've been through this. You don't work anything out when you're this upset. You back off, cool down, come back with a clear mind and talk like grown-ups.

I went to my desk and picked up Claire's offer letter.

I didn't say anything to Bethany, but she watched like an angry hawk, her eyes glued to my every move.

I still didn't know what I was going to do with Claire. I had two letters now. Resignation in my pants pocket, offer letter in my jacket pocket. And somehow, I was supposed to be gracious about this. Praise her for her good work. Let her know how much she meant to the company.

How was I going to swing that when my mind was so muddled I couldn't even have a rational conversation with Bethany?

I had to psyche myself into it. Think of it as another day in the ring, Freddy.

I put on my fight face, or tried to, anyway. Tried to gather my courage and summon my resolve for the long walk into the ring. This wasn't like the others though. For the first time I could remember, I dreaded the confrontation. Claire was the only opponent who ever had me beat before we even squared off.

On my way out the door, Bethany said, "What's your favorite food, Freddy?"

"I don't know. Get out of my way."

I pushed past her, went into the hall, hit the down button on the goddamn elevator.

She stood there in the office doorway, arms crossed, like my ex-wife when she was pissed off at me.

She said again, "What's your favorite food?"

The way she asked it, it was like a challenge. An angry challenge.

"I don't know."

Food was the last think I wanted to think about. I was going to a restaurant for a meal I knew I wouldn't be able to eat, and she's asking what I'm going to order? I felt sick. Heartsick and physically sick, and what was up her ass, I didn't know. She's usually not that thick. Usually, she can read me.

The elevator doors slid open.

"It's frutti di mare, Freddy. Think about it."

I tell you, I couldn't think about eating a goddamn thing.

This is why boxers don't bring their wives to fights. You're trying to focus on a difficult and potentially unpleasant task, and they're asking what you want from the menu.

What the fuck?

68

I got to the restaurant late. It was loud. Way too loud for conversation.

I scanned the tables, but I didn't see her. That was funny. It wasn't like her to be late.

Someone tugged on my elbow from behind. I turned.

Claire said, "Let's go somewhere else."

She pulled me outside. It was quieter in the open, but something was wrong. She didn't look right. I mean, she looked beautiful in a dark blue dress, more beautiful than any woman has a right to look, but she was anxious.

"What's wrong?" I asked.

"My stomach is in knots. I don't think I can eat."

She was worried about the job. Ed must have told her we were meeting to discuss her position with the company. He didn't tell her we were making an offer. After all the work she put in, her contract was up and she didn't know whether she was getting hired or fired.

"Come here," I said. I took her arm and we walked down to the boardwalk at the river's edge, where it was even quieter.

"You have nothing to worry about," I said.

She looked hopeful for a second, then doubtful.

"But I do," she said. "I have a lot on my mind."

"Well, let me lay it all to rest." I hated to see her like this. She, of all people, should not doubt herself—she who had everything you could ask for in a person. I handed her the letter.

I could see the line of her collarbone as she pulled the letter from the envelope. The bones were perfectly level across her chest. When she tilted her head down to read, her hair fell in the way. She pulled it back behind her ear, read the letter, then read it again. I watched her expression. Concerned at first, eyebrows knit together. That's also how she looks when she focuses, when she's reading through documents on her computer monitor, thinking.

Her posture relaxed a little. Not as much as I had hoped. I had hoped she would be relieved, that all her anxiety would melt away. That she wouldn't have to feel the kind of stress and tension about her job that I'd been feeling about her.

She looked up at me, neither excited nor relieved, but curious. And her tone was curious too. "Freddy, what's wrong with you?" She asked the way a child does, without accusation or judgment.

"I don't know."

"Yes, you do. You've been out of sorts for a long time now."

I couldn't remember a time when I was *in sorts* with her, if there is such a thing. Looking back, even to the time before she came onboard, even to our first two meetings on the Reisman case, I couldn't see her any other way than I saw her now. The face, the body, the voice were all infused with the mind and soul of this person I admired and wanted to be with. I couldn't separate my memories from the now of her.

And I couldn't look at her just as someone I worked with. This is why I didn't want to be there. She asked for a mentor and a chance at a new career, and I did mean it when I promised her those things. Honest to God, I did.

She slid her arm through mine. Innocent, unsuspecting, like the hopeful young actress in Hollywood, out to dinner with the movie producer whose heart she cannot read. She slides her arm through his because in her mind they're friends working toward a common goal. Her guard is down because, in this context, he isn't someone who has power over her. He's a mentor and she trusts him. She doesn't know he lies awake at night and thinks of her.

She was still waiting for an answer. I couldn't look at her.

I turned, watched the river flow beneath the silver moon.

She pulled me back. "Talk to me! Freddy, I was looking forward to this dinner. I was looking forward to having you all to myself for an hour. To having a real conversation. We're both off tonight, and this would suck a whole lot less if you'd speak."

"Sorry. I'm preoccupied."

"Obviously."

She thrust the letter at me, and her voice broke a little on the next words.

"This hurt! This really hurt, Freddy."

"What? That we offered you a job? Isn't that what you wanted?" I couldn't understand what she was complaining about. I had never seen her be ungrateful.

"Did you even read this letter?"

I hadn't actually. I just signed it because I was in a hurry and Bethany wouldn't shut the hell up.

"What's wrong with it?" I asked.

She held it up in front of me and pointed to a line. "This line, after the second paragraph."

She pointed to a sentence in italics, but I couldn't read it. I was heartsick and the break in her voice was like a blow to the gut of a fighter on his last legs.

"What does it say?" I asked.

"You can't read it?"

"No."

She turned the letter and read aloud. "Freddy, add your comments here."

Crap. Ed had put that in as a placeholder.

"You know, Freddy, I've always had confidence in my abilities, and in my heart, I know I've done good work. It was kind of Ed to say so, but I really wanted to hear it from you."

There was real emotion in her voice, and I just couldn't handle that. I had no defense against her to begin with, and now I'd hurt her feelings, let her down. The dam was breaking. The dam that had been holding everything back was finally giving way. I could hear the cracks, like I did that day in the woods before the water came crashing down and tore her away from me.

"When you asked me to come on board," Claire said, "I asked you to teach me. To guide me. And I've watched you, and I've listened, and I've learned. Your opinion matters to me, Freddy. It matters deeply."

I didn't know how to win this fight. I had no corner to go back to, no trainer to advise me, no one to reassure me. I didn't believe in myself anymore. The dam was breaking, and I didn't know what to do.

"Is it so hard to say, You did a good job, Claire? I mean, is that, like, beyond you?"

I started to lose the sense of what she was saying. I heard the words, but I was too far gone to make out the meaning. Her eyes told me though. Her eyes, dark and lively, full of wounded passion.

"Whatever you say," she continued, "whatever your opinion of me is, I accept it. But please just say *something*. I think the world of you, Freddy. I really do. And I trust you one hundred percent."

Before I even made the fateful move, I felt in my imagination the soft skin of her face between my hands.

"One hundred percent, Freddy, and that's something I've never said to any man."

The dam gave way at last. I grabbed her and I kissed her, and I knew right away I'd blown it.

After all the work I'd put in, the months of restraint, I had crossed the line and ruined everything. All I wanted to do was kiss the mind that took in everything and processed it all so brilliantly, the spirit that rose to every challenge and still wanted more, the woman who outshone them all and still didn't measure up to her own high standards.

She stood there with her eyes closed. She wouldn't look at me, and I knew I wasn't going to see her anymore. Not at work, not at her apartment or at mine, not anywhere. The resignation letter in my pocket would be on Ed's desk before I got home.

She was already removing herself from my life. She wouldn't let me see her eyes. She kept them closed to spare me the sight of what it looks like to be betrayed, to be lured into a job by a man who promises to train you, a man you trust one hundred percent, who betrays you with his desire.

It hurt her, I know, because her strength gave out. All that strength and confidence that attracted me every time I saw her, that made me admire and want her. It was all sliding away. Her posture slackened. She let out a long breath, her hands slid up to my shoulders, she pressed her face against my chest, and she whispered, "Jesus, Freddy! What took you so long?"

GATE 76

Freddy Ferguson, Book 1
Mystery/Thriller

A mysterious woman fleeing an unknown terror boards the wrong plane at San Francisco International and disappears into the heart of the country. Freddy Ferguson, a troubled detective with a violent past, believes she's the last living witness to a crime that has captivated the nation.

Sifting through the wreckage of her past, he begins to understand who she's running from, and why. Now he must track her down before her pursuers can silence her for good.

A modern crime thriller with elements of Raymond Chandler and the classic pulp mysteries of the 1950s, *Gate 76* weaves a deeply personal tale of witness and investigator, loss and redemption.

"A consummate thriller with some of the best characterization you'll see all year." —*Kirkus Reviews (starred review)*

"One of the year's best thrillers." —*BestThrillers.com*

- Named to Kirkus Reviews' Best Books of 2018
- Named to BestThrillers.com's best thrillers of 2018

THE FRIDAY CAGE

Claire Chastain, Book 1
Mystery/Thriller

Someone new has taken an interest in Claire Chastain. He circles her house when she's alone and follows her on errands across town. He tours her home while she's away, leaving little things disturbingly out of place. He may even be involved in the recent death of her childhood friend.

But who is he? And what does he want?

Claire soon discovers that, like Cary Grant in *North by Northwest*, she's caught up in someone else's dark conspiracy, and she has no choice but to play the game. The only exit from her troubles will be the one she makes, if she's smart enough to figure out when and how to make it.

A suspenseful crime thriller in the tradition of Hitchcock and Ross MacDonald, *The Friday Cage* features a tough, sharp-minded protagonist who must do some soul-searching in the midst of her quest to survive.

"Fast-paced and exciting... ingenious and gloriously unpredictable.... one of the most compelling and odd private investigators in literature today." —*Jack Magnus, Readers' Favorite*

"Anxiety, fear, grief, regret and the quest for survival and justice are constantly simmering under the surface... A deeply psychological crime thriller that perfectly captures the terrors of both murder and life itself. Highly recommended." —*BestThrillers.com*

THE REISMAN CASE

Claire Chastain, Book 2
Mystery/Thriller

A wealthy business owner asks investigator Claire Chastain to solve a simple case. Is his employee stealing or not? From the moment she's hired, subtle clues tell her something's wrong: the unbusinesslike business owner, the lingering scent of a woman on the stairs, the rustle in the curtains where someone watches from above.

Claire's gut tells her the case isn't about theft. Her investigation turns up a pathologically anxious suspect, a deeply dysfunctional family, and a murder that she herself appears to have committed.

"If I had known what this case would turn into," she reflects, "I never would have accepted it. No one walks into a burning house."

But she's in it, and she has to find her way out...

"Chastain is hardly a typical PI. She's clever and analytical, and yet she is quick-tempered, even volatile... Diamond has equipped her with a case that deserves a spot at the top of your queue. Highly recommended." —*BestThrillers.com*

"A gripping murder mystery... with the suspense and intensity growing with every page." —*Readers' Favorite (5 stars)*

"Diamond, who writes well-acclaimed crime, mystery, and noir fiction, is here exploring for the second time the mind and motivations of Claire Chastain, a daring, highly intelligent female who has her own secrets to repress... The twisted tale causes her to cross paths with some dark characters and dodge life-threatening peril, while maintaining a certain enviable inner strength and outer cool. *The Reisman Case* proves again that author Diamond has a mind for the malevolent scheming and shadowy settings that are the stuff of noir fiction, with a strong female lead to weave the crisscrossing plot threads into a rich, ever-shifting panorama." —*The Feathered Quill*

IMPALA

Thriller

After four years on the straight and narrow, Russell Fitzpatrick has a boring job, the wrong woman, and an itch for something more. All he needs to get his life going again is a nudge in the wrong direction.

When he receives a cryptic email from a legendary and slightly deranged fellow hacker—his old friend Charlie, whom he knows to be dead—he tries to tell himself it's none of his concern. But the guy who stalks him across town at night, the two thugs waiting in the alley, and a ruthless FBI agent let him know his days are numbered if he doesn't turn over the money Charlie stole.

The problem is, Russ doesn't have it. As his enemies close in from all sides, Russ slowly unwinds the mystery of his old friend's paranoid mind and finds that Charlie left behind something worth much more than the money. And no one but him is on to it...

- A Kirkus Recommended Review — September 2016
- An Amazon Best Book of the Month — Sept. 2016 - Mystery/Thriller
- An IndieReader Best of 2016 Selection
- First Place Winner — Genre Fiction — 24th Annual Writer's Digest Awards
- Gold Medal Winner — 2017 Readers' Favorite Awards

TO HELL WITH JOHNNY MANIC

Psychological Thriller / Noir

John Manis, aka Johnny Manic, isn't who he says he is. His money can't ease the burden of his dark secret. The high life, he finds, is a lonely life when you have to live it as someone else. If only someone could see him for who he really was.

Marilyn Dupree has a strange intuition, a spark of recognition when they meet. Her life isn't going right either. Johnny is reckless. Marilyn is passionate and volatile, with too much money and the wrong husband. She and Johnny have a chemistry like nitrogen and glycerin.

"The wiser part of me knew I should have left," Johnny recalls. "But knowing what's right and doing what's right are two different things, especially when you're at war with instincts you can't articulate and don't understand. The important thing was that in the grocery store that morning, Johnny Manic and the raven-haired Marilyn Dupree had found each other. The fuse was lit."

Watching them both is the wary detective Lou Eisenfall, who senses he's going to be very busy in the coming weeks.

A dark tale of deception, murder, and psychological suspense, *To Hell with Johnny Manic* is a throwback to the classic crime fiction of Patricia Highsmith, Raymond Chandler, and Jim Thompson.

"A feverishly readable psychological noir." —*Kirkus Reviews*

"Truly riveting... One of the year's best thrillers." — *BestThrillers.com*

WARREN LANE

Mystery/Comedy

Susan Moore is about to hire the wrong man to investigate her philandering husband, Will. There's something not quite right about that detective. Warren Lane drinks too much and has a hard time staying out of trouble. He's just the kind of guy Will's mistress can't resist. And everyone is starting to figure out that Will is hiding a lot more than his affair with a reckless young woman. With a bit of mystery, romance, crime, and suspense, Warren Lane has his hands full.

WAKE UP, WANDA WILEY

Comedy/Romance/Satire

Hannah Sharpe has been written out of all eighteen of Wanda Wiley's romance novels. A runaway heroine who won't conform to the plots laid out for her, Hannah has been consigned to a realm of fog deep in the recesses of the author's imagination.

Trevor Dunwoody, the protagonist of a macho action-thriller that Wanda has regrettably agreed to ghostwrite, is single-minded and obtuse, understanding only what he can beat up, shoot, or screw. Like Hannah, he's a character Wanda doesn't know what to do with. When he appears one day in Hannah's fog world, she can't convince him he's in the wrong story.

Hannah knows she'll be stuck in the limbo of Wanda's subconscious until the writer can find a suitable story to cast her in. But Wanda, trapped in a disastrous relationship with the philandering narcissist Dirk Jaworski, is sinking into a deep depression. The pot she smokes to self-medicate impairs her ability to write and thickens the fog of Hannah's timeless isolation.

As Hannah explains her predicament to the thick-headed Trevor, she begins to realize that she knows her author better than her author knows herself. If she can only break out of the limbo of Wanda's subconscious and nudge the writer in the right direction, she can free them both.

But how can Hannah penetrate the fog of her creator's mind from within? The answer is right in front of her in the form of the big, dumb, action-ready tool, Trevor Dunwoody.

"Diamond's prose is funny and barbed, particularly the dialogue between Hannah and Trevor... surprisingly compelling." —*Kirkus Reviews*

ABOUT THE AUTHOR

Andrew Diamond writes mystery, crime, noir, and an occasional comedy. His award-winning books feature cinematic prose, strong characterization, twisting plots, and dark humor. You can follow Andrew on Goodreads or on his blog at https://adiamond.me.